The Dark Eve: A New Recruit

By T. K. Thompson

Published By

To get more FREE books from T.K. Thompson, learn more about *The Dark Eve* **book series,** get updates on future book releases, and more.

Subscribe to our newsletter at
TKThompson.com

CHAPTER ONE
The Crossroads

Acantha's dark eyes burned out from the shadows of the second story balcony of the Three Crossroads pub. The tavern sign banged against the building, making her head pound, but her freshly opened bottle of rum would solve that problem soon enough. She peered down, invisible to the ground floor and its inhabitants. The shady faces, travelers from the dusty roads and those that ventured out only in the night, crowded the dank walls. An old grandfather clock chimed eleven o'clock, each ring bellowing as if it could be its last.

The vagabonds silently toasted to their pleasure. A stage spanned the room. Dancing girls kicked their heels for the whistling coins that flew their way as a man bounded out lively music from a piano box. The old tavern owner tilted his ear at the conversation near his bar.

"The Lady? What?" A large man at the table laughed.

The room went silent. Every head turned to the source of the disturbance and stared at the fool that dared voice the name. The piano player froze against the keys. The dancing girls stumbled. The old tavern creaked and groaned with the pounding wind.

The traveler relished another drink from his mug, spilling ale down his beard and gut. "Ha!" he chortled. "I can't believe you think such things! If such a fiend did exist…" His voice trailed off into another guzzle.

The two other blokes at the table sat wide-eyed and red faced, noting the response from the room. The old tavern man, Cornelius, paused in wiping the counter. He peered up at her in the shadows of the balcony. "I tell you, stranger," he said in a hush, "watch what you say. She be the devil if you ever meet her. Be warned."

The stranger twisted his expression, ridiculing him.

Cornelius squinted his weather-worn face. "What is your name, fellow, and what is it that you do?" He began filling mugs at the bar.

"I am Hurly and a tradesman. I've come to town on business." He pointed to the others with him, who shrank back under their hats. "These two are Hess and Sam."

Cornelius leaned over the bar, his voice gruff and deep. "They say she was born with the mark of darkness. A vixen and horror of the seas, she is. As tall as a man and curved like Aphrodite, but dare you gaze upon her and your eyeballs would be plucked from your skull with her twin blades." The bartender's voice grew louder. "Her three closest crew be the deadliest. *The Dark Eve*, her ship, be stained red with blood. Sirens sing at the helm, estrangin' men from their souls. And treasures—" Cornelius paused, his voice straining. "Mountains of gold, cursed by her blood, hidden."

From above she gripped her bottle of rum at the familiar legendary words. A sly smile crept up her face.

Hurly rolled his eyes.

"I tell you, be careful!" Cornelius paused and spat behind the bar. "She's not to be trifled with. Her crew will have no mercy on you." The air of the tavern had grown thick with the influence of the speech.

"Old crow, keep your tales to yourself. I have no fear of ghost stories. Nor do I believe that a woman could take the fury of the sea."

Gasps escaped from the women on stage.

"Beware what you say about the Lady." Cornelius gazed at her, trying his plea once more.

Hurly guffawed and hollered, "Do be serious! It's folklore!" He became aware of the stares boring holes in the back of his head and shifted his large weight.

Cornelius's voice remained steady, but a fearful intensity grew in his wrinkled face. "The Queen of the Sea." His words whispered with reverence. "She's real, as real as your worst nightmare."

The battered tavern sign's thumping ceased and the wind faded. As the tavern grew eerily silent, all eyes looked to the walls and roof. She leaned back in her chair and whispered to her sides, "Jennings, Scar."

The balcony creaked with their heavy footsteps. The front door at the bottom of the stairs flew open with a force of the wind renewed—crashing against the wall. Dust surged into the pub. The sign resurrected its pounding, harder now. The musician rushed over and forced the door closed at the bottom of the stairs. The startled room peered with flinching eyes at the dark staircase.

Their figures appeared halfway down the steps. Guests rushed from their seats to the opposing walls. Jennings's dark, massive hand gripped the railing and he ducked his bald head to avoid the beam. His bare chest inked with tattoos bulged in the low light. Scar was right behind, running a hand through his greasy, dirty-blond hair.

She stood and gripped the balcony railing, enjoying the fearful look that grew on Hurly's face. Jennings covered the gap to the door and pounded his hand against it, glaring at the piano man. The performer scurried back, tripping over his tall round seat. Scar leaned back against the wall, where he pulled out his knife to clean the underside of his nails. Hurly gaped at the large scar that traveled from his mouth to his ear.

A nervous whisper vibrated through the crowd.

"Acantha." Cornelius stepped back, gripping the bar.

The darkness of her shadow seeped down the stairs. Her tall black boots thumped against the worn wooden steps with authority. She sauntered to the center of the room. Hurly eyed her maroon corset and ruffled collar, avoiding her gaze. She brushed forward a lock of wild hair and traced her fingers down the silver chain to the large red pendant at her chest.

Hurly followed her lingering hand. His eyes widened and darted up.

Her dark stare burned from beneath the brim of her black hat. Hurly froze, the folklore burning into his reality. She shifted her eyes to Cornelius over the wide collar of her black coat. He wavered as he tipped his head toward her.

The Vixen of the Sea, tall as a man, curved like Aphrodite.

Her threatening glances darted around the room and then fell full upon Hurly. Sweat dripped down his forehead, which he quickly dabbed with his handkerchief. She spoke, her velvety voice cold and emotionless. "You were warned to take caution on mentioning my name and reputation." Her full lips pursed as she glided toward his table. Hess and Sam rushed to the sides of the tavern with the rest.

Hurly looked nervously around—almost pleadingly—as he sat deserted.

"I…" he stuttered. "Was just…"

Without warning her coat flew open. She unsheathed two long silver swords. In a lightning-fast scissor motion, she thrust them toward Hurly. Her swords were sheathed again before his head hit the floor and rolled back to the end of the bar. Small screams burst from the tavern women, quickly silenced. No one dared to breathe, the room awkwardly quiet. The men at the bar scurried from their places as Acantha approached Cornelius while Jennings and Scar guarded the entrance.

"What did you hear?" she asked, scanning the cowering crowd.

Cornelius kept his head low and spoke the truth as he nervously glanced away. "I don't know what was said. I just know that your name was mentioned." There was a shuffle. The companions of the deceased shifted uneasily, eyeing the exit where her men stood sentinel.

Acantha jerked her head and in a sudden sweep, Jennings and Scar were upon them. Both men struggled. Nobody dared to protest. The crowd looked away from their fear-stricken faces as they were dragged kicking and screaming into the night. The sounds of a wagon and horses roared outside, muffling the cries of Hess and Sam.

Cornelius took a small, antique-stemmed glass from the top shelf behind him. He filled it with a flask of wine from a reserved cupboard and placed it on the bar. Then he backed up, giving distance to the space between them. Acantha turned, noticing his actions.

She brought the glass to her nose, smelling the sweet aroma of the wine. She brushed the crystal against her lips before tipping it down her throat. With delicacy she placed it in the exact spot Cornelius had set it. "You didn't hear anything concerning Jennet?"

He shook his head. Acantha turned to the rest of the audience, darkly examining each face.

She leaned back against the bar. "I am in need of men." She addressed no one in particular, but allowed her message to sink in. "If any have the desire to live less than long lives and to be paid for them, then visit the south end of this bar come morning. My man Vaster will be there. You will commission yourselves to sail the high seas on *The Dark Eve*."

She stared hard at the man at the music box. He turned, pounding out a tune, prompting the girls to continue their dance. She stood straight and walked out, kicking Hurly's severed head before disappearing into the night.

CHAPTER TWO
South of the Three Crossroads

Acantha bolted out of the mouth of the cave, running in a dead sprint down the rocky gray mountain. She focused solely on the cliff face ahead. There the targeted crevice provided just enough space to squeeze through. With the dragon egg cradled in her arms, every moment was vital. She heaved a lungful of putrid dust as the screams of the dragon rattled the rock beneath her feet, shaking her very soul.

She dropped the egg, discarding its extra weight. It hit the ground with a deadening crack. The thundering steps judded to a stop, but only for a moment. The shrill cries of the dragon intensified, filling the air with fire. Adrenaline coursed through her veins to power each step. Her heart pounded in unison.

How did I get conned into being the bait?

Sweat dripped from her forehead. Every muscle in her body strained to move faster. *Don't look back.* She repeated this over and over in her mind. She threw herself into the fissure, just squeezing in as the enormous head snapped after her. Her knuckles scraped against the walls. The mountain groaned as the dragon collided into the rock, clawing and striking after her. She cursed her sister under her breath.

The cliffs exploded as the creature continued to nosedive in. Clumps of dirt and rock cascaded down. She heard the dragon suck in air. She threw herself into the open space and ducked to the ground. A fiery breath burst, filling the mountain to the core. She sheltered against the wall, but the heat singed her exposed skin.

"Now, now, now!" she screamed, unsure if her voice would carry far enough.

The top of the cliff rumbled. Her crew released the dam of boulders they had spent weeks preparing. The rocks poured down over their target. The fire ceased. Acantha scrambled to get up. She huddled against the farthest wall to escape the raining assault. Her heart sank. There was no escape for the creature. The avalanche buried the beast, breaking it underneath the weight. Dust billowed and clouded her sight.

Hacking, Acantha waited for the dust to settle before crawling from her protective position. She sprawled out on the rocks to catch her breath. Shouts echoed above.

"Acantha?" Tessa yelled down. "Did you survive?"

"You know she did. Why are you even asking?" her other sister Jennet snapped in her French accent.

"I'm fine," she growled. "Will you two idiots stop fighting and get me out of here?" Pain throbbed all over where she had been struck.

"You see? Now you've pissed her off," Jennet said.

Tessa snorted. "She was bound to be angry after that."

Acantha seethed. "Vaster," she yelled, "you get me out, now!"

A rope smacked her in the head. She cursed and whacked it out of her face.

"And send the crew into the cave," she ordered. The dead dragon's claw protruded out from under the rocks. She felt a sting of regret. It had been a magnificent creature. She would have never believed its fabled existence until she saw it with her own eyes. She drew a knife from her boot and cut off a claw.

She climbed the rope and rolled on top of the cliff. Both sisters hovered over her, blocking the sun. Jennet peered down in annoyance and Tessa's eyebrows pinned together with worry. In the distance, the crew hurried into the cave.

"Great, you're fine," Jennet said carelessly. "Let's go get my ring."

Acantha glared. "It shouldn't have been off your finger."

"How was I to know that a dragon would commandeer my cave?" Jennet griped as they made their way up the mountain.

Voices echoed. "I've got it!" Vaster's words resounded against the hollowed walls.

Jennet quickened her step. Vaster popped out. She opened her hand, but he hesitated, glancing to Acantha for permission.

Jennet's face furrowed. "Give me back my ring."

Acantha nodded to her man. Jennet snatched the large emerald and slipped it on with relief. Acantha peered at the exact replica on her own finger. Tessa displayed hers and punched Jennet's hand, striking their rings together.

"Don't take it off," Tessa barked.

Jennet yanked her hand back, scowling. "I left it with my loot. It was safe."

"It's an insult to leave it with common treasure," Acantha said.

"It was safe," she repeated.

Acantha shook her head, disappointed. "I don't think Solon would agree with you."

Vaster led to the location of the treasure. Heaps of gold littered the cold floor. Bags and bags overflowing with precious gems and golden antiquities piled everywhere—

Acantha's eyes flew open to the dark ceiling of her quarters. Her sheets twisted around her ankles. She shook the dream off and sat up. The moonlight illuminated the space, making it ethereal and all wrong. She scanned the details of her room and out the wall of windows. Everything looked in place. She checked her antique desk connected to the ship as if carved from the same tree. All the contents normally on top were there. She sprawled out on the oversized bed and brushed a hand against its thick red drapes.

Shaking the sleep from her head, she examined further. Everything was just as it should be. The dragon's claw hung on the wall. That event, a little over a year ago, had been the last time she had seen Jennet. She rubbed her head in frustration.

Why do I even try to sleep?

The ship swayed gently as she stretched her neck. She rose, walking over to the shiny metal mirror and water basin. Pale skin and tired dark circles under her eyes reflected back. She ran her hands through her hair and bent down to wash. Gripping the sides of the sink, she peered back into the mirror. A faint green tinted her skin.

Am I getting sick? Impossible.

She squinted suspiciously and examined closer. The greenness grew upon her face, flickering like the light of a candle. The rest of her room remained unaffected from the odd color that reflected in the mirror. Suddenly, recognition clicked.

Anger flooded her chest. Rushing over to her desk, she pulled one sword from its sheath. The emerald light expanded, blotting out her image in the mirror. Acantha looked down at her desk, where the light flooded from under the lid of her small box. She grabbed the box to save its contents.

An explosion of energy blew her backward through the door onto the deck. The green light erupted into flames, consuming her chambers. It spread out the door. She picked herself up, stunned but livid. Shards of glass were embedded in her back. Despite the pain, she stood straight and pointed her sword directly toward the chaos.

"I will kill you!" she screamed. "Come on, you crone!" Her hands shook. She had been waiting all this time for this moment. Rain poured on the empty deck. "I won't leave this world till I find you! You hear me? I will find you!" She yelled at the glowing inferno, searching for a figure to form among it—

Acantha sat straight up in bed, gripping her favorite dagger. Her breath panted out. Sweat dripped from her head. Disoriented, she glanced up at the clock. Two in the morning. Right on time, she thought to herself, bothered by the dream within a dream. In a rush, she moved to her desk and opened her box. Relief calmed her as she grabbed the large red pendant chained in silver. She let out a deep breath.

She placed the chain around her neck. The familiar weight rested upon her shoulders, releasing a flood of comfort, anchoring her to the ground. Strapping on her swords, she marched out of her quarters to find Vaster.

◇◇◇

Basile walked up the alley south of the Three Crossroads Tavern. A husky, dark-bearded man dozed, slumped against a wooden crate. He had a crumpled piece of parchment on his lap and a quill in hand. His legs rested on a neighboring crate along with a bottle of ink. A brown hat draped over the top of this face, camouflaging him with mud and fog.

Basile shifted his weight several times and looked around. *Am I in the right place? Is this who I am supposed to meet?* He leaned over examining the parchment. The word "Crew" was scribbled on it. *Guess I am just first in line.*

He rolled on his heels. A few more men finally appeared, which put his worrying at ease. The fog thinned as the sun inched higher. The group formed a line along the back corner of the pub. Basile held his knapsack firmly in place over his shoulder. He was the only one that stood out in height. The tattered, dirty line of potential sailors curved around the building now. He would not have been surprised if they lived on the streets and slept in the mud.

Surely these men didn't fit the bill.

A large ship needed hard-working laborers. This riffraff looked like their last day could be tomorrow.

He spun back to regard the sleeping gentleman. The temptation of disturbing him was too much. He tipped the man's hat up, but the bloke remained snoring. With both hands, Basile shook the crate. Quill, parchment, and person flew as the stranger jolted from his makeshift chair and glared through a dirt-encrusted face.

"Good morning, sir!" Basile lifted his hat.

The man stared up from the dust with a crazed expression.

"Wake a sleepin' man! What were ye thinkin', boy?" He swiped his hat from the ground and whacked at Basile's legs. Basile quickly dodged the attack. The man collected his parchment and quill and resettled on his crate. He noticed the growing line. "Ye all just got here, eh?" He wobbled his head. "Vaster's the name. Now I'll be takin' yers." He picked up his quill, dabbed it messily into the ink, and started scribbling.

"Audim Basile." The rest of the vagabonds in line made him look completely out of place. He squinted with worry. None of them looked robust enough. He had hoped for a higher quality crew, but what he saw was disappointing at best. He looked down at his clothes. They were clean and pressed, and his shoes shined.

"Have ye been a pirate before?" Vaster asked as he continued to scribble in illegible hand.

"No," answered Basile politely.

"Have ye done work on a ship before?" Vaster's voice sounded weary.

"Yes, on trade ships. I'm a good fighter, too."

Vaster peered up, amused. "Good with a sword, are ye?" He let out a chuckle. "Age?"

"Twenty."

Vaster glared, assessing his answer.

Basile didn't flinch. *Almost.*

"What has made ye adventure down the dark side of the world into pirating?"

"Adventure," said Basile quickly. This was his goal, a life beyond normal, away from regulations.

"Death would have been a better answer," responded Vaster, not bothering to look up at him.

"Then death," Basile agreed.

"Then ye made it." Vaster stretched forth his hand and Basile responded with a hearty shake. "Be at the pier tomorrow before noon and receive yer orders. Sign here by yer name if ye make terms." He pointed down to the spot by his misspelled name.

A strange wind gusted down the alley. The dust swirled up between the crates, whipping through the line of new recruits. Basile raised his arm to shield his eyes from the debris. He braced himself, feeling a tremor in the ground beneath his feet. When he looked back to confirm the quake, no one else was moving. They appeared frozen in time, completely unaware of the disturbance. Even Vaster stared unblinking in the dust storm around them.

Basile felt pause as he clutched the quill. He skimmed the contract, only catching a few readable words. *Morburn Kingdom, Three Hills, 1752*. He was taking a step that would change his life forever. It boiled down to the two arguments: he had the choice to live his own life the way he wanted or be controlled and have what his father demanded.

Ink spots littered the top of the crate. With a surge of rebellion, he jabbed the quill into the ink and elegantly wrote his name under the illegible paragraph of scratch at the top.

The wind ceased its torrent, drifting dust down around them like snow. He looked back to Vaster, who was now unfrozen and gazing at his signature. Vaster's words didn't look like a language compared to Basile's schooled penmanship.

The man gave a sarcastic smile while waving for him to move along.

"That's pretty. Now get out of the way. Ooh, 'n be sure t' say goodbye t' yer kin, as ye'll probably never be seein' 'em again."

As he left, Basile examined the line of crew he had just signed up with. They were nothing but evident scum with dirty, shabby clothes, unkempt hair, and rotten teeth.

"Next!" Vaster shouted out and they all shuffled closer in unison.

The man at the end caught Basile's attention. He had an eye patch and a mean, overly wrinkled face. The sailor grinned mockingly back, with only a few teeth left in his mouth. Basile disregarded him, but now without wondering if he really was missing an eye.

He continued down the road until he found himself in Top Side. He took extra effort to notice the whitewashed walls of the connecting brick buildings with their flower baskets. He strolled the cobblestone roads to the market. The sidewalk shops bustled with the energy of the working people. He heaved at their neverending hustle and observed them slaving away.

He took an exhausted breath at their work, like bees in a hive. He could never understand the happiness it brought them. As the fragrances of spices and cookeries lulled his senses, he reflected on all the days he had done this very thing. His troubles and fun felt like a dying memory.

If he died tomorrow, he would be happy. At least he had escaped the fate of this town. Born and raised here, he was determined not to die here too, like the rest. He pitied them. What more could they advance to?

His father's voice scolded his dreams in the back of his mind, endlessly lecturing about his responsibilities to home and family.

What family? Basile snorted. The two of them did not make a family. He reflected on the most recent argument.

Father had sent him to school for nothing. It was a waste of money and time. He was lazy and ungrateful. He had been given a paved road and didn't want it.

The endless trying to explain that not every person's reason for living was the same was useless. He had stopped caring whether or not his father understood. The yelling would continue, but Basile couldn't hear him. It was the same each time, and nothing changed.

Spitefully, he reflected on what his father's response would be to find his son's bed empty this morning. He imagined his red face yelling down at the clueless servants, who had all been fast asleep.

As Basile slipped out, he had relished one last moment to study his mother's picture: her soft, angelic face, just as gentle as he remembered, with her golden curls falling gently down her shoulders. It would be the last time he would see this picture.

"Don't live an everyday life," she had said. "Become much greater than that."

"I'm never coming back." He knew with a pang of guilt his father's words were in some ways true. He was ungrateful and had been given too much. He wished it could have befallen a more deserving person. But there was one thing he had learned in his years: wishing was useless. Action was his friend now.

He was different. His mother understood that. After she passed away, all the color had faded out of their lives.

When he heard of the pirate ship in the harbor, fate pounded in his heart. This is what he wanted: a life on the sea, no one around to order him about, no one to tell him where to be or how to act, to earn and spend his money where and how he pleased. Sure, he could have picked a more respectable lifestyle than pirate. He was certain his fortune lived out there. All he had to do was find it.

Besides, onboard a ship, he could forget this place.

As the sun was well into its descent in the sky, Basile found himself at the docks staring at the silhouette of the ships. Countless evenings he had come here waiting for the chance that his life might change, or maybe for the courage to alter it. The lights of the town sporadically flickered as they were lit, and a whole new world emerged. He started back toward town. While passing a fisher's hut, he heard whispering voices. One said, "Treasure!"

The single word cast a spell on his mind, making his heart skip a beat. He froze in his path. His conscience hesitated to eavesdrop, but his body dashed to a nearby bucket to be closer to the open window.

"She has it hidden," a raspy voice spoke. "Th' ole tavern dog spoke about it last night. Piles 'n piles o' gold, he said, 'n then th' Lady herself showed up."

Lamplight flickered from inside the structure, and a strong smell of sweat and tobacco poured out. "She has a map somewhere?" asked a deeper voice.

"I don't know how you'll get your hands on it," spoke the raspy voice again.

"I've signed up," replied the deeper voice. A long pause filled the room.

"Don't get caught. She was clear last night what she does to those that meddle," The raspy voice cautioned. "I've heard the things she's done to traitors, skinning them alive and dragging them along with hooks for the sharks to feed off." The old fish hut creaked with a gust of passing wind.

"The secret lies with her sister," whispered the deep voice. "I've heard she been missin' fer years now."

"Send us word when you port, and we will follow you. Keep your ears open for anything about the sister or the treasure. We need to watch her and then decide what to do. Figure out her weaknesses."

Basile strained to peek through the hut window but realized they were leaving and ducked back down. When he glanced around the corner, he couldn't catch their faces.

He pressed against the backside of the fish hut, his heart rapping within his chest. "Treasure." His mind was crazed with excitement. His eyes glazed at the thought of gold pieces mounded in piles as tall as him: precious jewels, rubies, diamonds, and emeralds. Gold cups, plates, crowns, and he sat in the middle of it. He reflected about what they said. *Who was this lady and her sister? Interesting*, he thought, but he had no good explanations. The sun burned down into the ocean as he headed back to the boarding house.

Just before reaching his destination, Basile heard a familiar high-pitched whistle. Spinning around he scanned the area. The cobblestone road was empty and the last light of the sun burned against the whitewashed buildings, lighting them in a golden tint. Two buildings down, a figure peeked around the corner. Basile bolted, checking over his shoulders for anyone who might see him. As he slipped behind the building, his childhood friend, Bernard James Strutter, leaned cockily against the wall with the same boyish grin that Basile remembered.

"Benny," Basile cried, arms wide.

"Bass," Benny responded. They hugged and pounded on each other's backs.

"What are you doing here? I didn't even know you were back," Basile said, shaking Benny's shoulders.

"Yeah, got back late last night. Had to help Pa with the rest of the load and then headed over to your place. I found you've gone missing. Figured I'd look in all the regulars before getting too excited." Benny squinted. "What are you doing staying in town?"

Basile stepped away, disappointed that word had already spread even though it was inevitable. Bernard's black, curly hair stood off his head and every inch of his flat, grinning face was covered with freckles. He had always been skinny.

Basile looked back in time to the child version of his lifelong friend and all their adventures. Though Benny looked happy, he failed to hide the concern in his eyes.

"I'm leaving," Basile announced with determination.

Benny's eyebrows furrowed. "Where are you going?"

Basile motioned for them to sit. They perched themselves against the wall with the sun's slivering light shining on them through the alley.

"I signed up on a ship," he blurted with excitement.

"No." Benny's eyes bulged.

"Yes." Basile felt a wave of disappointment. He was capable of leaving. "I signed up this morning. I leave tomorrow."

Benny squinted hard. "But where are you going? And why?"

Basile blinked at the question. He suddenly realized—he didn't know where he was going, but as for the why, he understood clearly. "I'm finally leaving, getting out of here. Going on a real adventure." He watched as Benny stared at the ground processing his words.

"I can't stay here anymore, Benny. I'm ready for something real to happen in my life." They both soaked in the silence as the light transformed into a darker red.

Benny finally broke. "Look, Bass. I know things have been hard for you, but that can change. You don't have to leave to be happy." His eyes wilted like a sad puppy. "What about all our plans?"

Basile shook his head. "If I stay here, things are just going to stay the way they are. I will end up in one of my father's stores, permanently, doing everything that he wants. I don't want to pretend anymore. I need to leave."

"What about Carla Jane?" Benny wagged his eyebrows.

Basile shot a stern look. "Carla Jane does not like me. She likes that I come from a wealthy family. If I didn't have money, she wouldn't be interested."

Benny rolled his eyes.

Basile released a huff. Benny was like his little brother, always around since he could remember. It was hard facing him like this. Basile secretly wished that there had been no goodbyes.

"Come with me!" he pled. "We can be chums on the high seas. We can divide and conquer through the Great Atlantic Northern Kingdoms. A grand adventure will be around every corner, perfectly free to do whatever we wish. We'll build up a great treasure!" His mind reflected back to the conversation in the fish hut. "We will become kings, the richest people in the world, and find our own place somewhere, where no one else can find us. We'll just live until we're old and rotting." He spoke wildly, painting the picture in the sky with his hand.

Benny gave a half smile, but the rest of his face remained serious. Basile knew he wouldn't come, just as Benny had known that someday Basile would leave. The reckoning was here. Basile held back his disappointment. He knew Benny didn't understand. He had grown up much differently.

Benny's family was close, always spending time together as they worked their farm at the edge of his father's land. Father did constant business with them for their goods, so naturally, Basile accompanied and observed this foreign family life. The empty dark hole surfaced inside his chest as he recalled his hated memories of his father and the first time he had met Benny—

The clock ticked. The fire blazed in the hearth. Everything was in its place within his familiar home, but Basile knew differently. Cleaner than normal, the home missed the one thing that made it home. It had been two days since the funeral. All the guests had finally left, but now the walls echoed with a penetrating silence. He sat at the wooden table across from his father, whose size was towering to a ten-year-old. An uncommon thick brown beard grew from his father's face and his hair drooped, covering his brown eyes. His broad shoulders hunched as he ate. The dinner was served for the two.

Basile looked miserably at his food. The servants had disappeared and the clock ticked endlessly, like the beats of his heart. Each beat pounded harder and harder. He felt the urge to rip the clock from the wall and smash it. A cricket chirped from the corner of the room near the fireplace. He tried to pinpoint its location among the cupboards, baskets, pots, and a broom along that wall. The sound of the cricket and the ticking of the clock escalated.

His father burst from the table. Basile jumped as his father stormed over to the corner and kicked repeatedly. The rampage spread. He broke everything within distance of him. The cabinets fell from the wall and all the clay pots shattered. He picked up the broom and split it across his knee. With one half, he batted the contents of the fireplace mantle, including the picture of Basile's mother. Basile shrank back, clenching the base of his chair. Servants peeked through the kitchen door. His father attacked the corner again, his face contorted with anger. He spun, picking up the broken picture frame, yelling at the servants. They scurried in to clean up the mess. He returned to his meal, tossing the picture on the table.

"Eat your food," he ordered as he sat. Basile picked up his fork at last. That night was the first time he met Benny. His family pulled up to the house later that evening.

"Wow, your house is like a castle." Benny's innocent face glowed at the sight of his large stone home.

Basile looked back with hollow indifference. "There's a monster in the basement."

Benny's eyes widened with shock.

Basile's heart leapt at his believing expression. "He comes out only at night." His voice dropped to a whisper. "He storms through the house, breaking everything in his path—"

The harsh memory fueled his conviction. Looking at Benny, he wished to portray the right picture, but words were useless at this point. His father was a monster and he had to break free.

"What ship did you join?" Benny asked, bringing Basile back to reality.

"I don't know, and it doesn't matter."

The sun was nearly gone and the light-blue tones of night seeped through the alley. Benny's face spoke the emotions that Basile felt: a mixture of excitement, contemplation, doubt, and disillusionment all wrapped into one.

"I'm going to find my treasure."

"And what if that doesn't exist?" Benny probed.

His friend's doubt bothered him, but he had to admit that he had asked himself that same question. They had spent their entire childhood dreaming of the places that existed beyond this dusty town. All the old stories that his mother had told him when she was alive powered their minds, sending them deeper into the glamorous places of their imaginations.

"I don't care if it doesn't exist. I'm going anyway. I'm going to find a different life."

Benny looked solemn. "I understand. But at some point, we have to wake up and realize that things are just the way they are and are not bad because of it."

Basile felt disappointed in Benny's lack of ambition.

"Promise me that someday you'll come back." Benny now looked at him with great concern.

Basile remembered his declaration before his mother's picture. He felt the sincere significance behind his words and yet now he was filled with regret for having meant them. "Of course," he lied.

A wide smile stretched across Benny' s face. "I will hold things together for you until you come. I will make sure Carla waits."

The guilt grew inside. "Oh no!" Basile protested. "I'll find someone better than Carla Jane! And don't go telling my father where I've gone."

Benny nodded happily. Basile jumped up with Benny following like always. "I've got to go." Basile's lips pulled into a line and once more they pounded on each other. He walked backward out of the alley, leaving his friend in the shadow. He waved one last time, spun around, and ran to the boarding house.

CHAPTER THREE
The First Adventure

That night Basile's dreams were filled with shadows. He ran in circles through the darkness in search of something important, but he couldn't figure it out. He didn't feel afraid, but panicked, which made it hard to breathe. The darkness spun like a thick cloud blocking his way. Still searching, he kept running, sprinting as fast as he could.

A deep coldness climbed up his arms and legs. Sweat poured off of his brow, but he pushed himself harder and harder as knots built up in his stomach. He had no choice but to continue. If he stopped, he would lose it all.

Suddenly, he found himself screaming out into the darkness. "Where are you?" Over and over again he yelled, waiting for someone to reply and end his suffering. A rumbling answered as the ground underneath him shook and collapsed. He slipped through the rocks. His stomach flew up into his throat and he choked as he grasped for solid ground.

Just then, Basile fell from his bed. He was twisted up in the blankets and dripping with sweat. The bright sun penetrated through the shutters of the boarding house. Sheltering his eyes, disoriented and lost, he collapsed on the cold floor feeling relaxed and relieved. It had only been a dream. He had never had a dream so vivid. It left him empty. He convinced himself that it would soon pass and rose to get dressed. He opened the shutters, letting the morning light fill the room, and felt warmer. It was time for his old life to die.

As he neared the dock, sudden uneasiness waded over him. His entire life was about to change. Each step he took felt significant. Soon his sheltered life on his father's estate would be nothing but a dream. He rounded the corner to the docks and paused. His eyes bulged at the sight of the huge black ship. It was unlike any he had ever seen, majestically grand. The wood was extraordinarily thick and dark. The bow swarmed with naked sirens entangled in the waves of the ocean. Their carvings were so immaculate that they looked lifelike, threatening to come alive and sing their deadly song. The mast held a large white sail adorned with two smaller versions in front and behind. He felt insignificant in comparison. An eerie feeling flowed through him. Disturbed, he walked down the rickety gray dock, suspicious. The dock stretched on and on before him, elongating his view.

A memory flashed. When he was a young boy, his parents had taken him to the south beach. It was his fondest memory, sitting on the shore, feeling the small sand stones beneath him. He loved the water and the way the waves rushed up to touch his feet over and over again. Their constant steady rhythm relaxed him. Slowly he breathed in the salty fresh air while the warmth of the sun glided over him. Looking up, he saw a big black ship dividing the ocean in two, shimmering like a mirage. It surged the shoreline. A menacing black flag flew above white, cloud-like sails. He gazed at it, lulled by its constant flicker. Strange music hummed in his ears, beckoning. His feet ran along the shore. If his mother hadn't rushed him away from the enchantment, he would have let it carry him off. He couldn't divert his eyes as she sheltered him from view, but squinted to see more.

There was a lone silhouette on the helm, gazing out to sea. The rest of the ship's crew bustled around—

Now as he stood on the docks as a man, the strange feeling grew in his chest. He recognized this same ship from his childhood. *Could it be?* He shook his head with doubt, but he felt almost certain as he gazed at it. Now his decision was propelled by more than just his desire to escape. Destiny had brought him here.

Men worked on and off of the ship, carrying crates and rolling barrels. Vaster stood at the end of the long platform leading into the ship. He watched carefully and coordinated all the oncoming supplies, checking them off on the parchment he held in his hand.

He looked up and met Basile's eyes. "What 'cha going to do? Stand there? Get going!" he shouted, annoyed at his lack of movement.

Basile jumped into motion.

"Put yer stuff up in *The Dark Eve* in the crew's quarters on the top level and get back down here! We've got work to do if we are leaving by on time!"

Basile walked right past him up into the ship, touching the wood as he passed. It felt alive, pulsating against his palm. He knew it was only in his mind, but sensed a feeling of belonging. It gave him pause, this sentiment he hadn't felt in a very long time.

The storage level was half-full with supplies already. A staircase stood in the middle of the room, dividing the ship in half. Men passed him angrily as he dodged their paths.

The next level also held supplies: an arsenal. Barrels and barrels of black powder along with cannons adorned the dark walls of the ship. He looked behind him and twitched with surprise. A large wall rose up, making the room considerably smaller than the lower levels. The wall was enormous, with a mural carved into it. Sitting in the exact center was a king in fish-scaled armor. He held a long scepter crowned with an orb that acted like the sun, radiating light into the other parts of the carving. His throne was made of mountains. A small shore lined the back of this throne and the waves curved around the edges of the mural. Strange creatures and elegant fish curved into the water's flow. The king's face was long and cold, with a full beard. His eerie eyes stared out into the room, almost hollow. In the waves of the mural, a ship resembling *The Dark Eve* sat on the left side. On the right was a small piece of sky circled with a crescent moon and a star in the middle.

Basile swallowed nervously. It was the most breathtaking thing he had ever seen. It took him a moment before he climbed the stairs to the next level, where he was shocked again to find two men locked behind iron bars. They didn't even look in his direction but sat hopelessly in their cage. Basile noticed several torture devices strung around the room. He wondered what they must have done to find themselves in such a position. He moved on, feeling a strange pang of guilt for not helping them. He couldn't imagine such devices being used. They must just be for scare tactics.

The next floor had two doors facing each other on opposite sides of the staircase: one was labeled "Mess Hall" and the other "Crew's Quarters."

As he entered the living arrangements, the foul scent of body odor overtook him. He held his nose, retreating back into the hallway. Standing there a minute, he tried to regain the strength and stomach to open the door again. He took a deep breath and looked in.

Endless hammocks hung from the ceiling. "This is not ideal," he affirmed to himself, thinking of his nice feather bed at home. His father had one thing right, but he shook this from his mind. *Sacrifices must be made.* But feelings of remorse pricked him as he entered. Filing down the lines of hammocks, he searched for one that didn't look otherwise inhabited. He found one at the very end of the ship, right next to a circular window. He couldn't believe his luck. This would be the most valued position in the room. He was convinced there would eventually be a squabble for the coveted hammock, but until then he would enjoy his claim. He threw his bag onto the hammock and opened the window before heading out, with hopes that the smell could lessen while he worked.

He hurried back down to the loading floor, trying hard not to look at the doomed prisoners as he passed. He was surprised to find the lower level was almost full. He got by the crew without an angry glance and found Vaster checking off his list back on the dock.

"Did ye get lost in the powder room?" Vaster rolled his eyes, and all the nearby sailors gave a chuckle.

Before he could make allowances for himself, his eyes froze, and he caught his breath. Walking toward them came the most beautiful woman he had ever seen. She was as rare and beautiful as a goddess, with black hair that flowed gently like the tide and dark eyes concealed under a wide-brimmed hat. Her smooth skin looked soft. She radiated a sense of mystery and danger. Gaping at the sight of her, he felt unable to turn his gaze. His pulse raced as sweat dripped down his head. Two men accompanied her. One was a large dark-skinned man that stood taller than him. The size of one of his arms was thicker than Basile's leg. Two one-sided battle axes protruded over each of his bare shoulders. Tattoos spiraled his arms, but the words were unreadable. The other was Basile's same height, but his face was disfigured with a large scar that traveled up the side of his mouth to his ear. His dirty-blond hair hung to the bottom of his ears. He was equipped with only a knife in his belt. The tall dark one was fit enough to be her bodyguard. The other didn't appear too menacing besides the scar and scowl on his face.

As she drew closer, Vaster waved his hand in front of Basile's eyes to wake him from his trance. "Have ye gone dumb or something?" He turned and saw the captain approaching. He slapped the back of Basile's head. Putting a stern finger in his face and with fowl breath he warned, "Don't stare at the captain if ye want to board the ship alive."

"That's the captain?" Basile asked confused slightly dizzy. *She's the captain? How could she be the captain?*

Vaster motioned for him to look at the floor, and he did so obediently.

"Vaster," she called after him. Basile closed his eyes and lowered his head as the captain stopped in front of them. Her voice was velvety smooth, but at the core it demanded authority. Just then, Basile realized what the men in the fish hut had been talking about.

"She," he murmured to himself. She was the "she," and the sister was her sister and they were the pirates they spoke of who had the treasure. He blinked through the realization that one of those men was on this ship and was planning to steal from the captain. His mind grew suspicious of all the crew members.

"Yes, Captain." Vaster stood, revealing his checklist. "Every man is accounted for now"—he glared over at Basile—"and the supplies are almost loaded." Basile glanced up toward her periodically.

She slightly smiled. "What about our prisoners?"

"They are comfy and cozy!" He saluted.

Basile noticed dried blood on her boot. She walked past both men toward the ship, taking no notice of him. He felt her move past and smelled the scent of lavender.

"Don't keep me waiting, Vaster!" she yelled back as she climbed up into the ship through the cargo doors.

"Aye, Captain," he responded faithfully. "Get 'er moving, ye dirty sea rats!" Every man picked up his pace.

Basile stood petrified. "That's the captain?" he finally asked when she was out of hearing range. Vaster blew the whistle around his neck, startling Basile, who was still gazing toward the boat where the captain had boarded.

"Get on the ship. We be a-leavin' now!" he yelled to the crew. He gave Basile a bewildered look and once again slapped him on the back of the head. "'Course she's the captain! Didn't I say captain?"

Basile fell forward from the force of the slap, which was much harder this time.

"Boy, I have a feeling..." Vaster said as he pointed to his own large belly. Basile's eyes followed his finger down his stained shirt. "...deep down in here..." Vaster gestured to himself, motioning to the pit of his stomach. He stepped closer, looking Basile square in the eyes, their noses almost touching. "...that ye ain't gonna live very long. NOW GET THOSE BARRELS ON THE SHIP!" He pointed to the rest of the supplies being loaded.

Basile felt like a child being scolded as he rushed over and helped with the cargo. He loaded barrels at what he thought was an impressive pace, instantly pleased as he worked alongside the crew. The same man with the eye patch from the tavern walked by, giving him another dirty look and spitting on his boots. Basile made a mental note to stay clear of him.

Aside from the two men who boarded with the captain—Scar and Jennings—the crew wasn't all that impressive. They wore dirty, plain clothes, and their faces were weathered from the sun. Basile nearly fell over by the scent of half of them. Not one went by his given name, and formal introductions were frowned upon. One spat tobacco juice in his hand as he offered it, and it took Basile all of his strength not to lose his stomach. He came to the quick realization that most people in the pirating world didn't bother with manners. His hope of sailing on a pirate ship with newfound friends faded, but it didn't defeat him. He tried to remember their names when he heard them shouted out. He repeated them in his mind whenever possible, memorizing faces, starting with a tall skinny bloke that looked less intimidating than the rest, Pole. He couldn't control their manners or hygiene, but he could at least try to be socially groomed.

◇◇◇

Acantha watched from the main deck as Jennings stood beside her. "What is he doing among the crew?" she asked.

"Captain?"

"That young chap." She nodded in Basile's direction. He stuck out from among the regular sailors as they loaded a stack of barrels onto the ship. His golden-brown hair was parted in the middle, hanging just above his eyes to make his square face look more angular.

"Who is he?"

"That would be Basile, Captain," Jennings's voice boomed. He was a tower of dark muscle and flesh next to her.

"He seems a little too wholesome for the job," she said.

Jennings nodded. "Yes, Captain. Shall I throw him off?"

She thought about this, but judged against it. "Tell Vaster to keep an eye on him," she said while watching him work. He seemed too content to be doing the menial tasks assigned him, as if the work were an escape from a prison—unaware that he was walking straight into another one. By the looks of him a crueler one. His appearance told clearly that he was not raised in a poor home. *Upper-middle class was more like it*, she thought. He was tall, golden, and not scrawny. A huge grin adorned his face. She felt the urge to smack him. No person had reason to be that happy, but reality would soon wipe his smile clean off his face. False moments of happiness were meant to be fleeting.

Jennings left to report her words. She watched him as he told Vaster, who looked up to her and nodded.

"I would hate to see him fall overboard," she said smugly to herself, hoping it would happen. Then she retired to her quarters under the helm of the ship. She longed to rest and forget the burdens inside her, but last night's dreams kept her awake and ready for action.

Basile reminded her of a time when she had been freed from restriction. Everyday tasks felt common enough to regular people, but to her they were liberation. The memories were as clear and sharp as the ocean around her, as vivid as when they had happened. Her memory flashed back to a town deep in the mountains, hidden behind some hills in the distance, an hour's walk away from the seaside village. Dome huts surrounded her, made of woven sticks and mud. The high grass between the huts stretched far. Two large mountains sat to the north, with a swamp separating them. She remembered how bright the stars were at night, constantly shining in her mind, as she lay in the tall grass, hidden from view.

She jerked back to reality before her memories went too far. While her mind was relaxed from the remembrance, her face showed no sign of it. She sat at her desk and pulled out her charts from the long drawer. Thousands of charts occupied the wall across from her, each in their own little hole in the shelving. Large red X's adorned all the maps on her desk, representing all the places they had searched. Her fingers gently touched the ones closest to her. All of those places represented failure.

"Damn her," she muttered and shoved the charts off the table. "I'm going to kill her when I find her." She reached down into her desk drawer and pulled out a bottle of rum, along with a small-stemmed glass.

Pouring her drink, she barely allowed it to fill before she emptied it, just to fill and empty the glass again, each time trying—with no relief—to fill the hole inside.

A knock rapped at the door. She put the bottle back. "Enter."

Vaster walked through, noticing the glass in her hand. "We're ready, Captain."

Acantha nodded. "Take us to sea."

"What course do we set?"

"It doesn't really matter," she mumbled, feeling all the pressure in her head, waiting for the rum to numb it.

"Captain?" He looked at her, bewildered.

"NORTH!" she shouted.

He took a step back, fearing her frustration.

"I'm not sure, Vaster," she said with defeat. Maybe it was the rum, or maybe she was just tired of looking. She held her head in her hands. "I don't know where else to look."

He picked up the charts on the floor and set them gently on her desk. She took her hands from her eyes and peered once again at them.

"I know we've looked hard every place that we could think—and not think—her to be. But maybe now we need to tread into unknown areas. We might have to go to a deeper source to know," he whispered. He didn't want to upset her, but the subject he was about to bring up was bound to.

She glanced up at him and then to the charts as if she hadn't been listening, but she had. She always listened.

"I mean," he continued, "more than just the two blokes ye have down in the prison cells. Captain, ye know they have nothin' to squawk." He held his hat nervously in front of him. They had been searching for a year for Jennet, and her trail was cold. There had been no sight of her in all their time searching. Not one hint of her whereabouts or of her ship, *Le Voleur*.

"You've been with me a long time, Vaster." She looked up at him.

"Aye, Captain, forty blessed years I have." He nodded with reverence.

"What is it that you are suggesting?" She gave him a stern look. "I know you do not know all of my secrets."

He nodded again in compliance.

"But you have been wise enough not to wonder. And I have left you alive because of that."

He did not dare say anything.

"Why can't I find her?" She slammed her hand on the desk. Vaster jumped, startled by her sudden reaction. "If she were dead, I would know." She pounded her chest, searching for something—anything—that would deter the feelings that her sister was alive. She had done this, time and time again, and each time she knew that her sister still lived, by no other evidence than her intuition.

He nodded, agreeing again. There had been times in their travels where she had diverted disasters based on her intuition alone. He had never once disregarded it.

She stood and paced the length of her quarters. Vaster watched, hesitantly taking a step closer and trying to reach out to her, though he didn't dare to. "Captain, what about a soothsayer o-or..." He stuttered, trying hard to not anger her. If he mentioned it, she would be mad. "The Seeing Eye," he finally spoke, flinching.

She stopped and pinched the bridge of her nose, cringing at his suggestion. Anger welled up inside, but to suppress it she took a breath, making herself relax. *Has it come to that?* she asked herself.

"I know," she replied, exhaling heavily, giving in to the last option she had ever wanted to use to find her sister. A flood of disdain overtook her, but in her heart she knew she needed help. She had already wasted enough time looking.

Jennet had not shown up at the last drop-off. The dragon raid had been the last time Acantha had seen her. If she had deserted, then it was her job to find out and bring her back. If she was dead, then to bury her. If she was captive, then to kill whoever stood in her way.

Vaster took a step back in shock. "I wasn't all too sure that oracles existed until just now." He stood in amazement at her response.

"Yes, Vaster, they do exist." She found his expression to be childish. "I know of at least one oracle that exists." Her headache was easing, but she felt a new tiredness behind her eyes. "You only need one."

"I've heard ye make mention of one before." He looked nervous, not sure what he would get away with talking about. "But ye seemed terribly angry about it."

"I AM! It goes against myself to go there and ask her for help!" She closed her eyes in defeat. Walking over to her wall of charts, she reached to the very top corner and pulled out a chart wrapped in a bamboo mat. She brought it over to the desk and gently unrolled it. Vaster shuffled to the desk, examining the map. The territory consisted of many islands that swirled around each other, making watery pathways in between them, much like a large maze. The entire region was surrounded by a mountainous guarding wall where there was only one entrance point.

The details of the map were intricate. As he looked close, certain parts of the islands swirled into animated motion. One small side of a little island had a picture of sirens, ghastly half serpent and humanoid demons that writhed, flickering like fire on the shore. Vaster almost touched the map to make sure his eyes weren't deceiving him, but drew back when a song vibrated from their tiny mouths. At first, it was sweet but then turned dark, along with their eyes. From behind their sweet lips, fangs emerged, and they jumped out as if they could leave the page, making Vaster jump back. Frowning, he looked up at Acantha, who watched him with amusement.

"Captain, what dark magic is this?" He slowly drew back, staring at the enchanted map. The Oracle's pointed, sheer mountain was in the heart of the maze, next to a cove with a flickering sun behind it. The island looked impenetrable with the large cliffs that guarded it and only a small shoreline to enter onto. The jungle around it was depicted as a paradise.

The map pointed out the many obstacles: rocks fell from the cliffs, a whirlpool drained down one of the paths, and another had pillars of rock protruding out of the water, making the way almost impossible to maneuver a ship through. He searched for a straight clean path to the middle, but there was none that he could tell would work.

She took out another map from under the first that charted their journey. "Take us to the Scattered Isles," she called it while pointing to it on the map, finalizing their destination.

Vaster replied, "I have a feeling this is one of those journeys that most don't come back from."

"Not many have. The maze is only the first challenge. If one survives, there are other trials that are in store on the main island."

"Trials, Captain?"

"No more, Vaster. I'll be the one to worry about it."

"Yes, Captain." He turned to leave, so many questions lurking in his mind, wishing to look closer at the intricate maps.

Acantha walked straight to bed and threw herself onto it. "Wait." Her muffled words were barely audible. He paused and faced her. She lifted her head from under her hat. "Do keep a close eye on Mr. Basile. I don't want to be bothered by his presence on the ship."

Vaster nodded and left.

It had been a long time since she had been reminded of her past life. She didn't like the idea of having someone on the ship that could conjure up her memories. She could very well just throw him overboard. This made her chuckle inside as she imagined the look on his face. But she hesitated to even consider it, which made her even more upset. It only meant one thing to her: change was coming. Just like a new smell in the air, she could sense change was coming. Now was the waiting game. To figure it all out, time would tell what importance of letting him stay on board would be. It all hit very close to home. Somehow, it was personal, and no good could come from that. Her mind swirled alive at the thought.

She would never fall asleep now. She needed to throw someone overboard.

She jumped to her feet and went to catch Vaster, opening the cabin door hastily. "Vaster!"

Both he and Basile stood right outside and jumped at her abruptness. She hadn't expected them there.

"Yes, Captain?" Vaster dutifully asked.

She paused to look at Basile up close for the first time. He glanced back but turned his gaze from hers obediently. She looked to Vaster. "Throw our captives overboard when we get to sea," she commanded. She looked back to Basile, his brow wrinkled with concern. "They are useless."

"Aye, Captain!" Vaster responded, delighted. Basile's jaw dropped. With no sign of showing it, she enjoyed his innocent expression. She turned back into her chambers to finally rest. Normally, she would have thrown someone off board for such a reaction as Basile's. He was like a child on the boat learning that the world isn't as polite as he was raised to be.

He's too good, she thought.

On the deck, Vaster directed Basile around the ship. "For ye to survive long enough to be useful, I'll show ye the ropes." He patted Basile on the shoulder. "Up there," he pointed to the helm, "is the captain's throne. She be sensitive about her area. Best not go up unless it's urgent or ye are summoned. In the second case, I would probably just throw myself overboard, 'cuz that's likely why she be a'callin' ye."

The elaborate staircase led to a large deck where Jennings was at the wheel. Near the helm stood a large table, which also served as a wooden shelf underneath that held dozens of nautical charts in little wooden square cubbyholes. Everything about the ship was thick and sturdy. Basile slid his hand over the smooth railing, marveling at the indestructibility of it. He could not imagine anything being able to sink it. He thought of the captain, a woman. A stronger type of person should be captain of a ship like this.

The whole ship was rich in detail. Everywhere he turned there were detailed carvings of the sea, strange fish, coral, and plants shaped perfectly in the doors and moldings, all of which said everything about who the captain should be. Even the half-naked sirens at the helm seemed alive with the movement of the ship. S*he definitely could be one of those*, he thought.

"What kind of wood is this?" Basile asked as he stroked the railing, the thick black wood smooth under his hand. He looked close at the very fibers of the grain. "How did a person as young as her get all of this? She couldn't be much older than I am."

He was answered by a swift slap across the back of his head. He looked up, astonished. His mind was sent back to being disciplined as a child, and he half-expected to find his father standing behind him glaring down in anger. He stared instead at Vaster, who shook his finger.

"There is one rule ye must follow while aboard this ship: no questions. NO QUESTIONS!" Vaster shoved him along for the rest of his tour. He introduced Basile to the bucket and the mop, which were to be his constant companions while aboard.

"Ye are the bona fide deck boy."

Basile scowled angrily at the word "boy."

Vaster sneered back at him. "Which means," he continued, "that ye do whatever we need ye to do. That means wash clothes, run errands, do this, do that!" Vaster's hand flew around the ship. "Sometimes there will be work for ye, and sometimes there won't. The only thing ye need to do in times like that is to stay out of the way." He turned a circle, looking around the ship. "This floor is yers! I want it to sparkle. The boat tour has ended."

Basile stared down at the cleaning tools and then at the other sailors readying the ship for sea. They worked simultaneously on the riggings and sails in silence.

Even though he would rather be doing something more exciting, he was happy to be on his first adventure. Vaster had foretold this would be his only quest, that he had just one adventure in him—whether it was true or not, he didn't care. He was free. The excitement of being on a large pirate ship surged through him.

The ship cut through the ocean, leaving the town he grew up in. Everything was the way it should be. The salty, fresh smell of the air, the sea gulls calling, the crew members busy at work around him.

He scrubbed the floors underneath the crew's feet, listening to their talk. Tall tales, he decided once he heard the word "dragon." All about finding mountains of gold, fighting demons in the sea, and conquering great storms—stories worthy of telling. He wrinkled his face in disbelief at the mention of their hidden gold. It must have been a metaphor: they looked and smelled too foul to have any riches among them. He still felt uneasy about the captain's orders concerning the two men in the prison. Locating Vaster on the deck, he casually mopped his way over.

"She didn't mean it about throwing them overboard, did she?" Basile stood and looked out at the ocean as he spoke.

"What are ye talkin' about now? Don't ye ever shut up?" Vaster rolled his eyes, annoyed, and continued to loop the rope in his hands, shaking his head.

"The two in the cell," Basile said, finding it unbelievable that he had forgotten.

Vaster slapped his forehead, "Oh, empty turtle shells! I forgot!" He shouted at Jennings and Scar on helm. "Need to dispose of the baggage!" They both left their posts and went below deck.

"What?" Basile's face stretched in shocked. "What did they do?"

"NO MORE QUESTIONS!" Vaster pointed a stern finger in his face again. "They be talkin' too much about the captain in public."

"That's it?" Basile was mortified, his face flushed. "They said her name in public?" The idea that she would put someone to death just for that was ludicrous. "There has to be more!"

Vaster stood face-to-face with him, squinting with annoyance. "Watch yer mouth, boy, or ye'll find yerself afloat as well."

Basile looked away, feeling that injustice was about to prevail. But he had no influence here. He was powerless. Others watched the scene, faces weathered and rough, no emotion of protest, even a slight amount of pleasure. He felt disgusted. Vaster's warnings were empty. After living alone with his father, he could distinguish an empty threat from the real. But he did sense he was wearing on Vaster's nerves. Basile did not appreciate being hit on the head like a child. Other than that nuisance, Vaster was harmless. So why was he bothering and bossing him so much? It must be that Vaster was accountable for him onboard.

Jennings and Scar emerged with the two culprits. The crew members cheered and gathered on the deck. The prisoners dragged their feet, exhausted and scared out of their minds. Basile felt sorry for them. They were brought straight up to Vaster.

"Did they spill their guts down below?" he asked Jennings and Scar.

Scar chuckled. "Like babies choking up milk."

"And…?" Vaster tapped his foot, waiting impatiently for their reply.

"They don't know anything about the captain or her sister." Jennings smiled. Both he and Scar were satisfied.

"Well, throw 'em overboard." Vaster waived his hand, as if discarding them was much like tossing scraps to the dogs.

The two men struggled against their captors. "Look, no hard feelin's," Vaster assured them as they were forced over to the railing. "We just have a weight limit."

Jennings and Scar dangled them over the boat. The two men screamed and wailed for mercy. One pleaded that he had a wife and children. Basile looked around for a merciful face, someone who felt the same as he did and could intervene. He found no one. As the two men wailed, the crew cheered even louder, feeding on their torment. He watched in horror as the men struggled for survival. But their fight was useless.

Just then, a voice pierced the commotion. "Wait!" Basile's heart relaxed in a flood of relief. As the crowd parted, Acantha stood against the far railing.

Vaster ran to her side. "Orders have changed, Captain?"

She nodded once and walked through the crowd toward the bound prisoners. Their faces filled with fear and hope.

"We need a new apprentice to the cook." She walked past them and leaned on the railing. She glanced behind Basile. He looked back at the door to the mess hall. A small, old figure peered out through the crack of the door.

"I will give one of you the chance to fill the position." Acantha nodded to Scar and Jennings. They let their captives go. Jennings ordered a few nearby sailors to work. They left and returned with the plank. After removing a portion of the railing, they fastened the plank off the edge of the ship. The two prisoners watched with a sense of impending doom as sailors cut their bonds and placed swords in their hands.

One, a larger man with a thick brown beard, stood forward to talk to the captain. "But we are family, Lady." His voice shook as he spoke. "I can't kill my own family." The skinny prisoner looked down at the ground. They both wore common clothes, nothing special made them stand out.

Acantha studied the skinny fellow as if she were diagnosing him. She walked around both of them and perched herself on the railing. "Hess and Sam, right?"

Hess nodded.

"Brothers?"

"No, cousins."

"Well, it's your choice. You both can either willingly jump off the ship, or one can stay." She said.

Basile felt sick. What point was there to make them choose? Why not keep them both? Hess looked to Sam, who looked scared out of his mind. The crew around them looked on edge, waiting for action.

"But I'm afraid to inform you," Acantha continued, "that your cousin doesn't feel the same."

Hess turned, his brow furrowed with worry, just as Sam pointed his sword to his throat. A look of compete betrayal and anger flooded his round face.

"We are cousins!" he barked.

"I don't want to die." Sam shook uncontrollably, backing Hess toward the plank. Hess threw up his sword in defense.

"You see, Hess," Acantha said from her comfortable place on the rail, "there is no trust between anyone, especially family."

Hess knocked Sam's sword away with his own. In the next moment, they were upon each other like dogs fighting over a bone. Basile gaped in horror. Sam consistently pushed Hess toward the plank, and Hess tried to fight back by blocking his strikes. The crew yelled, crazed as they batted at each other. Hess lost ground step by step, moving farther back onto the plank while trying to keep his balance. Finally, he willingly scooted to the end of the plank, far enough that Sam had no choice but to step onto it himself to reach him. The crew members cheered as Sam edged out.

"You're going to have to run me through, Sam, to get me off," Hess said. Sam carefully balanced his way out. As soon as he was a solid distance from the ship, Hess attacked. Between their swinging swords they worked hard to keep their balance. Hess used his weight to move the plank under their feet, but it did not throw Sam. In a striking attack, he caught Hess across the face with the tip of his sword. Hess jumped back holding the long gash on his cheek. Sam withdrew a step, and in that moment Hess charged him, knocking him clear off. He flew through the air. In the same movement Hess reached for his hand to catch him. Sam fell, face wide with fear, into the cold, icy water. The crew cheered at Hess's success. Basile watched in pain. Hess was full of heartbreak, demoralized by his own actions.

Acantha remained emotionless. She stood on the railing, holding onto the ropes. The crew quieted upon her movement. "You are welcome aboard."

Hess looked up to her with disgust, "I have a family." He looked out to the crew, judging them. Basile felt ashamed to be among them.

"You know the way off, then," Acantha said, uncaring.

Hess grimaced at the water and the moving ship, deliberating his choices. He took an unrestrained jump, flying out into the frigid sea. He cried out as he fell. Basile cringed as the screams silenced when they hit the water. Guilt filled him. He clasped his hand over his mouth, shaking his head. He glanced back again to the old man peeking behind the door, but he was gone.

Acantha turned to the crew. "There is no such thing as loyalty, not among family or friend. When it comes to life or death, all the cards are thrown into the air. To all of you new crew members among us, there is only one thing you can trust: if you cross me you will die. I will see to it personally. If you keep your heads down and do what is asked, you will be paid more than you can imagine. This job is not for the weak. If you can't handle it, throw yourselves overboard." Her voice was condescending upon Basile's ears. "Now get back to work."

All the men shouted and turned in the same moment. It was as if the interlude had not occurred. Acantha jumped off the railing and walked straight to the helm.

Basile shook his head, confounded. She didn't care about anyone. While he believed her words, he had a hard time imagining her killing anyone. She had the capability of ordering it to be done. She had dragged the evil out of two innocent men and made them a spectacle for the ship's entertainment. Basile looked down into the water for the abandoned figures, finding nothing but sea. "They weren't guilty of anything. They were just executed."

Vaster, who stood near him, placed his arm around Basile's shoulders. "Look… how do ye say this? Here," he waved around the boat, "we live by different rules than out there. Our principles are a little more rough around the edges." He curved his hands in the air making a silhouette of a lady.

He thought about it. "But solid, mind ye." Again he made a silhouette of a lady, but much fatter. "If ye want to stay alive, ye'd better learn to live by them. And that wasn't an execution. There would've been sharks if it was an execution. They 'could' make it back if they're good enough swimmers. Probably not the fat one, though.

"Plus, it's good for morale!" He lifted his arms and grumbled, "Arghhh." An echoing comeback rang from all decks.

Basile shook his head. "I'm in a crazy world."

"That is the first thing ye have got right!" Vaster said. "Now go get some grub."

Basile walked slowly away from the railing of the ship toward the deck doors. All of this was foreign to him but also unimaginably crazy. He had dreamed of working side by side with sailors who travelled as companions, adventuring into the wild unknown, swords in hand, with common camaraderie. He had never even thought principles would be a problem, and of all of this, she, a woman, a beautiful woman, was the captain of a large, stunning ship. This mystery was the grand puzzle of it all. "Never heard of her," he said to himself as he looked back at the captain on deck.

He walked through the deck doors into the narrow hallway that led to the stairs. On one side were the crew's quarters and on the opposite side was the mess. He opened this door to a large room with rows of tables and chairs. In the back, a small square window and doorway gave access to the kitchen. The old man looked up through the window, taking note of him and then going back to his work. Pole bent over his food, eating. He hadn't looked up as Basile entered. The gangly pirate had a narrow, less intimidating face and hair that resembled straw. A long table at the end of the room held stacks of plates, utensils, and a large pot.

Basile walked up to the table as the cook shuffled through the kitchen doorway. The old man was hunched over and the skin on his face drooped, spotted with age. He held a dead black-and-white-speckled chicken, whose head hung lifeless as he stroked its feathers. The old coot made his way behind the table to serve. Basile picked up one of the plates and met in front of the pot. The old man ladled a large portion of stew.

"Thank you." Basile's voice radiated against the silence and the old man squinted up for the first time. His eyes were glazed and fuzzy with no normal color. Basile almost jumped in shock. Could he see at all? The old man didn't speak but simply shuffled back to the kitchen.

Basile went to where Pole sat and plopped down in the chair opposite him. Pole paused and then resumed eating. Basile was hesitant to try the brown, thick stew at first, but found it to be surprisingly good.

He reflected on the captain's face as she ordered Vaster concerning the two prisoners, as she ordered their deaths—there was no emotion in her eyes and no immoral response. When she had turned her gaze on him, her dark, hard eyes demanded superiority over him.

How had such a person as rare as she become so hard and cold?

He felt instantly lost. He knew nothing about this world. He sensed the truth in his father's words, though pride still would not allow him to follow them. He had to be able to choose what he was to become, even if he ended up worse for it. He was starting to feel uncertain about his decision to become a pirate.

He studied the sailor across from him. "So how long have you been on the ship?"

Pole lifted his head and stared almost as hard as the captain had. Basile inwardly shrunk. Pole went back to eating.

"I've just signed up myself." Basile waited for some reaction. Pole continued eating and Basile took a bite. "This is a very interesting ship, don't you think? And I've never heard of a woman being a captain before."

This time, Pole looked up at him with seriousness. Even the old man glanced through the square window, but then they both went back to their business.

Basile sunk with defeat. "Well, at least the food is good."

A grunt answered from the kitchen.

"What's your name?" asked Pole.

His heart jumped with delight that someone was willing to talk to him. "Basile."

Pole looked him up and down. "You talk too much, Basile." Another grunt agreed from the kitchen.

Basile sulked down at his plate.

"And don't talk about the captain," Pole warned him. "Don't even think of her as a woman."

Basile's eyes widened. "But she *is* a woman."

"Not as the likes as you've ever seen," Pole said.

That statement rang true. Basile had not been interested in the girls back at home. They were plain and laughed all the time as if everything were funny. He found them fake and empty. There appeared to be nothing fake about the captain.

"Six years," Pole said.

Basile was pulled back to the conversation. "Excuse me?"

"I've been on the ship for six years." Pole continued to eat his stew. Basile looked back to the square window into the kitchen and caught the old man peering at them. The old cook ducked out of sight again.

Pole spoke again. "Mort."

"What?" Basile asked, confused.

"The cook, his name is Mort. Been here longer than anyone I know."

"Oh, I see." His head spun trying to grasp all the differences and awkwardness of his present situation.

"If you keep your head down and your mouth shut," Pole said, "you're more likely to live."

"I have all the intentions in the world to live," Basile stated. Pole looked again at his face. Basile studied his splotchy skin. He had to be in his twenties. And while his expression was as hard as stone, there was some feeling in his dark-brown eyes.

"Why did you sign up?" Basile asked.

"Didn't have much place to go. Mum died when I was young. Pop took hot iron to my mouth for crying." Pole stuck out his long tongue. The entire surface was smooth with massive scarring. "Don't taste nothing anymore."

Basile's eyes bulged. And he thought he'd had it bad.

"I've been around all sorts of ships," Pole said, "never staying too long in one place till now."

"That is horrible," Basile said. Pole shrugged it off as if it meant nothing.

How had these people become so unfeeling?

Pole finished his meal and left, dropping his plate in a bucket before exiting. Basile sat abandoned with the clanking noises of the kitchen in the background.

CHAPTER FOUR
The Dark Eve

The ship worked like a clock. After two weeks, Basile was getting the hang of things. Every man had his place and time. His rhythm meant staying out of the way of everyone else. He took in every word spoken among the crew. But mostly he found himself watching *her*.

When the day was over and it was dark enough that he could not be seen, Basile observed her. She was captivating. Framed by the evening sky, she took her post on the helm, like a queen upon her throne. She always wore a heavy ruby pendant around her neck and an emerald ring, all she need was a crown. Almost every evening she would be there, staring out, watching the sunset, always lost in thought, with her set-in-stone expression. It was the easiest time for him to get closer and watch.

What filled her mind? She was a total paradox, and the never-ending questions plagued him. Basile's suspicions of her grew. She was locked away from any interpretation. The only other place she went was in her chambers, where she spent long durations, even days. The three closest to her at any time were Vaster, Jennings, and Scar, but she still kept a comfortable distance. Her conversations were direct and to the point, never personal.

How could she be the captain of this ship? Why didn't anyone know anything about her? Why was it forbidden to talk about her?

Asking Vaster would just result in punishment. He was completely devoted to her, and lately, her patience was thin. Vaster was always tiptoeing around her trying not to ignite her anger.

Basile sat once again in the dining room of the ship. Pole sat across, assuming his defensive position above his food as he slowly ate. Stew was on the menu everyday, with slight changes.

"Well, this is monotonous," Basile said.

Pole looked up with a confused face and then back to his food.

A black-and-white-speckled chicken hopped up on the table. Basile jumped. The chicken bobbed toward him, pecking the table's surface. Basile tried shooing him away, but fowl continued undeterred.

Old Mort shuffled out. Pole and Basile watched as he wobbled up to the table with a large butcher knife, as though ready to swing it into a corpse of meat. He drove the knife hard into the end of the table, right next to Basile. Basile saw his own reflection in the blade. Mort picked up the chicken, which went completely limp in his arms. The crazy old cook shuffled again to the kitchen, stroking the chicken's back as he went.

"Is that the dead chicken?" Basile whispered to Pole.

"Don't bother Mr. Kinkles," Pole whispered back to him.

"Mr. Kinkles? You mean the chicken?"

Pole gave him a long hard stare. "Every person on this ship has their quirk. Leave it alone and you'll be better off."

Basile rolled his eyes and continued eating. Trying to understand anything here was a crime. "Why is everyone so secretive?"

Pole lifted his head. "You don't belong."

"I do too. I was approved to be among the crew."

Pole shook his head. "But that doesn't make you one of us."

"Well," Basile said, exasperated, "what do I have to do to be part of the crew?"

Pole finished up his plate and looked squarely at him. "You have to prove yourself first."

"I'm willing. What exactly do I have to do?"

"Time does it, for all the newcomers." said Pole as he sat back in his chair, relaxing.

Basile rolled his eyes again. Everything in life was subject and weighed with an amount of time to be paid.

The uninhabited chairs shifted. Pole instantly sat up. "We'd best get up top." He moved to the door.

Basile grabbed his plate and scarfed the rest of his food.

They both rushed through the deck door. The day had been bright and sunny with a strong breeze and blue skies. Now the wind thrashed the boat along with the water. Dark, billowing clouds furrowed overhead, and the deck crew scrambled to maintain control.

Vaster shouted orders while working on one of the riggings. "Reduce the sails!"

Pole flew into action among them. Basile followed. "What do I do?"

"Get out of the way, or go below." Pole shooed him.

Basile retreated behind the staircase that led to the quarter deck. The sky succumbed to the darkness of the storm, and lighting flashed thickly through it, followed by such a booming crack that the air shook around them. The rain pelted down. The crew scurried. He had never seen such fierceness, the wind and water trying to swallow them whole. Several men fell overboard, and the rest of the crew clung for life, trying to maintain their balance. Basile panicked and held tight to the stair railing.

But through all the chaos, the captain remained calm. She lay against the ropes looking out into the disaster. The violent movements of the ship did not shake her. She closed her eyes as the crew struggled against the turmoil. All the while, Vaster shouted orders.

"We're gettin' the sails down, Captain, but we should turn from the storm's path."

"No, Vaster. Keep the course."

He grimaced at her. "But Captain!"

She glared at him. "Keep the course."

Vaster left, looking back at her on the ropes with an uneasy expression. He shook his head, bewildered, and shouted into the fray. "Keep yer legs goin'! We head into the storm."

"It won't take us down," she muttered. The violence intoxicated her. She closed her eyes. The storm inside her had no end in sight. Soon this one would be gone and she would be confined once again.

CHAPTER FIVE
Wraiths Starboard

Basile woke the next morning by the staircase with someone standing over him. With the sun shining brightly behind the silhouette, he couldn't make out who it was.

"Rough night, Mr. Basile."

Her voice was smooth and firm. She rarely spoke beyond the helm. As inviting as she sounded, he could only steal a glance before looking away. She shifted her weight and the sun's rays bore down upon him, blinding. He squinted and brought his hand to his face to block out the light. He tried to speak but couldn't, his throat sore from the seawater. He tasted his lips. They cracked and bled with the slightest movement.

Sitting up, he brushed himself off. His legs were weak and every muscle ached. She backed up as he stood. The message was received clearly, and he took a half step back, dizzy as he gave her the distance she required. He glanced out to the sea: it was calm, unlike its tantrum last night. He stood straight, exposed. Her dark, judging eyes scanned him. He was weak and a liability, but still there he stood.

"Was that your first storm?" It was more rebuke than question.

He stood taller, facing the uneasiness, and took her gaze. He had never cowered, although he had never met a challenge like this. Fear crept up his chest, but he held his ground, trying hard not to show anything. The decks of the ship were empty and there he was, face to face with the most feared pirate captain in the world, at least according to the stories of the crew.

Their stories painted a dark and murderous spirit embodied in a beautiful goddess stature. And so far she was all those things. In that moment he decided to be someone of consequence instead of the scurrying rat who ran from the flooding water. He waited, half expecting her to pull her swords from their sheaths and thrust them into his belly. It felt like he stood in judgment before God himself. What consequences followed this judgement?

◇◇◇

It was refreshing to her for him not to shy away like a coward. He was bold, yet she could still see the apprehension behind his eyes. She read his mind like an open book. Why she felt the need to keep him aboard had been a great, silent mystery. She did not like the unknown, but she could see his character was good, a change from the rest of the bunch.

She dropped her shoulders, which was her only indication that it was all right for him to stand on the same ground as her. "If you haven't taken your stance before the storm comes"—she paused as he relaxed at the lack of anger in her voice—"you might as well just throw yourself overboard."

During the most ferocious storm of his life, she'd stood calmly in it, firm against the ropes, holding tight to keep her position, and yet peaceful amidst the rage. Against such persecution, she looked rejuvenated. *What was she implying?* Her stance in the storm was that she was equal to it. And while she had stood her ground, he had hidden behind the stairs.

She turned and walked up the grand staircase to the helm. His heart pounded as she left.

Vaster stood by her side, taking in every command as if God had given it. Basile found his mop and bucket and continued to observe her. Occasionally she caught his gaze and he would divert his focus to the floor. She was aware of him the whole time. Though she had never spoken to him until now, he felt a strange connection to her. Not romantic in any way, though she was more than beautiful. He felt suddenly loyal, as though he could trust her with himself and everything he had, including his life.

"Wraiths starboard!" shouted the sailor in the crow's nest.

Basile looked over the starboard side of the ship to the small speck in the distance. The captain, who now stood astern, walked across and peered through her looking glass. Once again she glanced down at him and slightly smiled, almost devious as she shouted the orders.

"Take it down."

Men flew to their positions on the ship's deck. Jennings turned the ship toward the wraith vessel.

Basile's heart jumped and lodged in his throat. He ran to Vaster, who now stood at the bottom of the stairs. "What are we doing? What is a wraith?"

Vaster looked at him, confused. "Wraiths, red-skinned savages. That wraith ship—" He pointed at it in the distance. "We are takin' her down!" he growled with happiness.

"But why?"

Vaster shook his head, baffled. "Because! We're pirates!" The men of the ship worked the ropes to maneuver the vessel.

"Ready the cannons!" Acantha shouted from the stern. Small flaps opened on the front, sides, and back of the ship. The cannons on the front and back had three linked together that rotated. Basile turned pale. He held to the ship's railing while everyone buzzed with excitement around him.

"What should I do?" he asked Vaster.

Vaster looked him up and down crazily. "Prepare yerself to kill some wraiths."

Basile's eyes widened. His mind raced. *I can't kill somebody.* He looked around for a weapon. The ship was a blur and he couldn't focus.

They followed the wraith ship. As the distance lessened, he could see the wraith crew scurry around. Their ship was old and tattered. The sails were white, but covered with a brownish-red dust. They were trying to outrun *The Dark Eve* and didn't stand a chance. The pirate ship overtook them in no time. The wraiths started to open their cannon doors.

"They're preparin' to defend themselves!" Vaster yelled to the crew on deck. They all cheered.

"Destroy their stern," Acantha shouted. Vaster gave the orders to the front cannons. They blew their hot iron with booming noise. Basile covered his ears. The cannonballs struck, and the wraith ship combusted in all directions. The cannons continued to fire. Wraiths fell from the decks until the ship appeared to have no life left. *The Dark Eve* surged up next to the wraith ship's port side.

"Board 'em!" Acantha yelled from the helm, but half of the crew was already over there, swinging across on hanging ropes. The red natives ran around in the chaos. Their faces fumed and contorted with anger. Basile shrunk back at their foreign, wild behavior as they battled. He could not move but only stood as witness to the battle and bloodshed. The natives attacked in any way possible.

A shadow travelled above him. Acantha flew, swinging on a rope overhead. She soared over, sliding onto the deck—rolling through a battling mate and wraith. The movement was so fluid, she rose up statuesque among the pandemonium. The combat swirled around her like time had slowed. A wraith charged her. She withdrew her swords and in a crossing motion ran them down his front. He hunched over and she spun, slicing his back as well. As the wraith fell to the floor, bullets flew past her face. Her expression was calm, swords still lowered from the last blow.

She was a dark angel, powerful, and untouchable.

She spun through the crowd, taking down anything around her. She could have destroyed every last man on that ship without any help. She lodged her swords into two wraiths on both sides of her, and they fell forward. She slid her swords out and decapitated a wraith in front of her.

A strange fear and realization dawned on Basile. Her expression was the same—no feeling, just a fierce, unbridled fury. Just like the storm. She was exactly what she appeared to be: a ruthless, feared pirate captain. No feminine gentleness, like he expected. That image would never come. She was what she was and nothing else.

Basile's attention was drawn to Jennings, who plowed through the crowd of wraiths, blocking them with his axes. A wraith swung a thick machete at his chest. Jennings flew back in limbo, escaping the blade. He severed the wraith's leg, sending him screaming to the ground.

Leaping into the air from a higher deck, Scar swept in on the wraiths with only a knife. As they charged, he dodged, easily ducking in and out while spinning around each attacker. He killed with sharp swipes of his knife, never there when the victim fell to the floor.

The scene was chaotic. Basile swallowed. Wraiths continued to advance with unbridled craze. They roared out like abnormal beasts.

Vaster rose out of the crowd. Sword in hand he heaved back three wraiths—holding them at a distance. Calculatingly, he took down each one by using them as shields against each other.

Soon there was a standstill. The wraiths surrendered their arms and the crew shouted victoriously.

Basile breathed relief and his heart calmed.

A huffing sounded from behind. An uncomfortable feeling crept up inside as he froze. He turned ever so slowly, hoping that nothing was there. A wraith stood behind him, bobbing back and forth with a natural tick. He must have been thrown in the water and climbed up the ship. He was dripping wet and in his hand held a thick machete. His dark skin and large face stared down without expression. Shards of bone pierced his nose, ears, and cheeks. His bottom half was covered with only a waist cloth, and he was bare from the waist up except for a small metal key that hung from his neck. Basile couldn't take his eyes off the completely out-of-place object.

The wraith looked to the reveling crew on his destroyed vessel. Incensed, he charged Basile like a demented animal. Basile scarcely moved quick enough. The wraith's blade penetrated the rail of the ship and stuck. The wraith worked to free it. Basile tripped over some rope and landed on his own bucket and mop. He jumped to his feet, searching for a sword. There was a barrel full of them next to the attacker. He picked up his mop and jabbed it at the wraith to keep distance between them. The wraith squinted confused, by his weapon of choice. He dislodged his machete and sliced the mop's head off. Basile dropped the stick and ran back, gaining some distance.

The members of the crew on the wraith ship cheered, egging him on to fight back. The wraith and Basile circled around on the deck. When the wraith would take a slash at him, he would barely veer away. Finally, he neared the barrel of swords. He grabbed one and went in for a stab of his own. The wraith dodged and swiped back, scraping Basile's arm. The pain stung. Basile grabbed his arm and glared as he charged. He had no idea what he was doing, but he knocked the invader down, running through to the other side. He caught a glimpse of Acantha watching. Her eyes told him to sink or swim. He turned back, and the wraith was on his feet. The wraith swung his sword to take off his head. Basile ducked and lodged his own sword into his opponent's belly. The wraith gasped.

Stunned, Basile released his sword, leaving it in the wraith. He fell backward and crawled to the railing of the ship, where he held onto the ropes tightly. The wraith gaped at him and gripped the handle of the sword lodged in his abdomen. Crew members returned from the other ship. The wraith collapsed in front of them all. They cheered and patted

Basile on the shoulder. He sat frozen. He had never killed anyone.

He dropped to his knees beside the dead native and slowly withdrew his sword, its tip stained red with blood. He removed the small key from around his victim's neck.

"Look at him!" someone shouted.

"Basile manned up and became a pirate!" another crowed. They all cheered as they lifted him onto their shoulders and bounced him around the deck. Basile was unnerved.

He was a pirate, a murdering pirate. He did not feel the least bit proud. He leapt to the floor and ran to the edge of the ship, where he lost the contents of this stomach to the sea. The crew laughed behind him. What had he thought would happen? He was on a pirate ship, but there had to be a bargaining system. Parlay? They could seize the valuables and allow the victims to drift and survive on the scraps of their ship.

Acantha swung over and observed, almost sympathetic as Basile hunched over the railing.

"Vaster," she yelled back to the wraith ship.

"Yes, Captain!"

The crew members roped the ships together for walking distance between them. The wraith ship was taking on water and would eventually sink. They patted Basile's back as they passed him.

"Raid the ship for any valuables and bring everything to the deck." All the crew cheered. She looked to Basile. "Go over there and help."

He nodded to her, still hunched over the side and wiping his mouth. He walked the plank between the ships. The wraith ship was in extreme disarray. The back end was damaged the most, water sprayed through the cracks. Vaster opened the doors on the deck into the cargo area. Piles of chests, gunpowder, ropes, and supplies lay in heaps below.

"Looks like they were heading back," he said.

"Back where?" Basile asked.

Vaster placed his hand on his shoulder. "Fair job!" he said, looking like a father to him.

Basile's eyes widened in disbelief. "Thanks," he said, but he didn't mean it.

"We don't know where the wraiths come from, but they be the captain's most favorite to take down. She hates them something fierce." He turned back and yelled, "Let's get going. We have a huge load here. Take all of it, and leave any captives below." Crew members swarmed to transport the supplies and chests to *The Dark Eve*.

"Come with me. We'll check the quarters." Vaster led the way and Basile followed. It wasn't nearly as nice as the Lady's. Everything was covered in the same reddish-brown dust and nothing had a place. A hammock swung against the far wall and a broken-down desk with charts stood in the middle, along with a mangled tin cup and a half-empty, dusty bottle of rum. Vaster took a swig from the bottle, swishing it around in his mouth and then promptly spitting it out. He set it back on the desk, his face scrunched from the taste. He examined the charts while Basile rummaged around the desk drawers. They were mostly empty, but one was full of ripped parchments. They had fancy writing on them, but had been torn to shreds. Underneath them all was a golden box no bigger than his fist, made of thick metal with beautiful engraved designs: strange birds and mountains up against the sea all around the outside of the box. He looked at the lock hole.

Just the right size. He reached into his pocket and pulled out the small golden key that he had taken from the wraith.

Vaster watched him. "Where did ye get that key?"

"I took if off the wraith that I killed."

"Open it," Vaster encouraged.

Basile gently slid the key into the lock. It was a perfect fit. The mechanics clicked. They looked at each other, perplexed, as Basile opened it. Thick, red velvet lined the inside.

"It's strange for them to have this hidden here," Basile said.

Vaster grunted his agreement. "Too bad there's nothin' inside." He took the box and looked it over. On the bottom was a strange crest with a large letter B. "Must be the markin's of a family or tribe. Not one that I've ever seen before." There was an indent in the middle of the velvet in the box, as if something were missing. "Oh well. It's just a box. Ye'll have to show it to the captain. Everythin' must be run by her before ye can keep it. But it has no value besides its gold and I'm sure she'll let ye have it if ye want. It is yer first treasure." He gave it back to Basile. "Let's get off this boat before it sinks."

"Why does the captain not like the wraiths?" Basile threw out the question quickly, hoping Vaster would answer without hitting him.

"Do you like 'em?" Vaster grabbed all of the charts from the room and went back out the door. Basile held the box close as he put the key around his neck, under his shirt. It was his first piece of treasure. They walked out of the quarters to find the ship empty of its supplies and all the crew back on *The Dark Eve*. The wraith ship sagged in the water. Basile quickly moved back over the plank to *The Dark Eve*. The new cargo sat in a large pile on the deck. The second Basile was back onboard, the plank was lifted and the crew set the ship back into motion

Vaster went to the helm to show Acantha the charts. She scoured them, completely engrossed.

They left the half-sunk wraith ship in the distance, along with the wraiths that had surrendered. Basile stared back at the lonely scene. He looked to the spot where he had defeated the savage wraith. All that remained was a puddle of blood.

Someone nudged him. He turned to see a fellow crew member, Booth, who had one eye patched and walked crookedly. He held out the mop and bucket. Basile rolled his eyes and took them. *Of course,* he seethed.

Later that day, Acantha and Vaster catalogued the spoils of the wraith ship. It appeared as if she was looking for something specific. Gold coins and trinkets spilled out all over the deck. Basile stayed close to them the entire time.

"How did they get all this treasure?" he finally asked.

Both Acantha and Vaster looked at him, taking real notice of him. His eyes sparkled at the beautiful treasures on the deck, just like he had imagined. He picked up a golden coin. Vaster hissed and he dropped it, remembering his place.

He glanced to Acantha. "Sorry," he muttered.

"They're worse than pirates," Vaster said. "They pillage villages, towns, collecting whatever they can where they can."

"How do you know?" He shrank at the glaring look both Vaster and Acantha returned, and decided to hush himself.

"Because we've been in a village they raided." Vaster peered out to the sea. "They don't leave anythin' behind or alive." He didn't sound angry, just factual.

Basile for the first time felt justified in killing the wraith, imagining the horror of innocent people attacked by such savages. But then again, he had taken a man's life. Could he trust the words and make them all savages? Surely they had families and worked the land in which their people lived. The image of the wraith's face growling and animal-like as he had attacked was burned behind all his thoughts.

He couldn't imagine that such a thing had a family, or loved at all.

Acantha broke his thoughts. "Vaster tells me you found a piece of treasure that needs examination."

Basile took out the box in this pocket. "We found it in the captain's quarters in a desk drawer and the wraith that I..." He paused, reflecting on his first kill. She noticed the key around his neck. When she saw the box she held her hand out for it. He complied, careful not to touch her.

Her lips pursed and her eyes flickered with familiarity.

She was holding her breath. She stared long and hard, as if the box revealed a dark secret to her. Vaster glanced to Basile, eyebrows lifted.

"Is this somethin' ye were lookin' for, Captain?" he whispered to her.

She let out a long, slow breath, her lips relaxing. She glared at Basile over the box.

"It was empty when I found it, my Lady." It was the first time he had ever called her that. It felt natural on his tongue.

She looked back to the box and her eyes glazed, her face still expressionless. Even Vaster was squinted, restless. They both stared at the box now with new eyes. The golden surface glimmered in the sunlight, making it look more valuable than when they first judged it. It looked ancient, the engravings like a paradise told of a place he would only see in a dream.

"I know." She threw the box to Basile. "You may keep it," she said, like it meant nothing to her.

He held it carefully as she turned back to the treasure pile. Vaster looked over at him several times, eyeing the mysterious box. It meant only one thing to Basile: that not even the closest to her knew her well. Would it be different with her sister?

It took them the rest of the day to go through the treasure. The gold coins were separated from all the other valuables, then bagged and taken down to the lower level with the mural wall.

Later, when Basile went down, the bags were gone, vanished into thin air. He searched around, but they were nowhere. They had been next to the mural. He put his head to the wall and listened, knocking to see if it was hollow. He ran back up to Vaster, who was again rolling rope.

"The treasure's gone," Basile whispered to him.

Vaster looked unconcerned, "Ye'd best not be caught snooping around."

"Aren't you worried that someone has stolen it?" His forehead wrinkled.

"No. Happens every time."

"What?"

"Don't worry, lad. Ye will get a piece of it when ye get to land." Vaster smirked at him. "Ye have nowhere to spend it while ye're here."

"That's not what I'm worried about," Basile said defensively.

"Don't worry, Mr. Basile." Vaster looked him up and down and divulged, "The ship takes care of it." And he winked.

◇◇◇

Acantha stood at the helm, hovering over the Oracle's map with Jennings, Scar, and Vaster. After a few more days of sailing they arrived at a cluster of small islands. Basile was relieved to see land. He longed to set foot on it.

"She'll be in the center of this mess," Acantha said.

"How will we be doing this?" Vaster stood right next to her, nervous, with Jennings and Scar behind him. The islands were sheer cliffs and held an impenetrable jungle. A small opening allowed for a ship to enter, and what lay beyond was unknown.

She looked down at the crew, the weight of her stare on Basile. He mopped around the floor, carefully moving closer to the conversation.

She didn't take her eyes off of him. "I know the route that will take us to the middle the safest." She pulled out her map of the islands. "The Oracle will be able to tell us exactly where Jennet is, should we survive the trip."

"This is a chart of just the islands?" Jennings leaned in to examine it.

"Yes, and this is the route we will take." The map again burst alive. Both Jennings and Scar jolted back. She curved her fingers around the entire chart. "It's like a maze. There are several spots that we will have to avoid. This path here, here, and there." Her finger darted around. "High coral reef will kill us here."

They all stared in disbelief at the intricate map. Its details jumped out of the chart, dancing with motion. "There are sirens on this side of this island. But we won't have to worry about them, even if we did go there." She glanced up at their dismal stares.

"What?" she looked almost annoyed.

"How do you know all of this?" asked Scar.

"I've been here before." She went back to the map and let her fingers circle the large island with the gulf in the middle. "A long time ago."

CHAPTER SIX
The Oracle

The three-week travel to the Oracle's island was long. Now, the dark night loomed around the ship, anchored mere miles away. The island was a large, mountainous silhouette in the distance. Basile watched as the captain, Jennings, Scar, and Vaster collaborated around the helm table in scattered lantern light.

Several times, Vaster came to report information vital to the journey through the maze. The crew listened intently for every description they could get. He ordered them to procure all the ship's long oars. Though confused, Basile did what he was told. He felt tugged from one conversation to another about the horrors of the maze.

"We'll start come first light and no sooner. We have until nightfall to make it to the center," he overheard Acantha say to the others.

In the distance, the shrieks of wild beasts echoed from the island. Swarms of bats circled the maze.

"The Tucaranda!" he heard from behind. Basile twisted back to a small gathering of the crew around the heaps of oars in the middle of the ship. Mort, the old cook, stood hunched with a lantern in hand, staring to the swarms above the island. He spoke in a raspy, shaking voice. "Long ago a large tribe lived, dark skinned and savage. They worshiped animals thinking they were gods, but most of all they worshiped the bat. Making sacrifices to it, they slew their own people to satisfy the animal god. Wars

50

broke out and in the end a great chief stood with a small handful of them left. One night the devil appeared in green flames to offer them a gift. The chief asked for his tribe members to become gods themselves." Mort glared at each of them. "The devil turned them into monsters, removing their eyes and blinding them. They only come out at night to search for prey. The devil cursed them with their own evil, set to stand guard against those who try to change their fate. Protecting the Light Oracle. She can see into your mind and future." He spat out his words.

Chills crept up Basile's spine. He looked back to the maze in the distance, his mind filled with the suspense of the unknown adventure before him. Up on the helm, Vaster had a solemn expression. The captain never left the helm that night.

Acantha stared out toward the maze, waiting for the sunrise to peek out from behind it. Only a few including Basile remained, ordered with stacking the long wooden oars against the walls of the ship and securing them with ropes. The light of the moon reflected shadows around her into familiar shapes. Long flowing clouds streaked across the sky like the balcony of a throne room. The wind blew gently through her hair, lulling her temperament. Moonlight flickered on the ocean waves like the orchestra swaying beneath the balcony staircase. Shadows danced as masquerade guests swayed around the room in a whirl of costumes and masks.

She closed her eyes, allowing the vision to come back. The tall, grandly carved doors of the hall stood before her. It was the first time she had attended such an event, though they should have been common in her life. Her black lace-and-taffeta dress draped off her shoulders and flowed thickly beneath her. A raven-feathered mask disguised her identity, though she did not know anyone there. The man she sought she had never met before, and after their encounter he would never want to meet her again. Her hair twined up in front and gently curled down her back, crowned and draped with lace knots.

Thank goodness for her jester. Her heart warmed at the thought of him as she walked into the great hall.

Servants adorned every wall, opening doors, serving food and wine to the colorful guests. Their crisp red uniforms stood out among the wildly decorated costumes. As she walked into the main room, it swayed with the orchestra's music, like the waves of the sea as couples danced circles around the extravagant hall.

Acantha glanced to the clock. It was only ten. The music from the strings vibrated inside her chest, moving her along within the crowd. The jester was to send his signal at half after ten if he was successful. She dodged around the ballroom, waiting for him, taking in the details of the party.

Fresh white roses with black feathers were draped with ribbons and beads, and candles dripped everywhere. She had never in her adult life heard such moving music. It made her want to dance. She could imagine a faceless figure guiding her flawlessly across the floor. She let herself go, closing her eyes as she spun in his strong arms.

At that moment, a hand grabbed hers. She spun around afraid to find the jester unsuccessful in their plan. Instead she found a tall man dressed in black. His short blond hair and crystal-blue eyes glowed against his velvet black mask.

Acantha knew exactly who he was. Her heart panicked that he would recognize her, but she held her ground, not giving any change in her expression. Here he was, holding her hand, the man she had been trying to hide from the entire time she had lived here. The only man who saw her come from the water and who had saved her from drowning, which was something she never thought possible. He bowed toward her, still holding her hand.

"Might I persuade the lady to dance?" He looked back up to her confidently, awaiting her answer.

She could run. It wouldn't take much to disappear in this crowd. Would he recognize her or had he already?

She nodded.

He stood straight and led her out to the dance floor. The crowd made a path for them, seeing as the son of the Lord of the Hall desired to dance. In the center of the room, he guided her, almost displaying her to the crowd. Then he firmly took her in hold. His hand was warm around her waist as he pulled her close.

Caution urged her to distance herself from him, but this would send a negative signal. She gently laid one hand in his and the other upon his shoulder.

Be as light as a feather, her mother had said.

As the orchestra's strings played, Acantha closed her eyes to the sweet ringing sound, and Lord Edwin Hugh Bracket danced her around the room. She felt weightless in his arms as they spun to the swaying melody.

"I don't believe I have the honor of knowing your name." His voice was deep and strong.

This will be our first conversation. He had an angular face with a pronounced jaw and nose. A crooked smile crept up the side of his face, causing her to look away. *I have to keep my distance.* She firmly looked back to him. He was attractive, which meant nothing to her. But in an odd way she felt drawn to him. Everything she worked for lay in the balance of her identity remaining secret. She could not get caught up in the noble crowd. There was no explanation for her being among it.

"No, sir, I believe you do not." She spoke without teasing.

Edwin drew his head back in surprise. Likely he had expected a humbler, kinder response. Her rejection fueled his curiosity. "Do you visit a noble family in the area? I'm sure I have never seen you before. You must be visiting. Might I enquire as to your family's name?"

"My family is not of this area or of any about here." Again, she spoke with no emotion.

Edwin squinted in disbelief. "Well, mystery lady, how does one come into favor enough to enquire of your name and origin?"

"I find that dancing hardly requires such information." Inside, she laughed. It took all her self-control to not smile.

They twirled around in silence for a moment before he petitioned again. "I feel intrigued with your game. Might I know the rules so I can better play?"

"What makes you think I am toying with you, sir?" She kept her face turned to view the room, avoiding eye contact with him, but it was difficult when she was pressed so closely against him.

"It is not often I find myself in such a lack of position," he said, searching for any sign of give from her.

"Maybe it is good to find alternate views every so often. I find it keeps the mind open." Acantha looked back to his face. For a moment, they both studied each other with the room spinning around them.

"I feel as though we have met before." His voice grew quiet. Her black eyes pierced through her raven mask, showing no sign of giving in. Her perfect lips pursed closed and expressionless.

He was drawn to her silence and beauty. Surely their paths had crossed before. Their faces stood so close. With just a few inches between, it would take little effort to close the gap. Yet, she felt so defiant in his arms. He was accustomed to women flocking for his attentions, pandering to his every desire and dream to gain his favor, which none had. For the first time his normal courage failed him.

Acantha heard the signal—the gentle cooing of the dove's call—and her eyes few to the clock. It was time. The jester had located the man she sought. But how was she to leave without the young lord's pursuit?

Edwin guided her out into a spin. It was perfect. The dancers swarmed around them. As he turned her, Acantha spotted a servant nearby with a tray of drinks. With a quick slip of her hand, she threw the tray up in the air, causing everything to clang to the floor. The noise and distraction was all she needed for him to look away. She slipped her hand from his, and before he had time to see, she camouflaged herself among the other guests, hiding from his view though ever so close. Pride bolstered her as he searched around, confused by her disappearance. It was too easy. For a moment, regret twinged, but she pushed it aside, unwilling to entertain any outside emotions.

She searched the balcony where her colorful jester peeked out behind a pillar, his vibrant ensemble capped with a three-pronged hat and tassels easy to find among the costumes. He pointed a crowned scepter behind to the thrones in the back of the room. Acantha darted that direction. A large dais supported the two grand thrones. The master of the house and his lady were not there.

Enjoying the guests, she thought.

Beyond the thrones, behind a staircase to the balcony, was a servant's door, and in front of that door stood the man she was looking for. He was wearing formal military robes, one of Lord Edwin's personal men. Her anger rose, but she did not allow it to change her appearance.

It was now or never.

Her charm came out. She sauntered toward the man. It took him only a second to see her. At first, he glanced behind himself, disbelieving she could be looking at him.

Acantha snickered inside. *What an idiot.*

As she walked directly up to him, he sucked in his breath and puffed out his chest. His thicker body type was exaggerated with his royal guard ensemble with its poufy hat and long, hanging feather. His round face grew bright red.

"Why is a person like you stuck here in the corner by himself?" her cool voice asked as she circled him.

He stood straight and stiff. "I am set to guard here. It's my post for the evening."

"All by yourself?" She brushed past his shoulder. He shuddered. "For the whole evening?" She faced him, leaving only a small gap between them. The guard looked down at her and then up to the ceiling, shifting his weight.

Acantha moved back, giving him some more room. "What's your name?"

"Jenkins, Bart Jenkins," he stammered.

"Well, Sir Jenkins, do you get a break?"

He looked out around the room to see if any other person was watching their conversation. The ball revelers swarmed, oblivious to them in the corner. "Yes, I do."

Acantha didn't say anything. She just waited for him to get the clue. After a moment, his eyes squinted in disbelief. But she answered with an intrigued expression. Bart looked through the crowd again, making sure no one was watching while he backed up to the servant's door. He opened it and beckoned her to enter. She sauntered toward the door, making him look more nervously about the room.

Before she entered, she glanced up to the balcony where the jester stood. His white hair flew out wildly beneath his hat and his crystal-blue eyes smiled at her success. She walked deliberately through the narrow stone hallway.

Wooden doors lined the right wall to the end where a staircase stood. He moved in front of her, leaning in for a kiss. Acantha moved back quickly shocked. He squinted, confused.

"Do you not have a more private place? I am a lady!" she said sternly.

Of course. She could see the words appear on his face. He held her hand and led her up the staircase. After two floors, they entered another long hallway lined with wooden doors. He guided her to the third one and opened it, allowing her to pass before him.

Within was only a small bed and a desk. It was clean and very simple. *Where could he have possibly hidden it in here?* She scanned the room. Bart closed the door behind him. This was the moment she had been waiting for the entire night—enough games. Bart moved close behind her.

"This is your room in the castle?" Acantha asked.

"Yes. I know it's not much, but love overcomes those types of things."

He sounded so hopeful. She rolled her eyes, disgusted. Before he could touch her, she pulled out her dagger, spun around, and placed it just under his chin. Bart froze.

"I don't understand," he spouted, frowning at her now-hostile expression.

"I'm quite sure of that," Acantha said. She twisted the knife, cutting his chin. He flinched back, but she kept her dagger firmly in place.

"What do you want?" His voice grew scared. "I don't have anything."

"Oh, I know what you have," she reassured him. "Where is my bag of gold and the ring that you stole from my hut in the village?"

He looked up at her confused, but she could see him calculating. "I don't know what you're talking about."

She would convince him of her seriousness: she cut open his chin. Bart yelled and charged her, but she used his weight against him, tripping him onto the floor. A swift kick to the gut knocked the wind out of him. He hunched over, bleeding and gasping for air.

"I don't have it," he said.

"You see, now we're getting somewhere." She paced behind him. "Tell me where it is and I won't disfigure your face anymore."

"I lost it, gambling at the Porter house." His words rang with truth and damnation at the same time.

All the anger now showed in Acantha's face. This meant a lot more than a "find you at the ball and beat it out of you" process. She kicked him to the ground. He fell with a huff and rolled to his side. With all her rage, she kicked him in the face. Her boot knocked him out cold.

She sat on his bed, calming herself and dissipating her anger. She forgot to threaten him not to tell anyone about her. *Too late now.* Maybe he would take that as implied. At that moment, she felt defeat. She closed her eyes, imagining what it meant if she didn't get her ring back.

NO. She shook the thought from her mind. She kicked him a few more times just for effect. Storming through his room she looked in every possible place. Disappointed, she fled out the back entrance to meet up with the jester at the designated place.

Her mind slipped from the memory before it went too far. She stood once again on the deck of her ship with the sun soon to rise. For a brief moment, she wished she could go back and change the past, but she pushed this feeling back with the endless storm that raged inside her. The silhouette of the Oracle's island loomed as the sun rose. Sunrise every morning awakened her soul, making her feel refreshed and renewed. It was the only thing that gave her peace.

Looking around, she once again caught Basile's staring gaze. How long would she endure his endlessly prying eyes without slitting his throat? How long could she suffer him to stay onboard?

Tiredness swept her entire body, as if her arms and legs had become as heavy as lead. She would need every ounce of energy she had to get through this day. It would make her more than happy to leave this place and never journey to the middle to find the Oracle. If everything she held dear was not threatened by not finding her sister, then she probably would have.

Vaster hurried up the stairs. "Captain, is it time?" He looked out to the rising sun.

Acantha studied his weathered, round, loyal face. "Yes. Wake the crew."

The morning light revealed the island. Mountainous walls protruded from the sea, rising straight into the sky, towering beyond description. They guarded the Oracle's peak, whose point jutted in the distance behind the fortifications. The map showed only one entry point: an opening big enough for the ship. The walls were impassible by foot, covered in tropical greenery, with waterfalls that poured down their heights.

The crew grew silent as they reached the entrance. The map revealed a swarm of waterways beyond. There they would decide which ones to take to lead them to the Oracle's mountain.

The sea flowed into the large gap. The outer walls turned inward, creating a watery tunnel to begin the maze. It continued for as far as their eyes could see. On the left side, the walls canopied over half of the water's path.

She spoke to Jennings, Scar, and Vaster at the helm. "We stay to the right. If we go anywhere near the other side, those cliffs above will break down on top of us and sink us."

"Starboard, ye lazy mules! As close to the right wall as possible," Vaster barked at the crew and they all worked their posts and ropes. Their silence set a nervous atmosphere on the ship. Basile held his breath like all the others as they entered the narrow pathway.

Acantha looked back at their gazing eyes and then upward at the hovering cliffs, waiting for the cracking noise that would send them down. At the first sound of the stone breaking, each man jumped in his own skin. The back end of the ship bumped against the rock wall and shifted over to the left side. Rocks crashed inches from the ship's railing.

"Straighten us out, Jennings!" Acantha ordered. "Hold us straight. Everyone keep your positions. It will take every man to get to the middle of this with our lives."

Farther in, a wall stood with watery paths continuing on to its left and right. "Take us farther and pull anchor there just before the next stage," Acantha ordered, and the men prepared for the anchor to fall.

Small spouts of cliff fell along their way to the opening. As they passed through, breaths of release poured from the men. Acantha felt a pang of pity and a treacherous stabbing spark of hindsight that no relief had yet been given. The crew flew to the sides of the ship, looking down the two paths before them. She knew both very well and imagined her men hoping and praying that they would take the calm winding one to the starboard side. A tropical forest grew thick on both sides and in the distance the wide river appeared smooth and calm, relaxing even, beckoning a gentle path. The crews eyes bulged at the port side, where a gaping whirlpool spun boundless and torrential. Beyond the impenetrable sucking hole was a rough, rocky path which appeared impassible.

The current of the whirlpool even at their distance pulled the anchored ship in its direction.

"We go straight into the pool." She pointed to the map as it moved, animating the scenery. "We have to catch the flooding current perfectly to push us around just past these safety rocks here on the other side. Then we must be ready to navigate past these rapids. We won't be able to miss them all." The four upon the helm looked out to the dooming path with apprehension.

"Only a mad man dare take that death path!" The voice shouted from the crowded crew. The captain, Vaster, Scar, and Jennings all turned. The crew split, uncovering the fool that dared to speak such words. He shook in his boots, a gangly man that Basile had not seen often on their journey, Potter. All eyes awaited the captain's reaction, but she gave none. Her stare bored down on the man. He did not look directly at her.

Instead, Vaster piped up in her defense. "She is neither a man, nor is she mad."

Potter muttered at the floor, "You take us all to our deaths down that path. This is the way we should take to the middle." His hand flew to the opposing path that serenely flowed far away from the whirlpool. His fingers shook as he pointed, his eyes pleading that he spoke common sense.

Acantha walked very slowly to the railing that overlooked the crew. "There is only one pathway through this labyrinth, and that is the one we will take." Her voice condemned every man who dared speak against her.

"You'll kill us all here, that's why you brung us. I won't take that path and no sane man or woman would." The remainder of the crew might have been thinking the same thoughts, but they did not strike up the support Potter had hoped. He looked around, but for nothing. Basile itched to console the man into reason, but he himself doubted in silence.

"I have a right to take that path!" Potter's voice now shook with fear. He walked over to the starboard side and pointed to the small boat below. "And any man is free to go with me if he chooses." He fiddled with the rope to the small boat and ores. He worked in haste and didn't notice the slow and solemn movement that Acantha took from the helm and through the crew. Like a snake in the grass, she moved toward Potter.

"All who want to come with me can! We have a choice!" he yelled over his shoulder. Silence answered him. He turned and found himself face-to-face with the captain. He flew back toward the railing, the small boat floating at the same level by the side of the ship. He flinched, scared and trapped like a rat.

Acantha glanced back to the crew. "Does anyone else wish to take the course that Potter has chosen?" Her voice was solemn. Several men shifted their weight, but none spoke. Potter looked around desperate for any other protester to take his position, but none did. The suspense rose. Acantha pulled a dagger from her side seamlessly and laid it to rest into Potter's gut. He let out a cry and, stunned, peered down at the weapon. Acantha closed the gap between them and talked silently into his ear.

"There is only one path through the maze. Only a fool thinks the easiest path takes them to their destination."

Death crept into his eyes. Basile looked to her, expecting hatred, rage, and disgust, but there was no expression. She pulled back and pushed Potter over the side of the ship into the small boat. Then she unsheathed her swords and cut the ropes. The vessel fell with a splash and then gently the current took it down the calm path that Potter had chosen.

She turned upon the rest of the crew as the small boat floated away in the morning sun. "There is only one way through this maze. If anybody else wishes to protest my judgments, you know what will come. Either we all work together or we all die here and now. It's not a hard choice."

"Every man at his post!" Vaster yelled and the crew scattered to their positions.

Acantha sheathed her swords and returned to the staircase.

Basile stood there, still in shock.

"Young Mr. Basile," she called.

He looked to her soulless black eyes. "Yes, Captain?" He held her gaze. She probed his soul, looking far beyond what any normal person was capable of seeing. It sickened him that she could kill an innocent man who only wanted to escape the doomed path that even he felt they were on. She was a monster and yet as he looked into her pitiless eyes, he didn't believe her lack of feeling. He felt loyalty toward her on some strange level, and he hated himself for feeling it.

"Hold on," her velvet voice spoke. She turned and went up, shouting at Jennings to move forward with the plan. "The moment we catch the other side, be prepared to navigate the rapids and rocks. All hands to the oars. You will have to move as a group side to side and push us."

Basile grabbed his oar, bracing himself for the whirling water.

"Don't pull the anchor until the surge!" she shouted.

"The surge, Captain?" Jennings questioned.

"Look closely down the path." She pointed. A waterfall poured into the whirlpool opposite of the safety rocks. A surge of water rushed from the cave under the falls.

"That's our ticket to the other side," she said.

Vaster asked, "But how do we time it, Captain?"

"We cut the anchor at the next surge. It's timed to work perfectly. Once we reach the edge of the whirlpool, it will happen again and push us to the other side." She stood at the helm, watching intently.

Basile clutched the banister, praying for it to work.

The water gushed through the cave, flooding the whirlpool.

"NOW!" the captain yelled and the sailor closest to the spare anchor cut the rope with his sword.

The ship surged toward the treacherous pool and gained speed every second. Basile held his breath as the rapids increased. They entered the whirlpool. He gripped tight. The water in the middle gaped open like an endless funnel. He imagined other ships torn down its path.

There is no way of escaping its current.

But the torrent from the cave gushed again, pushing the ship against the far outer level of the whirlpool and directing them back enough to go behind the rocks. The crew held tight. It was almost too easy.

He was jerked out of his thoughts by the crew yelling. They had sailed into a rocky, rapid path. The walls of the mountains made a narrow alleyway. Rocks staggered down a long stretch and the crew had their oars up. They pushed against the port side of the mountain, shifting the ship to the starboard side to avoid an outcropping of boulders before them. They barely missed the protruding disaster.

Vaster directed them to the other side. Basile joined the party as they ran back and forth to guide the ship. Water sprayed up onto the deck, causing a dozen of them to fall. A cracking sound followed the crash—they hit a pile of rocks, throwing every sailor to the ground.

Acantha clutched the railing. "Back to your feet! Port side! Port side!" But it was too late. Even she fell as they collided again. The crashing noises and splintering sound echoed through the watery canyon.

Vaster jumped up and looked at the path. "Port side again!" Enough men got to their feet and pushed against the rock walls, avoiding what could have been their end. Basile ran back and forth several more times before the rapids ended. Once again the waterway opened up into a pool where three paths branched.

"Anchor us!" Acantha yelled and relief filled the crew as another anchor was dropped. Every man was soaked and panting.

Basile hugged the railing that supported him. The three paths couldn't be more different: the middle one looked the easiest, having a few rapids, but it disappeared around a mountain wall. A strange fog filled the starboard path, but the water was smooth. The third had dark, thick jungle seeping into it. Treetops grew out toward the opposite bank, making a tunnel of brush above the water. Long vine-like ropes dripped from them. It was darker than the other paths. This last one, he was sure to be the path they would travel. He thought back to Potter and shuddered.

"Ye alright, boy?" Basile turned to the familiar voice. Vaster stood on the other side of the staircase railing.

He felt heavy. "Yes. Do you know which path we take?"

Vaster cocked his head toward the jungle, the third path, thus validating Basile's premonitions.

"What waits for us in there?"

"Who knows," Vaster answered in a fatigued voice.

"Why did she kill him?" The question popped out before Basile could stop it. He clenched, ready for the slap on the head. But when no punishment came, he opened his eyes. Vaster gazed up toward the captain.

"Ye can't always understand why the captain works the way she does." His eyes once again glowed with admiration. "She has her reasons to keep order. She preserves us all in the end."

While his words ringed with truth, that her decisions protected them all, Basile found her actions brutal.

"But she didn't need to kill Potter. She could've just let him go."

Vaster snarled out his regular scolding voice. "Look around. Does this place look like paradise? One direction has more horrible terrors than the other and just because yer naked eye can't see 'em don't mean that they don't exist."

Basile lowered his head.

"She directs our course." Vaster glanced around to see if anyone was listening. Basile leaned forward to close the distance between them. Vaster whispered, "The map mentioned somethin' worse than death down that path. Creatures that will eat a man alive, peelin' the flesh from their bones." He delivered a solid nod. "What she did was merciful."

Basile squinted in disbelief, not from the treacherous path, but from the fact that the Lady had shown Potter mercy. It was a foreign concept that he could not pin to her character. He looked up to where the captain stood. The sunlight bore down on Acantha's dark figure. It lit her face as she wiped her neck with a cloth. Awestruck with her beauty, he tried to find her capable of supposed mercy.

Just then she looked down upon them.

Vaster turned his face, but Basile didn't.

"Pull anchor," she yelled without taking her eyes from him, "and arm yourselves."

The men scurried, pulling their weapons. Jennings directed the ship to the jungle's path. Basile clenched his teeth as they entered.

The sounds changed. The air didn't move through the area, and the calls of hidden beasts echoed around them. Buzzing noises spun as huge insects flew past. Jennings guided the ship around several corners. The hanging vines draped down into the path.

"Cut 'em away." Vaster motioned toward several men, including Basile. The treetop canopy grew thicker, shielding the sun. The men climbed the riggings on both sides of the ship, cutting the vines closest to them. The sounds from the jungle intensified the deeper they went. The crew looked out, eerily suspicious of the area and distancing themselves from the sides as they brushed the jungle walls.

Basile worked next to Blain, an older, more menacing sailor, careful not to tread in his space. The oversized leaves of the jungle brushed against them as they passed. He focused on his task, dodging the foliage. The jungle poured down on top of them. He touched a leaf the size of his torso. Its surface was smooth.

Just then, he spotted movement on the twisting bark of a passing tree. He squinted, drawing closer, but nothing was there. A shrill cry sounded out. A stick-like creature resembling the surface of the tree struck out at Blain, its legs still latched to the tree. Its claws pierced through him, drawing him completely off the ship and into the jungle.

Basile fell backward. He looked to where Blain had been. He scoured the jungle ridge for him, but he was gone. Basile jumped to his feet, his heart racing. Movement flowed through the jungle. Blain's cries flailed out and ended with a crunching, snarling noise.

Basile's insides crumbled at the sound.

A pair of eyes blinked on the nearby leaf. Basile held up his sword as the camouflaged creature jumped straight at him. It was the size of a dog striking with a flat, smooth, leaf-like head. Its wide mouth gaped opened almost completely vertical as it extended its pointed claws to snag him. Basile moved his sword in the nick of time, severing one of its arms. It streaked back, clinging for safety with its legs still attached to the tree. A gurgling call vibrated its throat and movement streamed above. The silhouettes of creatures dove out from the jungle tops down into the ship. Basile could hardly see as the chaos swirled around him. Men instantly disappeared, their struggling, dangling figures caught in the creatures' grips. Basile panicked at the snarling faces. Each creature distorted to the likeness and texture of what it was connected to.

Jumping to his feet, he grabbed one of the struggling men. The creature's grip on the tree held firm as its bark-like jaws snapped out at him. A shot fired out into air striking the beast. Its claws unlatched dropping monster and victim on top of him. The weight crushed him against the floor. He struggled uselessly to get free. Looking sideways, he watched the battle.

Acantha stood at the helm, guarding Jennings at the wheel. She held a smoking pistol. She threw it to the ground and pulled out two smaller pistols, one from her boot and the other from a holster on her thigh. Jennings flung one of his axes over her shoulder, striking a creature mid-air as it launched toward her. She didn't even blink as both mini-pistols fired, striking down more creatures and captives.

Crew members swirled around with swords in hand. Madness circled the surface of the ship as creatures fell from the trees. The end of the jungle path opened around the next bend and the creatures retreated, snagging a few more sailors before the ship emerged out from under the treetop canopy.

Vaster shouted out orders to discard the bodies overboard. Finally, the weight of the carcasses lifted from Basile, and strong hands hoisted him to his feet.

"Get up. This isn't over yet!" Vaster yelled toward him. Basile peered back to the jungle's edge, disoriented. He could still see movement within. Ahead, rolling sandy hills lined both shores. The mountainous walls were visible in the distance. It couldn't have been anymore different from where they had come. The ship's crew relaxed in the absence of imminent danger.

Basile examined the winding path and noticed the way split into six. Each path looked the same. At the helm, Acantha directed Jennings where to go for what felt like endless hours. She guided them in and out of different paths. The scenery never changed. A penetrating heat radiated upon them as they moved past the sandy shores. The sun intensified and Basile felt as though he were being cooked to death. He wandered to the edge of the ship and looked out. The landscape was dead, with patches of yellow grass spread out among the hillside, not a single movement of a bird or animal. Skeleton bones lay upon the sandy shore without a single footprint in the sand around them. The figure was sunk halfway into the burning surface. The skull looked in the direction they traveled. Its mouth gaped open with sand pouring out of it.

"This is it!" Acantha yelled. Basile's attention returned forward. The floor of the waterway was covered with red plants waving in the current, as though the bottom of the river were covered in blood. A rocky mount as tall as the walls of the maze loomed before them and the path curved around it. It was the break in the scenery.

"Now on to our last trial," she said to Vaster. Basile's heart shook with the mystery of what else they could possibly face. As they neared the last bend, the shore was cluttered with rocks. The opposite side of the hill was sheer rock again, but small caves hid behind the tall boulders. The rocks spread out into the water toward the ship, making a pathway to the shore.

Basile looked closer. Claw marks and bloodstains scattered the rocky shore. Between the cracks were bones, not those of any animals, but of men. Chills shot up his spine and he jumped back from the edge.

Acantha, noticing his motion, focused on the shore. A strange fog poured from the shoreline. She jerked her head back, alert.

"Everyone tie yourselves down!" she yelled. The crew paused—then it was a race to any open end of a rope. Vaster scurried to her for clarification. Basile waited, itching for her answer.

"She's changed the maze," Acantha said under her breath, annoyed. She paced back and forth. The fog thickened as it billowed toward them.

"Changed the maze, Captain?" Vaster stammered back.

Acantha stormed over to the map on the deck table. It swayed with animation. The tall hill looked like nothing but that, and then suddenly the rocks appeared, forming on the side of the hill with the fog rolling out. Red, glowing eyes appeared from within the caves.

"I don't believe it!" Acantha glowered. "They wouldn't dare attack my ship!" Then she glanced to the fog. "But they won't know whose ship they're attacking."

"Captain?" Vaster questioned while tying his leg to the railing.

Basile found a rope at the bottom of the stairs. He picked up the end and panicked as the fog smoldered toward them. Low singing radiated from it. He gazed deeply, looking for the approaching danger. The fog frothed, curling and spinning. His mind felt hazy and his ears started to ring.

The next thing he knew, Acantha had grabbed both his hands and was tying them tightly to the staircase railing. Her hands were soft. He felt confused, but held still. The low song spread out, echoing off the rocks toward the ship.

"She told me she would do this. She said if I ever came back there would be consequences."

Vaster snorted. "And ye didn't think to mention this earlier?"

Acantha finished tying Basile's hands, tighter than he thought necessary.

"What about you?" he asked her, though he couldn't see very well. His eyes felt heavy and his mind numb. It felt strange for him to speak of concern for her. He wasn't really talking to her, he decided. It wasn't real. She wasn't looking at him anyway.

It was like he didn't exist.

She spoke defiantly to him. "Their song doesn't work on me. Prepare yourself for the song of death!" she yelled to the crew. They were all poised in their tied positions scattered upon the ship.

Soon the fog was upon them, with heavy moisture in the air. It thickened, smoldering around them. Basile could hardly see in front of him. The captain had disappeared. He looked around for any other person, but found only fog. The voices lulled his senses. His brain was falling asleep, but his eyes still blinked awake. Sharp pains burned his wrists, the stinging unbearable. The captain had done too good of a job tying them to the railing.

The song kept building and building inside his mind, making him feel as though he swayed to the sweet sound. The stabbing pain grew in his wrists. They were bleeding. The torture grew deeper and deeper. He couldn't even feel his fingers anymore. He opened his eyes, unaware that they had closed. Movement flickered in the fog. The pain in his hands traveled up his arms to his shoulders. The sweet song rang painfully in his ears.

"Please," Basile pled, "loosen the ropes."

He could hardly tell that he had spoken. His mouth felt dry. A figure stood beside him. He jumped back, his heart racing. He expected a monster from the rocks, but it was Bowen, a husky crew member with eyes glazed in a sort of trance.

"Bowen." Basile could hardly hear his own voice. "Bowen, are you all right?"

But Bowen didn't respond. He turned his face. His eyes glowed with a low, bluish tint and looked as though they had been turned back in his head. Basile fell back against the railing, his hands throbbing. He scrambled to his feet. His wrists were covered in blood. Panic filled his mind and his hands felt as though they would fall off. Movements jerked through the fog all along the deck. He focused hard to see the monsters that attacked. A cry sounded above him.

Vaster writhed in pain at the helm. He jerked his legs in their ties to the point that they rubbed raw and were bleeding. Basile looked back to Bowen, whose leg was also bleeding where it was tied. But the end of the rope had been cut, freeing him from the ship. A long dagger hung from his hand, poised to attack. The fog thinned near the railing next to them. A figure crawled up the outer wall. Basile braced himself for the creature to attack, but as the figure rose, soft, gentle blond hair swept into view. It shimmered and sparkled, shaking his mind from the danger he expected.

A gentle, angelic face appeared from behind the railing. Basile's heart fluttered and his knees weakened. Her perfect lips moved soft and slow as she sang a sweet tune. His eardrums ached with the vibrations of her voice. Her golden hair hung gently down, hiding her scaled naked front and giving a teasing view of her curvy feminine figure. She curled herself upon the railing and a three-pronged fish tail flipped up, caressing the outside of the ship. Her eyes fell upon the two of them, cleared from the fog. Basile's body twitched beyond his control. His hands pulled on the ropes that bound him, making his wrist bleed more. He stopped, finally realizing he was the cause of his own pain.

"Don't listen to the song!" Vaster cried above him. He gazed around wildly, holding his hands to his ears. Basile bent his head down to his roped hands, trying to block out the creature's song.

Bowen stumbled toward the singing beauty, his body twitching and jerking uncontrollably. Basile looked back to the naked creature curled outside the ship and jolted at the now hideous sight. She had transformed into a scaled demon. Beautiful golden hair was now protruding dark-black, in twisting knots. Harsh green scales covered her entire body. Her eyes glowed red. She opened her thin, scaly mouth, hissing out the now-distorted song.

Bowen continued to her. A long, snake-like tongue flicked out from the monster's mouth. Her teeth were sharp and jagged. Her jaw gaped open wide as her long tongue stretched over the railing toward Bowen. Her long claws gripped the ship as her voice radiated out, summoning her prey.

"Bowen, stop!" Basile cried. But Bowen shuffled toward the beast. "Bowen, don't listen. Cover your ears!"

The singing creature wiggled in delight as he stepped closer and closer. More snake-like figures crawled beyond her on the rocks leading up to the ship. Their red, glowing eyes pierced the fog. As Bowen continued, the monster's jaw unhinged, jerking wider and wider.

From the churning fog, Acantha flew past. She thrust her dagger down, piercing the demon's tongue, pegging it to the railing. The creature screamed. It flopped wildly like a landed fish, and before it could tear free, Acantha pulled out a large three-pronged hook attached to a rope. As the beast's tail whipped around, she sank it deep into its hind. The creature screeched again. Acantha threaded the rope though a pulley and hoisted the monster up, tying the end to the ship.

She stood back and watched the beast struggle in the air outside the ship, its tongue still pierced to the rail. She slowly walked toward the creature, and bowed down to whisper in its ear. "You chose the wrong ship to board," she hissed, spitting in its face. The creature's eyes widened with fear and sudden recognition. Acantha's swords were out. In one descending blow, she severed the head of the beast. Its body writhed upon its fishhook, and the head hung from the railing by its tongue.

The captain kicked Bowen back from the ship's railing. She retrieved her dagger, and the monster's head rolled, spilling crimson-red blood out onto the deck. She picked it up and pointed it out to the remainder of the red-eyed demons. The fog instantly dissipated. Dozens of the scaled creatures headed toward the ship, but as they gazed upon the captain's trophy, their tune changed.

The sweet-sounding song turned into a blood-curdling scream. The piercing vibrations penetrated Basile's attempts to blot them, as though his inner ears had burst. All the men on the ship flailed around on the deck, trying to shield their ears from the sounds. The demons retreated to the rocky shore and caves beyond, and soon their screeches stopped. The air cleared and the sun once again appeared, revealing the watery path.

The crew got to their feet, holding their heads and shuffling slowly around the ship. Basile's head pounded from the endless ringing in his ears. Some crew members had blood dripping from their ears.

Bowen lay motionless on the floor. A crowd had gathered around him. Acantha and Vaster shouldered through. Bowen's eyes still rolled in the back of his head, his tongue hanging from his mouth.

He was dead.

"Throw him overboard," Acantha said.

All the sailors held their hats over their chests for a moment before sentencing him to his watery grave.

"What happened?" Basile asked Vaster as the little crowd disposed of the body. "He was alive, I saw him."

"His heart couldn't take the siren's song," Vaster said in a reverent tone.

"Sirens. That's what those creatures were?"

"Aye, that they were."

"Why did they stop attacking the ship?" Basile looked perplexed. "They could have taken all of us with how many there were."

Vaster smiled, amazed at his ignorance. "Have ye not seen what stands at the helm of our ship, lad?"

Basile's eyes flew to the sirens carved into the ship's bow. This was supposed to answer the question somehow. But how had carved figures in wood retracted such horrible creatures? He looked back to Vaster, squinting with misunderstanding and disbelief.

Vaster shook his head, annoyed. "For a person who spends most his time observing, ye sure are ignorant. The fog hid the ship. They didn't know who they were attacking. They wouldn't dare take on the queen of their own kind." He watched for the understanding to take light in Basile's mind.

"The captain's a siren?" Basile was still unsure of his meaning.

"Not everything is a literal meaning." Vaster stormed off, abandoning his attempt at a subtle explanation. "A killer!" he yelled. "A natural-born killer! Higher on the food chain!"

Just then, the captain appeared. Basile and Vaster fell in among the crew, who had gathered, exhausted from the journey and ready for relief.

Acantha could feel their heaviness. The sirens' song had drained their energy. It was a good thing that the hypnotizing attacks only worked on a man's mind. But she could still count on her crew's greed and self-preservation. Knowing her men was key to her success, because the worst was before them.

"Our journey is not yet through." Her voice was grave. "Soon we will enter a cave, and your only instruction is not to make a sound—or even breathe, for that matter. If you do, that breath will be your last. Each man find his place and stay there." She looked to Basile, who had no real place on the ship. The crew scattered, tired yet obedient to the captain's words.

A slope in the river dragged them down toward the cave, its entrance like a monster's face with no eyes. Sharp, jagged teeth hung down, gaping wide after them. After the sirens, Basile felt nothing could ever scare him again. He had seen the deepest of evils.

But even the sirens were afraid of the captain. She shouted out now at the men, but every word fell silent to his ears. Even shouting she looked beautiful, perfectly poised, her raven-black hair gently flowing with the wind. Her lips were the most natural color of red. He didn't feel at all afraid of her. He knew he should be. Vaster would threaten some fear inside him if he knew. He didn't love, hate, or even despise her as she did to him.

The darkness of the cave loomed just above them. Basile held his breath and looked again to where she had stood. Once again she had disappeared from his view as they passed into darkness. He looked back at the opening, but the walls blocked out the light. The boat creaked as it followed the river around a bend.

Basile couldn't even see his own hands in front of his face. An eerie silence swept around them and nothing but the sounds of the ship in the rushing water could be heard. Soon his eyes adjusted to the cave. He could faintly see the deck of the ship and those closest around him. A strange clicking sound echoed off the walls.

As soon as they entered the cave, Acantha poised in the darkest corner of the ship, just behind where Basile stood. He stared out toward the cave's entrance until the darkness covered them, his face wrinkled with worry. It could be the last light he would ever see. This would be the case for some of the men. There was no keeping the natural sounds of the ship quiet while passing through.

She closed her eyes, allowing the darkness to change her vision. The beasts would come. She meant to minimize the damage if she was to have enough crew to sail out of here. She looked to Basile, who cocked his head as he listened to the sounds of the cave. His breathing was shallow and still. She had seen so many men preparing for doom and waiting for the signal that would set off when danger was in view. But the danger here was not one that revealed itself. A man was more likely to be dead before knowing danger was upon him. Once again, she felt the pang of responsibility for his life. She flexed angrily at the reminder. It was confounding not to have reason beyond her feelings. But those feelings meant more even if she didn't understand them.

The movement on the ship changed, though slightly. Taking her time, she scanned the outer railings and sails. It was only a matter of time. Like blind worms in the dirt, the creatures would soon find one of them. Acantha spotted movement on the mast. One crawled toward the deck. Its gangly, thin arms and legs with thick claws slowly inched forward searching. It was the size of a small man, but with flap-like wings extending between its arms and legs. Its face was skinned over at the eyes, blind, with two holes in its skull where a normal nose should be, and its mouth extended out from ear to ear above a pointed chin. It gaped, feeling its surroundings with its tongue. Its stealth did not surprise her.

They were about halfway through the cave as the creature moved down and out toward the deck.

Basile watched for any signal of attack on the ship. The air changed around him and, like a vision appearing before his eyes, he saw the devil's dog. Up on the mast not ten feet from him, it slithered like a snake toward the deck. Just then, a sailor who crouched near the railing, Popper, sniffled in his hiding place. The creature struck out toward the noise, clawing, and ripping. Basile moved to his aid, opening his mouth instinctively to avert the creature, when a hand grabbed his mouth and another pulled him deeper into the staircase. Her face grazed his while she held him firmly. She signaled with her finger for him to be quiet. Popper's screams radiated through the cave. Basile cringed inside and held his hands to his ears to blot them out.

More of the dark creatures crawled toward the ship. Popper's screams soon were silenced by the clicking shrieks of the devil's dog. The captain moved toward a cluster of demons ready to jump aboard. Before Basile knew it, she had slid near the devil's dog on the deck. As it raised its head to greet her, she sliced it off, ending its clicking noises.

Light appeared at the end of the tunnel, and another scream burst from the end of the ship. Basile pled to the light to save them, but there was still a distance until the ship touched its rays. Another devil's dog jumped up onto the railing, squatting like a cat. The creature stood blindly, almost face-to-face with the captain. Acantha held her ground, motionless as the beast sniffed the air around them. It lowered its head to the dead creature under her feet. Bloody remnants of the dead sailors were strewn around the area. Then the light hit the front of the ship. The devil's dog jumped back to the wall, away from the burning rays.

Basile's eyes were blinded from the full force of the sun, as though he stood next to it. He threw his arm over his eyes, shielding himself. As his eyes adjusted, a tropical paradise opened to his view. The ship moved into a gulf surrounded by a beautiful island with a large mountain spiraling straight into the heavens. The entire crew gazed at its wondrous size, entranced, as if the sand on the shore were nothing but gold coins piled in heaps. Echoing noises of wildlife burst from the lush jungle and a single small pathway led up from the golden beach toward the mountain. The sheer cliffs cut through the foaming clouds in the sky. There was no evident way up, but at the top, a cave led into the depths of the solid rock.

"Look there!" One of the sailors pointed to the middle of the gulf. A large metal rod stuck straight out from the water.

"Sail up to it, Mr. Jennings," Acantha ordered, "and anchor us there."

Jennings steered for the rod to come starboard side. An oversized corked glass bottle with a message inside was strapped atop it.

"What is it, Captain?" asked Vaster. The crew murmured, gathering near the rail.

"Instructions," she answered without looking at them. She walked past, uninterested, up to the helm, where she dropped her pistols with their wrappings on the floor.

Vaster followed on her heels. "Captain, shouldn't we read it?"

"I already know what it says." She jumped up on the railing, preparing to dive overboard. She crouched and looked back at the curious stares of the crew.

Basile walked to the edge of the ship. The gulf was deep and crystal clear. A ship graveyard lay below them. Hundreds of vessels adorned the rocks. A creature swam among the wreckage, a red squid double the size of a full-grown man.

Acantha spoke. "Only one person can go overboard. The rest must stay on the ship. Those are the rules. I will go."

"How long should we wait till we come a lookin' for ye?" Vaster asked nervously.

She smirked at him. "Stay on the ship."

He stared back with worry and abandonment, and she fed on this torture. The devilish smile on her face alarmed him. "What do you mean? I think we should read the instructions before ye go." Panicked, he ran toward the staircase. Before he could finish his sentence she dove into the water.

"Captain?" he shouted down at her, but she ignored him and swam to the shore. "Captain!"

Vaster turned on his heels. "Fish out that message!" he shouted at the men. They fastened themselves on the ropes, extending their bodies far enough. Basile helped anchor them as the note was retrieved and handed to Vaster. Basile read it over his shoulder.

Both men's eyes bulged as they yelled in unison: "WAIT!" toward the captain.

Soon she reached the shore. As her feet left the water, a loud rumbling started. The sea boiled, and the boat shook like an earthquake were onboard. The crew held to the stable parts of the ship as the water foamed around it. Some of the men looked as though they might jump overboard, but Vaster stopped them just in time.

Water shot up around the ship like fountains flying straight into the sky. It spread out, curving around the boat in a thick, hollow dome, flowing continually, until it had trapped *The Dark Eve*.

Angry shouts protested from the men as they ran frenziedly around the poop deck.

"Stay onboard if ye want to live!" shouted Vaster—as he and Basile dragged them from the railings.

"You'll die if you jump!" warned Basile. The men backed away to the safe center.

Jennings and Scar joined them. "What do the instructions say?" Jennings demanded.

Basile answered, "Only one person can go onto the island to see the Oracle. If any other man gets off this boat, they'll die." Both Jennings and Scar looked at each other. "We have to wait here until she enters the water again, and the dome will disappear."

"And if she never comes back?" a nearby sailor asked.

"As long as she is alive, we stay alive. If she dies," he paused peering through the crystal-clear water dome, "we die." It was the conundrum of the whole maze—she needed them to get to the center and they needed her to get out.

Acantha smirked and turned to the path that led up to the mountain. A mangled sign stood at its base warned visitors not to leave it. An instant death was rewarded to those that did, like most obstacles of the maze.

When she reached the mountain it was sheer cliff straight up to the cave. Her energy lulled. Calmly, she laid her forehead against the cold rock, allowing it to cool her brow. Then, she started up.

At first, the cool temperature affected her skill, but soon her body heat caught up with the strain of the climb. Several times she almost lost her footing. She scrambled to keep hold and get stable again. She looked back at the bubble that covered the ship and continued. Her hands ached with pain and were beginning to bleed. The opening to the cave was three-fourths the way up. Halfway there, she stood on a narrow ledge to catch her breath, allowing her legs to hold her weight. The sun was starting its descent in the sky.

As she reached up for the next ledge, it gave way, throwing her off balance. She reeled back onto her other hand, and her foot slipped. She skidded down, catching a safety spot she had last chosen. Cringing, she once again pressed herself against the wall before searching for an alternate route.

For hours she labored every muscle in her body. Sweat dripped from her face, and her limbs shook with exhaustion. Just as the sun was setting, she heaved herself up onto the cave's floor. Panting, she lay there to catch her breath upon the cold rock beneath her. Though she was dripping with sweat she was also freezing. The cave's path spiraled down into the mountain. Strange torches with white flames guided her. She dodged the bats disturbed by her presence.

The downward slope was gladly welcome after her climb. After half an hour, it finally opened up into a great room. A pond of lava boiled in front of her. It blocked the path that led to the opening on the other side, where a faint blue glow radiated.

She sat on a rock to rest. Skeletons with their clothes still on them adorned that side of the pond by her. She leaned over to the one lying next to her. "Got all this way and chickened out?" She tipped her head to him as though he spoke to her. "Instead of lying there starving and dying, you should have just thrown yourself in and got it over with." She stood up and walked up to the pond. "You see?" She stuck her hand down by the lava. "From here it feels like it could melt your flesh off! But," she waved her hand at the skeleton before putting it into the lava. It was freezing cold. "It's not hot at all!" She pulled her hand out and showed him. She shook the lava muck off her hand and started the small trek across the lake to the door.

"You know," she shouted over to the opening on the other side, "you didn't have to make it so cold!" A humming relayed from the doorway. She slogged to the rocks and stomped the muck off. On the other side, the skeleton's jaw was dropped in a deathly pose.

She gloated and proceeded downward. The rock walls faded to a smooth blue shell. Light from an underground water source illuminated the walls, making them flicker as the path spiraled. It was nothing like the doom-and-gloom skeleton lava pit above.

"You've got quite an illusion here. How many poor fools make it across that fire pit, only for your words to send them straight to their doom?"

Her voice echoed off the walls. She stopped at the bottom of the path where it leveled out, heading straight for the lake and dock. There, the most glorious ship she had ever set eyes upon lay in the underground harbor. The radiant blue light from the water made the ship more magnificent and large, twice the size of her own. "I see you got a new ship." Her words echoed off the walls. The entire vessel was a monster-sized king's crown seashell, manipulated and bowed. The defensive spikes stuck out at least seven feet and curved around the front of the ship to a long sharp point. "What did you name her?"

A quiet female voice, vibrated behind her. Acantha did not look to the source. "It's the same ship, just transformed." The cavern walls hummed with her speech. "It was a gift, from Solon."

The room was huge, and at the far side sat a large throne of seashells glowing brightly with the purest white light. The gentle voice flowed like the glow of the water.

"Good to see you're getting along with the family," Acantha said without looking at her. "Well, I think you should rename her. *The Elizabeth* doesn't suit her anymore. If you ran that thing directly into another ship you could split it in two." The sheer pleasure of this intriguing idea made her insides tingle.

"I see your sense of humor is still intact. Even after all these years."

Acantha turned away from the ship and slid down the small ridge from the pathway toward the Oracle. "Yes, well, I'm always in need of a good sense of humor. You already know why I'm here," she said dryly, stopping just shy of the throne.

Behind it, the wall moved like a camouflaged curtain. The Oracle stepped out. The source of light rippling off the water radiated from her. It glowed from within her white porcelain skin. Her features were dimensionally perfect, and with the illumination she was majestic. The blue of her eyes were the only real color on her, like a tropical ocean after a storm. Her every movement was slow and calm, an angel of the sea.

The Oracle sat upon her throne so light, like she didn't even touch the seat. Her white gown flowed to the ground. "You still have to ask," she said.

"Where is Jennet?"

The Oracle paused and looked down almost sympathetically. Then her eyes closed and light shone from under her lids. A small hum radiated around the room. The sound built as the light from her eyes intensified.

The cavern grew brighter as if she pulled her power from the room itself. Her voice boomed when she spoke. "She is captured!" Her eyes fluttered open and nothing but light flowed from them. "And held by the Sea Snake at the home of the sea wraiths. Her life hangs on a balance that must be filled." The Oracle's words were solemn. "By the king of the wraiths. He sits upon a throne of skulls, piled high." She paused. "You will find her in the center of the Basilisk's sea, past the mountains of blood. The wraiths flow like fire ants upon the earth there. Your last breath will be her only hope."

Acantha could see the vision the Oracle spoke of in her own mind, as clear as if she stood there. The red island, smoldering in dust, rose out of the sea. A large native man sat on a throne of skulls with a big fish scale pendant around his neck. Her sister's face flickered in the shadow of cell bars, and deep through the jungle a lake stood eerie with marsh and a small center island covered in human bones.

Acantha wiped the sweat from her brow, though she didn't fear the Oracle's words. "I was hoping for good news." She shifted her weight as her mind broke from the vision.

Finally, she knew the wraith's homeland and the source of their endless presence on the sea. Now, she could put an end to them.

The Oracle blinked, and the light disappeared, leaving the gentle blue color of her eyes again. "Why do you choose this enemy?"

Acantha did not answer. A small tingle started in her brain. "Prying where you shouldn't be?" She tilted her head away.

"I sense a deep hatred in you for them. I could simply take the memories from you," the Oracle said.

"I'd like to see you try," she barked out.

The Oracle looked away. "Do you not wish to know your end?" She spoke emotionlessly.

"No," Acantha answered with venom in her voice. "Though I am sure you would be glad to tell it to me." She turned to leave. "We both know why it won't happen."

"I do not feel as disappointing to you as you do to me," said the Oracle.

"I will choose my end someday," Acantha promised. "As I am sure you will."

The Oracle gazed upon her sympathetically. "My forever lives in a world where eternity exists."

Acantha's face tightened even more. "An unchanging one," she said through clenched teeth. "I see you continue to fool yourself."

"As do you," her quiet voice responded, "in a forever-changing world, when you do not change yourself. Is there any amount of treasure that will fill the emptiness inside you?"

"No. I don't see why you argue with my life when we serve the same person."

"The same arguments still hide within you," the Oracle accused back. "My service is fueled differently than yours."

"That may be, but it is my deal to live." Acantha's tone grew deadly. "Your life, however, is pointless."

The emotionless face of the Oracle looked gravely down at her.

Acantha softened, "R—"

"DON'T SPEAK MY NAME!" The Oracle's temperament changed and the cavern vibrated. The flow of her body burst into quick streaming movements that jumped like flames.

"Fine." Acantha rolled her eyes. She turned back to the path leading out, but before she started up the spiral road she faced the Oracle again. "Continue to keep all that anger bottled up. I'm anticipating the fire show. In the meantime, enjoy your prison."

"Acantha, I can have whatever I want here." And with her smug words the walls of the cavern distorted. Like a mirage, piles of gold the size of hills appeared around her. The smells of mint and vanilla flowed in a gentle breeze through her hair. Acantha closed her eyes and memories flooded in. She opened her eyes to see the familiar mountain in the background and a winding sandy beach. Two figures walked side by side in the distance toward her. It was too far to see their faces, but she knew them well. Her heart pounded as they became clearer and clearer...

"STOP!" She fell to her knees as she covered her eyes from the vision. Her head pulsed, and an emptiness filled her chest, as though it would collapse. Slowly she opened her eyes checking for any sign of the vision, but the blue flickering light was back. Her heart pounded harder than it had in a long time.

Acantha pointed to the Oracle. "You are still subject to the rules! Don't cross me!" She lashed out toward her, but the Oracle stood still. "Because the only reason you do stay is for him!" she yelled out to the cave, as if the words would go beyond the walls. "And you don't have him!" she said solemnly before she left.

CHAPTER SEVEN
Jennet and Le Voleur

The watery dome crashed down from around the ship, soaking the crew. They cheered as the captain swam back to them. With the sun burning in the sky, they had precious little time to get out of the maze before night fell. Vaster, Basile, Jennings, and Scar stood at the helm. A ladder was thrown over the side and when Acantha was on the ship again, they handed her personals to her. She joined them at the table nearby and summarized her encounter with the Oracle. They all stewed, but not one complained about her leaving the way she did.

She gave a little laugh. "Didn't enjoy the theatrics of the island?" She pulled out some charts from beneath the table. As she unrolled one, it diffused a reddish dust. Glances shot off between Vaster, Jennings, and Scar.

"She is here." Acantha pointed to the blood-red mountain on the map. The map had a tall red mountain in the middle of an island and a large oversized snake circled the bottom of it.

"Captain," Jennings said, "to the heart of the Blood Mountains? We only have a map of the island not the location."

"They will sink us the second they see the ship," rasped Scar. "We have destroyed too many of theirs."

"We don't know anythin' about their leader," Vaster said.

"Naulkiendum is his name. The Oracle showed him to me." She sighed, tired of the lack of options. "Once again, I go alone on the island." They all shook their heads in disagreement. She put her hand up to stop them. "Jennet's ship will be somewhere around there. I don't know if her crew is still alive, but I know she is. I need you to stay on board and keep *The Dark Eve* ready to sail at any moment." They all still shook their heads.

Basile just stood silently. *Did they not know that he was there?* As of yet, nobody had yelled at him to leave. Perhaps his presence was all right.

"There is no discussion," she said. "I've seen it. I know where to go. I know what to do."

It was hard for the three of them to disagree with her, especially after making it through to the Oracle. Her every command had delivered them to the middle of the maze with minimal losses.

Scar looked to both Jennings and Vaster. "We don't have much choice." His raspy voice was hoarse, like he had a cold. Basile had never heard him talk before.

Both Jennings and Vaster relinquished their hardened positions.

Acantha searched the eyes of her three most trusted crew members. Each had proved their loyalty to her, earning their place on her ship. "This last year has been different for us. I promise we will get back to our treasure hunting soon."

Jennings's deep voice boomed. "It's not that, Captain. We feel the winds are changing."

Acantha nodded her understanding. So she wasn't the only one who felt changes coming upon them. It built like water behind a dam inside her chest, threatening to burst. Her eyes flew to Basile.

All of the sudden he felt like he was in the wrong place.

"It will happen soon," she said, her expression accusing.

Basile spoke in defense. "I don't want things to change!"

All four of them stared at him like the idiot he was. Vaster slapped his own head with disappointment and scooted him off the helm.

When they were away from hearing distance, Jennings piped up again. "It's him, isn't it?"

Acantha assessed his understanding. "Yes."

"Do you know?" he asked.

"No," she replied. They all stood in silence, watching as Vaster thrust the mop at Basile while scolding him for his lack of propriety. Basile leaned on his mop and endured the reprimand.

"Explains why you haven't killed him yet," huffed Scar. Jennings nodded.

"I don't know," she whispered. "All I know is he must stay. I'm leaving you two in charge of making sure he doesn't die."

Basile looked up, noticing their gazes. He stood straight, paying more attention to Vaster, who still yelled at him.

Déjà vu.

"Steer us out of here, Jennings," Acantha ordered. "As the sun sets, it will reveal the crack in the end of the maze. It can only be seen from the inside."

She left them on the helm and went below to sleep, barely capable of holding herself upright. Inside her room she collapsed against the wall. Fumbling at her belt, she tossed it toward the desk. The bed was too far away as she staggered toward it. It didn't take her long to slip into unconsciousness—

In her dreams, the snow fell heavily around her face as she walked up the tall hill. She was constantly catching her step on the slush. There was nothing worse to her than snow. The heavy cloak covering her body from the weather hardly worked. She stopped, assessing the directions that the townspeople had given her. The small road led up and over the hill. As she reached the top, in the far distance, a tall, dark building looked just like her vision. She had found the right place. Her wrestling with demons did pay off in the long run.

Sounds came from her left. She trudged up a small hill and gazed down at the scene. A frozen pond sat between two more hills with no trees in sight. Snow and frost and ugly winter misery drenched everything. Down on the banks of the pond were piles of wood. A canvas tent stood barely tethered to the ground and moving in the wind. Just outside the tent were three boys, their ages ranging between eight and ten. The eldest boy stood on a crate in front of the tent talking to the other two.

"This is our new home now! We'll live out the winter here, and then in the spring we'll find a better place."

A black lad spoke up. "How will we eat?"

The older boy glared down at him. "We'll steal, of course."

A smaller blond boy stood next to the dark-skinned lad quietly, making no objections. All three boys looked like they hadn't eaten a good meal in their lifetime. Their faces stretched tight, with dark circles under their eyes. The clothes on their backs were tattered and worn—one didn't even have shoes.

The black boy piped up again. "I don't know about this." He shook his head with concern at their meager situation.

The older boy jumped off the box in front of him. "Well, Mr. Smarty-Pants, what do you suggest?"

"I don't know."

"Then I guess you'll have to listen to me. Don't worry. I know what I'm doing."

The other two just looked at each other.

"Now get some wood together and we'll start a fire."

They collected the wood around their pitiful campsite. Acantha watched with great interest. All three would die. Their frozen figures would be part of the frigid landscape in days. She looked forward in the distance toward the dark structure ahead. Smoke billowed out of its chimney. It was the only place they might have come from.

Maybe their existence would not be so worthless?

She walked down the hill toward their encampment. The older boy saw her first and stood straight from his position in the snow. The other two noticed his alertness and stood as well, watching her approach.

The older boy spoke firmly to her. "We won't go back."

She glanced again to the dark building. She nodded in its direction, a mute question.

The older boy nodded back, confirming. The other two stood freezing, eyes wide and pitiful.

"What is it?" she asked the older boy.

"An orphanage to outside eyes," he said. He motioned to the other two. "We escaped."

"And why is that?" But she knew why. Her visions all made sense now.

The boys looked to the ground, unwilling to speak. She walked closer, towering over them.

"I am looking for a man who they call Joseph Brigham." All three boys shared glances. "To most he would look like a regular man. But to others, closer to him, he might appear darker and strange."

The older boy judged her words. He pointed to the building in the distance. "It's a death house, lady. If you go in there, you won't come out."

She pulled her cloak off and covered the boy with it. "Tell me how you escaped."

She found the underground gated entrance, just as the older boy described. It was solid iron. All three of them had wiggled through the bars. It stood ten yards back from the weathered three-story house. All the shutters on the windows were closed and no light came from them.

She rattled on the gate assessing its strength. The lock holding it shut was old and rusted. She took out her pick and tinkered. Soon, she threw the lock out into the snow. The gate opened into an underground pathway to the basement of the house. She stepped over small, shallow graves. Roots hung from the dirt above.

The basement was large and square, with tall, molding walls. A narrow wooden staircase stood against the far side. She followed the path and quietly stepped into the upper level, with its gray, bare walls. The wood floors warped with age. She walked into the main room. There was no furniture, but a grand staircase wound up the side of the room to the next level. Creaking sounded from above. She hid beneath the staircase.

Footsteps thudded across the top floor and down the stairs. A tall man dressed in black appeared. His black hair fell straight to his shoulders and his hands were unnaturally white with a gray tint. Instantly, Acantha knew this was the man she sought. His evil tingled against her insides.

"I know you're here," the man said, his voice dull. "I can smell you." He spun, looking under the stairway only to find it empty. "Tricky, and much better than the rest."

He walked into the next room, which had a large fireplace as tall as him. He looked inside for the trespasser. "There aren't many places here for you to hide. Please reveal yourself so we can speak." He strolled to the door that led to the basement and listened for any sound. Then he returned to the great room with the staircase. The front door stood slightly ajar. He stepped close and examined the landscape. Finding nothing, he bolted the door and walked into the middle of the large room. "I have to admit, I am at a loss." He took several more steps toward the staircase, looking up to the second floor.

"That's strange," her velvety voice spoke from behind him. The man spun, his eyebrows raised high. She braced herself on the windowsill, one leg against the opposite side of the frame and the other dangling to the floor. She was spinning her knife in her hands staring out the window into the winter storm.

This was the window, she thought.

"Most people knock," he said.

"I'm sure they do."

He was much older around his eyes and had an oblong head with a pointy chin, balding just around his hairline. His eyes were sunken and dark around the edges, as if he never slept. He stood straight with his arms clasped behind him, his dark coat covering him well.

"Joseph Brigham, I presume?"

He looked confused that she should know his name. "Might I inquire as to who is visiting me?"

"I am quite sure introductions are not necessary for such dealings."

"I insist. I like to know the name of my company."

While his voice sounded cordial, she was starting to upset him. Acantha stood from the windowsill placing the dagger in her belt. She faced him straight on with her fingers poised in front of her face like she was thinking. They both stared, searching for all the unknown information between them.

"You're very brave to come here."

It was a warning. She remained expressionless.

"Brave," he repeated, "but foolish as well." He gave a small, crooked smile. "I can see you are no ordinary guest. What do you want?"

"I'm looking for something that I heard you have." She did not take her eyes off of him.

"I see. What is it you seek?" He now bored down on her, squinting.

She spoke delicately. "A key."

He looked to the ceiling, smiling. "You might have to be more specific than that, my dear."

She treaded closer to him, and his smile widened at her foolishness. "I think you know which key I'm talking about." She stopped just feet from him. "It's made of bone."

His eyes lit up with recognition, judging her seriousness. "I don't think you understand what you're asking for."

"Let's test that." Delight sprang to his face as she set the challenge. "But before we do," she said firmly to him, "let us strike a deal."

Joseph looked intrigued. "And what would that be, madam?"

"If I defeat you, then you tell me where the key is?"

"And if I win?"

"I guess that it won't matter, will it?"

A wicked smile stretched across his face and he lowered his head like a dog right before it attacked. The white of his eyes turned black. Veins like roots grew out from his eyes around the sides of his face. Acantha stood unmoving. His thin lips curled back to reveal his dagger-like teeth. When he spoke, it rasped out.

"Might I now inquire of your name?" His fingers had grown sharp claws. He crouched to the floor.

"Acantha," she replied just before he sprang at her. She spun out of the way, pulling her dagger from her belt. He landed across the room in a crouching position. She held her dagger horizontally and flickered her eyebrows up at the vampire.

He clapped, applauding her effort. "I am impressed."

She blew a piece of hair out of her face. "Do you always go straight for the kill? I enjoy the hunt more."

He bobbed his head back and forth like an animal stalking its prey. He leaped at her, and they both rolled backward toward the stairs. She landed on her back with the monster on top. She held both of his hands at the wrist straining to keep them from her face.

Strange lights flashed where their skin met. His face winced at the contact. She expected them as the unnatural effect of her run in with abnormal evil. She kicked her legs against his torso and sent him over her head. Once again, they crouched face-to-face. Her knife lay three feet to her left.

He lunged again. She rolled and grabbed her knife just in time to slice through his arm. He retreated several feet, examining the wound. Around the edges, the skin turned black and flaked like ash from his body. He looked up at her, stunned but fueled with anger. He attacked again, throwing her against the far wall. It knocked the wind out of her and dropped her straight to the ground. He grabbed her foot, throwing her across the room. She rolled several times and lay motionless on the ground.

As he approached, her heart beat rapidly within her chest from the adrenaline. He picked her up by her hair and neck, dangling her in the air above him.

"I think I will enjoy you very much, my dear." He caressed her bulging veins.

With the click of her heels, a blade popped out of the toe of her boot. She lodged it firmly in his shin. He dropped her, and she used the force of her descent to drive the knife into his shoulder, near his heart.

He screamed as his skin burned like the sun spreading through his body. He fell to his knees, almost incapable of moving.

"Didn't your mother teach you not to play with your food?" She knelt down to his level. "This must have been quite a challenge to you in comparison to children."

Pure hatred smoldered out of his eyes. "Fortunately for me," he hissed, "there are always unwanted children."

"You're finished," she said walking around him. "I had that knife made especially for you. It took only the first cut to condemn you. The poison is in your bloodstream now. Soon it will burn you from the inside out."

Searing pain moved through his body to all of his limbs. His shoulder disintegrated like ash floating away. He watched it, panting like a dog as sweat dripped from his brow.

She towered over him. "Where is the key? A deal is a deal."

He gasped in air. "Top floor, main room, behind the picture," he hissed. The rest of his body disintegrated into ash, circling the area before drifting to the ground like the snow outside.

The house burned in the distance as she returned to town. The three boys stood on the top of the hill, watching the large fire. She walked straight past them. As she was about to descend the hill, she stopped in her tracks and looked at the village several miles off. She turned back to the three frozen figures.

"You take orders from me now. If you have a problem with that, you can stay here and die. If I get any trouble from any of you, I'll kill you myself." She spoke harshly so that they understood her well. "What are your names?"

The older boy stood forward. "John Vaster." He then pointed to the black lad and then to the smaller child, "Bowen Jennings and Timothy Long."

◇◇◇

John Vaster stood on the helm of the ship. Jennings was at the wheel as normal, and Scar plotted their points upon the map. Vaster scanned the ocean scenery. The captain had not been up in four days. Worry filled him when he was not able to assess her mood. If he could find a wraith ship or anything of interest upon the sea, then he had reason to disturb her. He didn't dare do it without reason.

"I think I might go down and check on the captain's meals for the day." He tried his hardest to sound casual. But he didn't fool Jennings and Scar. His tone portrayed his guilt. They barely looked at him.

"What? Just want to be sure they are on top of things!"

"Leave her be," Jennings warned.

Scar's hoarse voice piped in. "It's not uncommon for her to leave to herself for a good amount of time."

"But what if she needs somethin'?" Vaster asked.

"Leave her be," Jennings said for the last time.

Vaster, defeated, leaned against the railing and once again diverted his attention to the ocean. A calamity shouted from the deck below and he barged away.

His heart skipped an angry beat as he observed Basile flat on his back on the ground. Frank Carter, a large, broad-shouldered new recruit stood over him snarling like a dog. A crowd already clustered around the two. Both Jennings and Scar shared glances as Vaster shoved his way to the middle.

"What is goin' on here?" he yelled. Basile was propped up on his elbows. Carter kicked him down again, and Vaster flew up into Carter's face, even though he stood feet below him.

"What are ye doing? Have ye gone mad? Fightin' just feet from the captain's door?"

Basile thought he had seen Vaster's angry face, but this expression actually scared him. He was livid and fuming.

Carter, a large, white, muscular man with a bald head, stood undeterred by Vaster's threats. Vaster did not back down.

"This rat hit me in the back. He's an idiot!" Carter's face was stiff. "I'm just teaching him a lesson on how to stay out of my way!" He glared at Basile over Vaster's shoulder, expressing his apparent hatred of him.

Basile scrambled to his feet, brushing off his clothes. Though Carter was larger, he refused to feel threatened.

"I don't care!" Vaster yelled out. "Get back to work!" He pointed to the deck doors.

"And if I don't? Seems to me this is between me and him." Once again he scowled at Basile. Jennings and Scar presented themselves on deck among the crowd. Carter stepped back at their presence. "He doesn't belong here. I'll be doing the captain a favor by getting rid of him."

Anger stabbed at Basile. He had traveled the same road as Carter. He had survived the maze and killed a wraith. He was earning his right onboard.

Jennings piped in. "Captain says he stays. He's not to be harmed, her orders."

Shock crept up Basile's face as he looked to Jennings. The captain had ordered his safety. He wasn't a baby. He didn't need anyone's protection.

Carter smiled. "She must fancy him, then. No other reason would exist for allowing him on the ship." The nearby sailors chuckled.

This set Basile off. He threw himself at Carter, though Vaster was still between them.

Basile yelled as Carter tried to attack. "Shut your mouth."

Vaster held him back.

Jennings spoke again. "Captain's orders are captain's orders."

The crowd opened up. Acantha stood on the outskirts of the fight. The crew became silent.

"I have the right to challenge this man." Carter pointed to Basile.

She nodded in agreement. The men cheered and readied for the fight. Vaster gaped at Acantha as she walked up to the helm. Jennings and Scar followed her, but not before throwing their muted looks in Carter's direction. Carter took off his vest and grabbed a sword from a nearby barrel. Vaster prepared Basile to fight.

"I don't understand what's going on here," Basile admitted. "Why was she protecting me?"

Vaster answered with a look of annoyance as he strapped a sword to his waist.

"But now she's gonna make me fight this raving lunatic?" Basile looked up to the captain. She was squinting at him in judgment. Both Jennings and Scar watched from behind her.

Basile stopped Vaster from buckling the sword on his waist. "What's going on?"

Vaster looked confidently back at him. "Ye'll have to learn to trust the captain." This was the first time he had talked to him like he was an adult. "Ye have to earn yer place onboard like all the rest. And when ye do, yer questions will be answered."

Basile looked to all the weathered faces on the ship. In the beginning he had seen them as old and weak, broken by age and appearance. But each worked harder than he, and in such unison and conformity.

He felt like an outsider. As though he was pretending to be among them. This angered him even more. He wanted most of all to be an equal among them. All of his dreams of finding his ultimate treasure and retiring to a lost island in peace dissolved. He looked back up to the captain, deliberating as he soaked in Vaster's words. The only position he had on the ship was to clean the floors. Yet she had preserved him several times in their journey.

Carter was ready, towering before him. "Let's get this going!"

Basile flinched with recognition. "Wait, you are the guy from the fish hut?" His mind traveled back to that incident the night before they left port. He had been so preoccupied that he had completely forgot.

Carter squinted at him, confused. And Basile looked away, recognizing his foolishness but also delighted at solving the mystery.

Vaster smacked him across the face, hard enough to bloody his lip.

Basile recovered with betrayal and shock. "What the hell?"

Vaster looked back at him seriously. "Wake up, or this man will run ye through. Will ye do the same?" With a nod, he ran up to the helm by the captain.

Basile shook the pain off his face.

"What if he dies?" Vaster asked Acantha in a hushed, skeptical voice.

"Then he dies." She spoke as if she didn't care. "Can't fight all of his fights for him."

Carter circled, and Basile followed his steps. The men looped around them.

Basile held his sword out, keeping distance between them. Carter smiled, as if he were going to enjoy killing him. He clinked their swords together, toying with him. Basile held his grip and continued to circle.

Carter lunged in jokingly, causing him to jerk back. Carter laughed. "He's afraid."

The crowd chuckled around him. With greater firmness, Basile held tight his sword.

Carter genuinely plunged at him. Basile blocked his blow but felt Carter's overpowering strength from above. Carter swiped again, this time to the middle. Basile once again blocked his blow. And then the sword fight started.

Basile kept on the defense, blocking as Carter delivered continual strikes. They glided around the deck of the ship. Carter was much stronger and persistent, but Basile was faster. He had never been in a serious fight before killing the wraith. Though he had been trained in sword fighting, it was never directed toward killing. Which did not serve him now.

With each blow Carter struck down harder and harder, knocking him back. He swung for his feet. Basile jumped up on a barrel and hopped to the other side of the ship. Carter turned and ran at a full sprint toward him, a craze in his eyes. Before they could collide, Basile spun out of his way—just as he had seen the captain do—down the line of Carter's body, and pushed him head-on into the side of the ship. Carter crashed into the railing knocking him out. He came to with Basile standing over him, sword pointed at his neck. Carter glared up with loathing and then glanced to the other crew members.

"Give me a sword," he yelled, but no one moved to his aid.

The captain still stood expressionless to the ongoing scene. Basile waited for whatever she should order. She nodded to him, giving him leeway. Basile lifted his sword above his head. Carter's eyes bulged in shock. He closed his eyes as Basile brought his sword down. A large thudding answered, and a moment passed.

Carter opened his eyes and blinked at the sword stuck in the railing just above his head. He scrambled heavily to his feet, coming face-to-face with Basile once again. With murder still in his eyes, but he turned away, headed to his post. The nearby sailors patted Basile on the back and went to their posts as well.

Power flooded Basile. He looked up to the helm to find Vaster's pleased face. Acantha turned away.

He went straight to his hammock in the crew's quarters by the window, shaking from the adrenaline that pumped through his veins. The cool sea air brushed his face, calming him. His mind raced. What game was she playing with him?

He drew out the golden box from a pocket he had sewn under his hammock. Lying back, he looked it over just as he did every night before going to sleep. The sun through the window struck against its glimmering surface, splaying golden rays throughout the room.

This piece of treasure meant more to the captain than she would ever tell. And still she threw it away as if it meant nothing. What had it contained? When he had given her the box, it was the first time he had seen emotion in her eyes.

A spark of recognition overlaid the images on the box, like two puzzle pieces finally fitting together. Basile rolled out of his hammock and rushed out of the door, down the stairs of *The Dark Eve* to the mural. He held the box up to the jungle terrain carved there. The carvings were exactly the same. The same strange fire-like bird existed in both places.

If the box reflected the same images as her ship, it originated from the same place. The crafters were the same. She knew it.

So where did it come from?

◇◇◇

They found the wraith island easily. Acantha had every step burned in her mind and after that last raid she now had a map. It burst into view like large spiked teeth covered in dark red dirt.

"Damned wraiths," she muttered. The movements upon the island flowed like ants. There would be no escaping recognition. She had taken too much pleasure in attacking their ships and watching them sink.

Memories of fires building high in the tall grass, screams from the villagers, and their fleeing movements blurred in her vision. Confusion and panic filled the air. The wraiths swarmed a seashore town with machetes, killing anything that appeared. Their faces distorted like wild animals.

It had been the first time she had seen one of them, and her first time to kill one as well, long ago, before *The Dark Eve*.

A port stood at the bottom of one of the steepest red mountains. A long, curving dirt path led upward. Acantha was surprised by the lack of attention she and her ship received. The wraiths bobbed back and forth on the island, working. She stepped off the boat and onto the island, half expecting them to attack, but they continued like she didn't exist.

She started up the red mountain's path alone. It wound up a cave at the very top. That's where she would find Naulkiendum.

The opening to the cave wasn't even guarded. She glanced back upon the spectacular view of the sea. On the other side of the mountain was thick jungle, just as the memory given to her by the Oracle. Out there was a lake with shores covered in bones and a monster lying in wait.

The dark wraith king sat on his bulging bone throne, fat and swollen, rotting in his own filth. He spat out his words. "I heard that you had come to my island." Spikes impaled his skin and stuck out all over his face. He looked like a giant blowfish. "The dark mark!" he called her.

"I'm here for my sister," Acantha said. While the Oracle might have provided her every direction, it could not have prepared her for the smell. The whole cave stank. It took all her concentration not to throw up.

He shook his head hard. His fat belly jiggled with the movement.

"I know you have her," she said. "I'm here to negotiate for her release." Negotiating with this pig was beneath her, but necessary.

"I don't know why you vouch for your sister. She brings nothing but misery."

"I see you've come to enjoy her sweet personality while she's been here." She gave him a mocking smile. "She is still my sister, regardless."

"I killed all my family." He pointed along the side of the wall to a dozen skeletons that were hung and dressed in clothes, and even adorned with jewelry. "I can keep a good eye on all of them! HA!" He broke out in a ghastly laugh, swaying back and forth. "Maybe you should do the same!"

"I'll think about that." She relaxed her position, folding her arms. The cave was hot. Sweat dripped from her forehead.

"This is not going to be easy." His oversized fingers strummed his beard.

"It never is," she muttered. "Stop being coy with me and tell me what the deal is."

"No man dares talk to me like you do." He glared at her.

She stared straight back at him. "I am not a man, and I do not fear the same as one does."

He eyed her, coveting. "And you are beyond equal to one. I know of you and your wretched ship. It takes from me all the time." His fists crashed down onto the table in front of him, jolting everything that stood upon it. She didn't respond. He pointed his swollen finger at her. "You have crushed my trade ships. I'm surprised of your appearance. I didn't expect such a beautiful woman. You and your sister both are interesting. She, though, is conceited." He licked his chapped protruding lips.

"Let's not pretend here," she replied. "You are no tradesman."

He stood, threatening, but she wasn't tricked.

"I'll warn you not to jest with me. You're a menacing, no-good wraith of a pirate," Acantha said.

He sat back down with a pleased grin. "I take everything by the rules. Everybody has a chance to kill me just as I do them."

Disgust washed over her. *Who would want to get close enough to kill him?*

But she lived by the same rules. What a man can't protect he can't keep.

"Your sister has stolen something from me."

"So why haven't you just killed her and taken it back? Why am I having this conversation with you?"

"She lost it. And now I require something in its place." He stamped his foot and stood again. His half-naked body jiggled, and the foul smell stirred. "This was not a mere trinket that I keep around like the rest of my gold. It was special, my looking pendant. Made from the scales of my Sea Snake and framed in gold. It can see beyond the eyes of a regular looking glass." His nose flared.

In her mind, she could see the pendant hanging around his neck just as the Oracle had shown her. She now understood what enticed Jennet. From the top of this mountain, a view and pendant like that would be quite helpful. Jennet was always after rare treasures.

"Naulkiendum." She was tired of the smell, tired of the mess, and tired of standing. "What do you want for my sister?"

He shook his head childishly. "You're not getting out that easy, lady. I want something greater. If I don't get it, then I get your sister. I'm sure she will improve the audience." He again gestured to his skeleton family.

Her face hardened at his words. Her blood started boiled and her hands itched for her swords. Only five steps, a quick blow, and it would all be over, but she knew better. Naulkiendum might appear to be a fat, old, smelly pig, but he was a powerful man and probably the greatest match she would ever see. He had known she would come for Jennet; it had only been a matter of time.

"What do you want?"

"I want the Golden Eye." The words echoed off the walls.

She shook her head at the ridiculous request. "The Golden Eye is a myth."

His face widened in a sparsely toothed grin, probably in delight at putting her on a wild goose chase that she would lose. "You had better hope it's not, for your sister's sake."

In the end, what choice did she have? "I'll need my sister back. Alive and unharmed."

He shook his head again in his childish way, an absolute no.

"If I'm to go to the ends of the earth to find some stupid nonexistent pendant, I will need my sister." Her words were absolute.

He strummed his fingers against the table. "Here is the deal. You can have your sister back. You have three months to find me my Golden Eye, and at the end of the three months you will deliver it to me here, or I will unleash the Sea Snake, and you will die along with your sister."

She reflected on his words. It was nice to have the games out of the way and the threats out in the open. "No."

He staggered in surprise. His face clenched in anger. His hand reached over to a large leather-hilted sword by the table.

"I don't trust you," she said. "I, *and* my sister, will find your pendant, but I won't bring it to you here, and I need six months. I'll meet you at the

Doors of Hell." She smiled inside.

If she ventured back to this island, she would never leave it alive. The Doors of Hell was the perfect meeting place, a small enough island that he wouldn't be able to take a lot of men. One side was sheer cliff, jagged and sharp and the pathway small. It plateaued at the top, where ancient ruins sat. It was a place disturbed with great energy. Those who strayed from the path found death on the cliffs below.

He sat back in his throne, pondering her changes. "You have four months. I will meet you at the Doors of Hell. Go back to your boat, Captain. I will deliver your sister there. Her ship will be released on the other side of my island, along with what remains of her crew."

She didn't bother to shake his hand, it was meaningless. Plus, that meant she would have to touch him and then cut off her own hand for touching something so disgusting. She just started for the fresh air outside. Even the musky rotten egg smell of the mountain was refreshing.

The trip down was a lot easier. When she reached the ship, a herd of wraiths bobbed back and forth like apes. In the midst of them was Jennet, tall and proud even after a year of captivity. She was as tall as Acantha, but with dark straight hair that flowed down her back. Her eyes were a shade lighter, her face wider and her lips thinner. She was dressed in only a stained, dirty shirt and tight brown pants.

As Acantha approached, Jennet lifted her hands, which were bound. The closest wraith drew his jagged knife and cut through the rope in one stroke. Jennet rubbed her raw wrists and squeamishly squeezed past.

Stuck up to the very end. Acantha boarded *The Dark Eve.*

All of her men were alert.

"Vaster, take us to the other side of the island, to *Le Voleur.*"

A quick "Aye-aye," answered from him. She simply walked into her chambers. Jennet followed.

The door shut.

"You gold-digging idiot! I should kill you now and get it over with!" Acantha cried out. She paced the length of her cabin, warring between irritation and relief.

"Stop boring me with your threats." Jennet's thick French accent pulsated. She leaned back in the chair behind Acantha's captain's desk and pulled up her sleeves, investigating her arms, "I need a bath."

Her accent always pinged Acantha's every nerve, their complicated relationship cursed anyone that even reminded her of Jennet. "How many times am I going to have to dig you out of your messes?"

"You are so dramatic!" Jennet yelled.

Acantha drew her knife from her belt and sent it flying. It barely missed Jennet's face and pierced the wall behind her. Jennet didn't flinch, but her eyes burned.

Acantha returned the expression. "You stole from him and you got caught. He murdered most of your crew and now has claim to your life. So either we find some crazy idea of a pendant, whose wearer will be able to control men's souls," her voice swooned with melodrama and her arms waved in the air, "or after four months, he'll release the Sea Snake and we're both served for dinner."

Jennet waved her hand carelessly. "We'll just find the Golden Eye and give it to him." She sat up, her voice thick with mischief. "Maybe we could trick him and keep it for ourselves. I'm sure it was next on my list, anyway."

Acantha burst. "Do you ever stop? Even if the Golden Eye exists, we are no match for the beast he has out there!" She pointed toward the mountain and paced again. "If we fail, we're going to need a backup plan."

Jennet leaped to her feet and leaned over the desk. "If the pendant controls people, wouldn't it control the Sea Snake too?"

"The Sea Snake isn't a man." She bit down on her thumb, meditating.

"I've seen it." Jennet's voice went serious. She was rarely serious. Her lifestyle hid the real conflicts inside her, the things she allowed no one to understand. Her eyes glazed over and a far away look filled her face.

"If this soul-controlling pendant does exist——" Acantha paused, stressed. Jennet's eyes didn't show any sign of strain or wear. She was far too carefree, a trait that cost Acantha more and more each time she encountered her.

Naulkiendum's greed knew no bounds. No innocence found mercy from him. Acantha shuddered to think what he could want with the pendant, but it wouldn't be for anything good. "We cannot give it to him. Either way, we're up against him." She eyed Jennet seriously. "And the snake."

Jennet's shoulders sunk before she replied, "At least it won't be boring."

"I hope this doesn't have anything to do with us."

Jennet's smile faded from her perfect face. "It doesn't," she said firmly.

"What could he possibly get from an average person that he doesn't already take? Make them slaves? He has enough damned creatures to do his bidding. He has his mind set on something and it involves us."

"No," Jennet said. Her expression was distant.

Acantha walked over to the desk and slammed both hands down. "What have you told him?"

"Nothing, nothing," Jennet anxiously responded, still searching her mind for anything that might have piqued the old fat goat's interest in them. "I told him nothing! You know that, Acantha."

A long moment was quiet between them.

Jennet softened her voice. "Acantha, we will have to go to her."

Acantha closed her eyes. "I just got back from there!"

Jennet found an apple in one of the drawers and pulled Acantha's knife out of the wall behind her. "So what did the old bag say?"

Acantha decided not to mention that the Oracle had said her last breath was their only hope. "She told me where you were." She unlatched the northwest window of her chambers. It was close to dusk. She then went to her desk and nudged Jennet's legs off of it. She grabbed her quill and a piece of parchment and wrote a small note. This she rolled up and stuffed into a canister at the end of her desk. She withdrew a key from her bootlace and opened the locked top drawer of her desk. From a black velvet pouch within, she took out a solid gold whistle smaller than her fifth finger. A twine of golden ivy revolved around it and a shy red ruby sat at the top. Back at the window she blew the whistle's silent sound into the sunset. Half the sky adorned the night with stars, the other half painted the last of the day. A bright star streaked across the heavens.

"Go to my closet and get my leather."

Jennet sauntered over to the closet doors, flinging them open almost hard enough to break their hinges. She shuffled through the top, found the leather piece with straps, and threw it to her. Quickly, Acantha strapped the leather to her arm securing it tight before peering back out the window. The falling star curved its path straight toward the ship. The sky grew darker as the light from the star grew brighter. In the distance, a golden hawk glided gently above the water, streaming light behind it.

Acantha held out her arm as it neared. Its wings flapped wildly as it navigated its landing. She braced herself for the bird's weight. When it calmly sat upon her forearm the golden glow coming from the bird went out like a candle and its brownish-golden color bronzed. She gently moved the majestic creature from outside the ship into her chambers and shut the window.

"I hate that dumb bird," Jennet said. Its wings flapped open and it snapped its beak at her.

"I'm the one holding Taro, if you don't mind." Acantha kept her arm firm as the bird calmed itself again.

"Well, last time, it didn't give you two my message!" Jennet crossed to the bed and fell backward onto it.

"She showed up over a year ago, but she didn't have a note. That's what tipped us off that something was wrong. When you didn't show up for the drop-off…" Silent understanding passed between them.

"Yes, but it took you a whole year to figure it out. They came right when I was finishing the note. The stupid bird should have found it on my desk and given it to you."

Acantha rolled her eyes. There was no point in arguing with the irrational. She held the canister up to the bird's view. Taro fluffed her feathers and gazed at it. "For Tessa."

Taro flapped her wings, blowing papers from the desk. "All right, hold on!" Acantha opened the window and the bird's claws clamped around the canister. It flew out of the room. In the night, Taro glowed like the moon again.

"That stupid bird only loves Tessa," Jennet grumbled. "Useless."

Acantha shook her head. "We should almost be to your ship by now." She started for the door.

Jennet was on her feet at this news. "Good. I need a bath and some decent clothes. But we'll have to split your crew."

"Don't worry. I just acquired some new recruits before I came."

"I saw that new deck man you got."

Compared to all the sea dogs on ship, Basile's face was refreshing.

"He is a pain in my side," Acantha said with a stern glance. "You'd throw him overboard. You're too pompous."

"He can't be that dull if he can get a rise out of you and not be thrown overboard…" Jennet's face twisted with curiosity.

That Acantha freely admitted he bothered her and he was still in her service meant something.

"It does intrigue me, Sister." Jennet flirted with the idea in her head before she spoke. "Is there a soft spot in you for him?"

The idea was futile and Acantha expressed that upon her face.

Jennet shrugged. "You will forever be boring."

"For the rest of eternity, Jennet."

"That's what I'm afraid of."

A knock pounded at the door. "CAPTAIN?" It was Vaster.

Acantha whispered to Jennet, "We still have this year's drop-off to do."

Jennet rolled her eyes.

"Come in," Acantha called.

He opened the door. "We've come upon *Le Voleur*."

Jennet stood quickly. "It's about time!" She walked to the door. Vaster took his hat off and lowered his head, stepping out of her way. She arrogantly left.

He gave Acantha a weary look. "How long be she with us, Captain?"

"I don't know." She followed her sister. The sunset burned on the horizon, letting the last bit of night fall over the sky. The blood island smoldered. In the distance of the jungle sounded a horn, and the shrieking cries that had to be the monster echoed through the entire island.

The Sea Snake was probably vexed that it didn't get to eat Jennet. At that moment she sympathized with it, feeling vexed herself.

She walked up to the helm. *Le Voleur* sat in the cove. It had a black bow, but the upper part of the ship was a dark wood, with a red strip between the two halves. The bow was adorned with a black dragon whose mouth gaped wide to show carnivorous teeth. The dragon's massive wings splayed across the front of the ship. The large white sails were dropped and only four figures appeared on deck. Falke, Jennet's second, had just as many brilliant ideas as Jennet did and was always dressed in the French styles, and usually ruffled and curled to every tip. Nash was a massive native, scary as hell, but mute. His large silhouette made the other three look minuscule. Parnell and Raffles, the identical French twins stood next to each other—the troublemakers.

She had hoped they were dead.

"That's your whole crew?"

Jennet shrugged. "Only the important ones are left."

"We'll meet just outside the Scattered Isles. We'll leave two ships out to circle and take *The Dark Eve* in." Acantha was ready to throw her sister off the ship.

"Fine." Jennet stormed off the helm.

"Vaster!" Acantha yelled. He bounded up the stairs. "Split the crew and send half of them to *Le Voleur*!"

"Yes, Captain!" He turned to go back.

"Vaster!" she yelled again.

He turned on his heels halfway down. "Yes, Captain?"

"Keep Basile onboard," she whispered. "He'll be on ropes now."

Vaster nodded obediently and left.

Those who remained with *The Dark Eve* secretly cheered the moment Jennet left the ship, and laughed at the poor saps going with her. They reveled that night in celebration upon their success. Acantha didn't join them. She gave orders to sail toward the Oracle's island again, and for the rest of the evening she stayed in her quarters with her own bottle.

Something besides the new turmoil that now threatened them bothered her. The Oracle' words played and replayed, echoing in her mind.

"Your last breath will be her only hope."

Acantha poured herself another drink and sent it burning down her throat. Since she hadn't died in rescuing Jennet, there had to be more, and she didn't feel it would be while looking for the Golden Eye. So many times she had flirted with danger. Death had always been a possibility, but she never felt it, thanks to her preserving deal. She understood the rules and what she was not immune to.

◇◇◇

Deep in the jungle of the Blood Mountains stood Naulkiendum and a dozen of his wraiths on a shrine dock decorated with bones; the only light flickered from their torches. The obese king peered out into the black lake. A small triangle island stood out in the middle. A totem pole of a massive snake's head and torso with stone human bodies enveloped throughout it sat on the island.

A horn blew from one of the natives. The sound penetrated the whole island. It sounded two more times before movement flickered in the distance. The whole bottom of the small island set into motion and swirled, moving almost silently into the water. The wraiths behind Naulkiendum bobbed more.

The water spewed out. Up through the spray thrust the head of the great snake. Cries pierced into the night sky as its massive pillar of a body flailed.

Naulkiendum laughed, his belly jiggling up and down. "No worries, my friend. You will get to eat her."

He moved his hand up and down to calm the giant snake and it turned its head, looking down with one of its great yellow eyes.

"We will take a trip soon and you will have all three witches," he said gently. The reptile cocked its head and a heavy gurgle moved in its throat.

He grinned. "Until then, why don't you have a little treat?"

The snake attacked the wraiths behind Naulkiendum. They scattered, but it snapped them from the ground, waving them around in the sky before throwing them into the lake. When every last one of them had been broken into submission, the basilisk went for his feast.

CHAPTER EIGHT
The Deity

The Deity appeared like the breaking sunrise on the water. The ship glimmered gold like a mirror on the horizon. As it neared it dazzled, splitting through the water majestically. The bow and stern had immaculate gold carvings of horses and soldiers. On the helm stood Tessa, her hair as golden as her ship, waving down her back. She wore a soft gray captain's suit, fitted tight to her curves and defining the gentle features of her face. Two Great Danes sat at her feet, salted and peppered with large black and white spots.

"Pull up beside her, Vaster," Acantha ordered.

Within no time, the three ships were close enough to place boards between them to walk across, with *The Dark Eve* in the center. Both Jennet and Tessa came from their ships to her.

Basile gaped, unable to divert his eyes from the golden sister. She caught his stare and smirked before turning away.

"Jennet!" Tessa ran and hugged her. "You look wonderful." She elbowed her playfully. Jennet was now dressed in a bright red jacket with long white cuffs.

"Well, it was about time you two idiots found me!" Jennet pushed her away and brushed straight her black striped vest and tight pants. Tessa bobbed back at her, playing around more. "Stop it." Jennet tried to slap her away. "You're already annoying me."

"You have no idea how I feel," Acantha said.

Jennet responded with a sharp look.

"So," Tessa said as she bounced around the helm, pretending she was crossing swords with the two of them. "What's the plan?"

"It's hardly a plan," Acantha said, with Jennet disdainfully glaring at her.

Tessa noticed the exchange and sobered. "Well, it can't be that bad, can it?"

"In a nutshell," Acantha said, "our foul, thieving sister here has stolen and lost a precious medallion of the Wraith King. It was a looking pendant that allowed a person to see miles away." Tessa's eyebrows shot up in surprise. "I found her locked up in his prison."

"Were they accommodating?" Tessa teased.

"It was horrible," Jennet replied contemptuously. "I had to demand fresh food."

"Anyway," Acantha brought them back to the subject. "He is requiring that we replace it."

"How?" Tessa asked. "What was it made of?"

"We can't make it. He wants it replaced with the Golden Eye."

Tessa shook her head, astonished. "But it doesn't exist!"

Jennet replied hopefully, "In theory. But what if it does? Think about that." Trickery flickered in her eyes.

"We are not going to look for the Golden Eye." Acantha pulled both her sisters back to reality.

"Then what are we going to do? Run?" Tessa frowned in disgust at the very thought of her own words.

"No," Acantha and Jennet said in unison, which also aggravated them.

"We're going to see the Oracle," Acantha said, revolted.

"*Ohh.*" Tessa tried to hide her excitement. "That sounds like a plan," she said. Then her face turned somewhat restrained. She looked harder at Acantha. "You must think this is a serious threat."

Jennet stared. Acantha walked away to the helm and the two of them followed. "This is different."

Her sisters shared looks, judging her concern.

"We have been up against hard things before," Jennet said.

"That snake isn't a normal enemy," Acantha argued, "and I don't think our boundaries extend to being eaten or ripped apart." She lessened the gap between them. "This might not be covered under our assurance. We might be accountable to this."

Tessa, catching up with the situation, read the uneasiness in both her sisters' eyes.

"He knows about us," Acantha said.

"How do you know that?" Tessa asked.

Jennet huffed. "The Golden Eye couldn't possibly affect us."

Tessa snapped back, "We don't know that."

"It could backfire and we could use it on him," Jennet said. "That's what it does, controls people."

"IN THEORY!" shouted Acantha. "And even if it does exist, we aren't going to give it to him, and we're not going to find it and use it on him, because we don't *know* what it does." She eyed Jennet. Something didn't add up. "Are you sure nothing happened that made him suspicious of you?"

Defiance and resentment shone in Jennet's eyes, along with a moment of truth.

Acantha leaped at her throat, but Tessa quickly jumped between them. Jennet scurried away.

"What!" Acantha drew her swords, pointing them at Jennet over Tessa's shoulder.

Tessa drew her own and held it firmly against Acantha's, keeping the blades away from her face. "Shhh, you two!" She looked around at the crew, wary of an escalation. All of the crew members' eyes were on high alert, and their hands on their hilts.

"I did *not* tell him!" Jennet shouted.

"But what *did* you tell him?" Acantha scolded. "You led him to believe *something*."

"I said nothing that would compromise us!"

"I feel compromised!"

Jennet sneered and said in her snottiest voice, "So?"

In a quick movement, Acantha flipped Tessa's sword from her hands and sent her flying across the helm. She was on Jennet in a flash. Jennet unsheathed her own sword and thrust at her, but to no avail. Acantha crashed into her, pinning her against the railing with one arm. The other held a sword against Jennet's neck. Tessa scrambled to her feet, but she didn't move beyond.

"Now," Acantha whispered into Jennet's ear so no one else could hear. "I want to remind you of something: I can undo you. I am the head of this family." She glanced between Jennet and Tessa. "If either of you want to challenge that, go ahead." Tessa was inches away from her sword, but she didn't move. Jennet's weapon was pinned, her face heated but submissive. "You both will follow the rules, or I will send you back."

Jennet widened her eyes. Acantha threw her away, and Tessa picked up her sword. They both sheathed their weapons. Vaster, Jennings, and Scar stood alongside the captain. "Take us back through the Scattered Isles, Mr. Jennings."

Jennings immediately took the wheel. Tessa faced Acantha. Jennet, humbled but still snobbish, nodded.

"We will take my ship," Acantha told her sisters. "Set your commanders on your ships to meet us at Woodmor. We will go there after we see her."

"But Captain, only one person from the ship can go ashore," said Vaster nervously.

Acantha gave him a mute, severe warning to mind his own business before stalking down the stairs to her chambers.

Jennet went aboard *Le Voleur* and shouted orders in French. Her crew cheered and then she stepped back across, going into Acantha's chambers.

◇◇◇

Tessa walked down to the bottom of the staircase on *The Dark Eve*. Vaster slipped by her side.

"Has she been this cranky for a while?" she asked.

"Yes," Vaster responded almost guiltily.

"I wonder why." She looked to her own ship. Monier, her first, awaited her orders by the cross boards. He stood upright, alert from the events. "Monier!"

He darted over.

Basile watched his exact and proper movements. He looked legitimate wearing a black and gray naval suit. He was tall, his long brown hair bound in the back. His sharp face was intimidating, yet kind and loyal. Tessa apparently ran her ship in a more refined manner. It was hard to even consider her a pirate by looks.

"Take her to Woodmor," she ordered her first mate.

A wicked smirk grew on his face. "Yes, Captain." He drew his fingers to his lips and whistled a high note. Over on *The Deity*, the crew buzzed. "Do you want a bodyguard?"

Tessa smiled.

Just then, she felt like someone was watching her. She turned to see Basile winding rope upon his arm. His blue eyes swept through her like a warm breeze. She turned back to Monier. "No, I won't need one." He bowed and quickly returned to *The Deity*, ordering the boards to be removed.

"So." She glanced back at Basile, who was winding faster and trying to divert his gaze from hers. "Who is this?"

Vaster looked to see to whom she was referring.

Basile discovered them staring at him. He lurched forward, his feet had tangled in his own rope, making him lose his balance and topple over. He fell into the mop bucket. Water flew all over the nearby crew. They barked at him as he jumped to his feet shouting his apologies.

Vaster rolled his eyes. "That would be the oh-so-talented Mr. Basile."

"How charming." Tessa laughed as he scurried around cleaning the mess. "He seems too good for Acantha to let on her ship."

"Yes, and even though he's been annoying as hell, she's kept him alive on purpose." Vaster shook his head. "Can't stand all of his never-ending questions."

"That's very strange of her." Tessa tilted her head. "Did she say why?"

"No. And I don't question her."

"Interesting." Tessa looked back at the illustrious Mr. Basile. "Wonder why?" She walked down the steps and around the deck to meet him. He was mopping up his mess. As she neared, he turned and slopped the mop onto her gray boots. He looked up slowly to greet his mistake.

"I'm so sorry, My Lady." He removed the mop and grabbed a nearby cloth, frantically wiping her boots.

She let out a gentle laugh. "Get up. Please stop."

He rose and drew back from her, perplexed.

"Please stop?" he asked in an amazed tone.

She eyed him, knowing full well what it was like working on Acantha's ship. "My sister is the Lady. I'm Tessa. Be sure to remember the difference." She walked past him to the rail of the ship. The sun blazed in the cloudless sky and would soon set. Her own ship and Jennet's faded into the horizon.

Basile followed her and stared straight out to sea.

"You don't seem like the type to join up for pirating," she said not looking at him.

He glanced at her and then back. "I'm adjusting well."

"But why?"

A strange peace flowed through him. He opened his mouth to talk, but then remembered all the slaps his head had endured. He gazed at the sun as it touched the water's edge. While he felt easier in her presence, a strange suspicion grew in his chest.

She could sense his apprehension. "Don't worry. You have permission to talk freely here." She smiled, coaxing him.

This sent a flood of relief through him. He had been under too much pressure not to speak his mind or to ask his questions. He never realized how restraining it had been until this moment. "This is too unreal," he blurted.

Tessa jolted at his outburst. "What?"

"Your sister, your other sister, and you! This ship. These situations. How did she become a captain of a ship like this at my age?" He spoke fast, wary that he could be shut down at any moment. Her face was emotionless, but not like the captain's. There was kindness in her hazel eyes. "And you." His nerves danced and his palms sweat as he stared at her.

She peered back at him keenly.

"Who are you?" he asked, calmer.

She turned back to the setting sun. "We're all sisters. Acantha leads us. Jennet is the oldest, but she's too immature for the job. Acantha is next in line, a natural leader, and then me, Tessa. I'm the littlest, but much more sophisticated when it comes to our profession." Her words were light.

"That's for sure." The statement just blundered out. He covered his mouth. "I'm so sorry! I didn't mean—"

She motioned for him to stop. "I know, I know. You don't have to apologize. I know how it is."

"I don't understand. Why are you so different? And your sisters are so..." he looked for the right word: *horrible, angry, mean.* He chose the safest option. "*Different.*"

"Well, Jennet is self-centered and French. Acantha's been around the world more then we have." She paused. "This," she continued while waving her hand around the boat, "is all her doing. She holds it all together." She smiled happily.

"But why?" It was almost a plea for sanity and then he thought about what she had said. "How are you sisters with Jennet if she's French?"

"Jennet was born and stayed in school in France. She liked it a lot more than home."

"I mean, piracy?" He looked for the words. "You're not—" He stopped short of the word "*men.*"

She knew what he meant. "We were born and raised on the sea. Who said women can't have a piece of the world too?" She elbowed him and he relaxed, feeling rather boyish.

"I just wanted to get out," he said. "My father owns a lot of land just outside Three Hills in Morburn. Just south of England."

She squinted. "Yes, I know where it is."

"I didn't want to become him." His voice dropped. He looked out to the sea, feeling almost guilty for the way he had left home. He breathed deep. When he had set out, he was sure he wouldn't miss the comforts of that life. Now he felt pangs of regret.

"Well, you definitely got out."

"Yes, and confined to a janitorial task." He kicked the bucket, spilling the rest of his mop water. "But I'm moving up. Now I work ropes. I'm with one of the maneuvering teams."

He looked up to the helm. Vaster was staring at him hard. Basile turned back away. "She's having me watched. She thinks I'm useless."

Tessa smiled. "It is hard having a puppy onboard."

He laughed, but mostly for feeling ridiculous. "I'm on my adventure and I'm the baby aboard."

"I'm sure you will find your real place here soon." She gave him a reaffirming smile.

Basile's face twisted at her sweet nature. "What kind of pirates are you?"

She squinted. "Complicated ones."

Acantha walked out of her chambers. "Tessa," she called out. When she saw her on the deck with Basile, she stood alert at the proximity between them. "I need you."

"Have to go." Tessa spun away without explanation.

Basile watched her leave and then caught the captain's evil glare. He dropped his eyes to his rope and mop mess. Even her sisters didn't challenge her, though they acted like family.

Family with swords.

He shook his head and he started working again.

When the captain's chamber door closed, he stopped and looked out to the setting sun. The weight of the world had lifted off his shoulders. For the second time, he squarely stood on even ground as events happened around him. He wasn't sure if he belonged to this world, but he felt more willing to stay now. The excitement for tomorrow built up and put a rejuvenated step into his mopping.

◇◇◇

Night fell. Basile finished his shift and sat around, antsy for something else to do. The captain and her sisters had been in her chambers the entire time. He had unconsciously stared at her door through the rest of his shift. Now he stood in his regular spot waiting for them to emerge.

His earlier conversation with Tessa was like she had taken a thorn out of his hand. He stared at the fogged diamond windows of the captain's doors. Lights flickered inside.

Scar strolled down the stairs from the quarter deck and walked every edge of the deck. Basile diverted his eyes to not connect with the mauled sailor's strange nightly ritual. Scar stopped at the captain's door and brushed his hand across the broken embellishments there before moving on and disappeared into the belly of the ship. Basile released a breath of relief.

After hours of waiting, he finally succumbed to defeat. In disappointment, he headed for the sleeping quarters. As he passed the mess hall, he heard Mort shouting and clanging pots and pans, but this did not divert him. He entered the crew's sleeping quarters ready for the horrific smell of body odor. He crossed through the rows of men to the very back where his hammock stood unoccupied. The nearby circular window was closed. He quickly opened it and hopped into bed. The stars burned bright, hypnotizing his mind as he fell asleep.

In his dreams, Basile ran through town, darting around all the people in his way. Benny trailed behind him. They sprinted toward the bakery. A great cry made him stop. Looking back, he spotted Benny lying in a heap of baskets that had fallen from a nearby cart. Basile laughed, pointing at his misfortune. Benny smirked and jumped to his feet, racing to his side as they continued.

The bakery rose into view. Basile and Benny ducked behind a wall of vegetable crates. They both peered over their hiding spot.

"There she is!" Benny pointed to a young woman dressed in a fancy yellow dress. She walked toward the pastry establishment with a laced umbrella covering her perfectly pinned light brown hair. Her brown eyes were a little too close with a small nose, and her thin lips smiled with delight as she skipped a step into the shop. She moved to the corner of the store, looking out the window as if waiting for someone.

"Wait for it," Basile said.

"What?" Benny probed.

The baker approached her inside. She spoke, pointing to the only table and chairs. Carla Jane sat down most proper and peered out the window.

Just then, little James, one of Benny's younger siblings, climbed from the roof of the bakery through a window and onto the beams inside.

"How did you get him to do it?" Benny asked as the child disappeared.

"Promised him access to all the books in my house." Basile smiled mischievously.

A note, scrolled up and tied at the end of a string, dropped in front of Carla's face. Both Basile and Benny hit each other with excitement. Carla jolted. She examined the note dangling on the rope all the way to the upper beams of the ceiling and looked around for an explanation. In the end, she took the note, but the rope bound it. She yanked harder and harder, but it would not budge. Finally, she gave a heavy pull. James released his grip on the rope and allowed a bucket of flour to pour down. A cloud of white filled the entire front of the shop. Basile and Benny shook with uncontrollable laughter.

Carla stumbled out of the bakery shop drenched in flour. She choked furiously, batting off the flour on her face and dress. She screamed. "Audim, I'll get you for this!"

They both ran back and away from her cries, laughing. They collapsed in an alley to catch their breaths.

"Oh, she is never going to forgive you for that," Benny panted out.

"It doesn't matter." Basile fell back against the wall. "She'll be in the same spot tomorrow pretending that she isn't waiting to run into me. But this time, instead of her insistent giggling and staring, I'll get her mad face." He laughed.

Benny shifted his head. "Why are you so mean to her?"

"I hate her," Basile confessed.

Benny rolled his eyes.

"She follows me everywhere. She's so predictable. I have to change my route every week to avoid her. She shows up with her group of giggling friends to stare at me. Prancing around like dressed-up dolls. I hate her. Nothing is ever going to happen. I'd rather cut off all my toes."

Benny laughed at that. "That would be funny, you without toes."

Basile stood straight. "I need to go."

"Where?" Benny stood to follow.

"No." Basile's voice was firm. "I have to do this by myself."

Benny furrowed his eyebrows with concern. "Why?"

"Look, I need to go by myself. I'll tell you why later." Basile ran off, leaving him there.

The road under his feet was uneven. He took large steps and soon darted off, up the large hill to his left. As he reached the top he looked back at the town now in the distance near the sea. He headed to the other side of the hill. His home arose into view as he strolled. The tall, two-story stone house had smoke coming out of the chimney. Lights beamed from within.

His father was home. His heart sank. He was supposed to be gone for at least two more weeks.

Basile took his time. When he reached the house darkness shrouded the sky. He opened the door to the regular scene: his father sitting in the large front room in front of the fire. He could not sneak past, so he didn't even try. He gently walked through, starting up the staircase on the opposite wall.

"What did you do today?" his father's deep voice asked, halting him.

Basile sulked back, standing in front of him. "I ran the usual route."

"I think you did more than that."

He knew better than to play games with him. He waited for whatever volcano would erupt today.

"I hear that you rejected and invalidated the contract with the Smiths."

Basile shifted. He had hoped it would take longer for his father to receive that news. "We have a supplier. Benny's father supplies our vendors with produce."

His father stood abruptly. "I made the deal to switch."

"Well, I didn't agree. We're loyal to their family for our produce. To switch would destroy them."

"Don't you ever think of anyone else besides yourself?" his father yelled, getting in this face.

Basile held his ground. Benny's father had broken his leg several months earlier, delaying their crop.

"No, I think of others. Especially those that have been loyal to us."

"You don't know *anything* about loyalty. This is not personal. It's business."

"No, this is you being greedy and taking the opportunity to make more for yourself without the care of others around you," Basile yelled back.

His father gave him an incredulous look. "How dumb can you be? I wasted all that money sending you to school. I should've just let you out into the yard to graze with all the other stupid cows."

Basile rolled his eyes. His father instantly struck him across the face. Basile bounced back with surprise, tasting blood on his lip.

"I care more about the people here than you do. Do you really think that it doesn't affect the vendors to not get their produce? Produce that I supply to them? How do they feed their families? And I repeat the plural, *families*." His father paced. "I'm not in charge of just Benny and his family. I manage many people and their welfare. But I don't expect you to understand, because you're loyal to only one person: yourself."

Basile's face was hard as he took in his father's words. Guilt gnawed at his insides, but he still felt justified in what he had done.

"Why don't you talk to the Smiths again and fix it?" Basile asked dryly.

"Because *someone* made sure that they couldn't sell their daily crop to anyone. It's hard to sell vegetables that have been mysteriously dumped in a manure pile."

He stood silent and still.

"Get out of my sight," his father said.

Basile woke and shook the dream away. The horizon, visible through his little window was starting to lighten. He sat up in his hammock and wiped the sleep from his eyes. Half of the men had already left. He returned to the deck. The men moved around to maneuver the sails. The levels of sailcloth on all three large masts sagged limp and then flapped filling with air. The salty sea breeze woke his senses. Jennings held the wheel and beside him Jennet glared straight down at him with a disturbing, mischievous smile.

Basile fought the overwhelming desire to retreat and diverted straight for his bucket.

CHAPTER NINE
Drop-off

All three of the sisters stood in the cavern of the Oracle after explaining again and again to Vaster that they were an exception to the only-one rule. "We have history." Was Acantha's only explanation. Both Tessa and Jennet admired the Oracle's ship.

"You have to be kidding me!" Tessa exclaimed. "How did they do this?"

Jennet glared spitefully. "It doesn't matter how they did it. It will never leave here," she whispered.

"I've been waiting for you." The Oracle flowed gently from her throne. Her feet barely touched the floor as she walked to them. Her long white gown waved around her as if the wind blew. "When was the last time we were all together?"

Both Tessa and Jennet reflected on her question. Acantha leaned back against a nearby wall away from the crowd. Her whole body was tense and rigid, angry for having to return, but not only for that. There was a hidden back entrance that nobody thought or cared to inform her about. They hadn't gone through the maze this time. This, most of all, had Acantha fuming.

She spoke menacingly. "We need more information. How are we supposed to defeat the snake?"

The Oracle walked to the water's edge. All three followed. She barely touched the surface, making it ripple. The crystal clear water clouded. A wavering image formed, with flashings of a dark island. Fog churned around the terrain. Everything appeared void of life and cold. The vision spun aerially around the island and sharp pointed mountain. A single untrodden path switchbacked up the sharp gray rocks. It all magnified into view as the Oracle spoke.

"The path you have chosen has no measurable end." Her voice vibrated. "And you have no choice but to take it."

The three of them exchanged glances.

"Acantha," the Oracle thundered to her.

Acantha felt defiant. She didn't like someone controlling her choices.

The Oracle continued, her face grave. "Your last breath is your only hope against the enemy you face. The Basilisk is born from a curse in the sea, its venom deadly, its scales impenetrable armor, and no mortal man stands alone against it." Pausing, she looked with concern toward the three of them.

Acantha turned to her sisters and met their faces. This, of course, was not news to her.

The Oracle continued. "She will need both of you to complete this task. First, you must find the black island of Death, where nothing stands against it. Its location is far beyond the southern ridge. Follow your compass south until you hit the black water."

This troubled Acantha. She had already sacrificed everything for them. Now her imminent death would be required for their lives and secrets to remain intact. She still had unfinished business before she could die.

"I don't understand how this defeats the Basilisk." She stared at the Oracle, asking for the puzzle pieces to be put together. "How does us going to this island and me dying stop the snake?" But asking for all the details would be useless. The Oracle only understood as much as her visions allowed. "Are we looking for a weapon of some kind that will kill the snake?" All harshness was gone from her voice now. The truth of the Oracle's vision ran chills up her spine.

The Oracle faced her, a strange pull on the air between them. Her eyes closed, glowing again. When they flashed open with light this time, an unseen force attached itself to Acantha's mind. It pulled her like the strings of a puppet. She couldn't close her eyes or move from where she stood, frozen in the Oracle's grip.

"You will be tried." The Oracle's voice quivered almost with pain. "If you are found worthy, then the power you seek will be given. Facing death is payment." Her face tightened. "In the mountain you will find a black door."

Tears fell from Acantha's face, but she had no control over them.

"Acantha!" The Oracle whispered in her mind the words that would open the door. "After this, there is no turning back."

Acantha felt her lips answer, "Yes," but she didn't hear her own voice.

"You must be found worthy." The light disappeared from the Oracle's eyes and Acantha's legs fell from underneath her. Both Tessa and Jennet grabbed her before she hit the floor, pulling her up by her arms.

Acantha shook her head trying to recover. "What did you do to me?" Her chest felt tight.

"I looked into your direct future," the Oracle answered. She leaned against the nearby wall, strained from the experience. "You are touched by darkness."

Acantha did not react. "Some things are better left unknown. You know that if I don't succeed this affects you too?" Her eyes warned.

The Oracle gave no reply, but she understood. She directed her attention to Tessa. She took her hands. "My blessings are upon you."

This confused all three of them.

◇◇◇

Back on the shore of the island, they made their way to the water. "What was that all about?" Acantha asked Tessa.

"Your guess is as good as mine," Tessa answered.

"It hasn't happened yet," said Jennet.

Acantha rolled her eyes. "I hate guessing games."

They entered the gulf. The second all three of them were treading in water, the watery dome released *The Dark Eve*. The crew cheered.

"What do you think about what she said?" Tessa asked. "About what we do next?"

"She said face death, not die," responded Jennet defensively.

"I don't know," said Acantha. "We'll just have to see." She could feel all their apprehensions and casually talking about it wasn't helping. The Oracle had confirmed that if they didn't go through with this, Naulkiendum would win.

Acantha shook the worry from her head. She needed to focus as much as possible to handle their situation. She had to stay in control.

As they swam back to the ship, the Oracle's voice sounded in her mind like a haunting ghost haunting. *"Your last breath will be her only hope."* The dark mountain on the island loomed in her vision, and a cold wind swept through, chilling her bones.

A strange voice whispered to her, like a breeze brushing the inside of her ears. She peered around for the source, but found none. Her sisters continued swimming back to the ship and hadn't been disturbed.

She swam again and it came once more, sending shivers down her spine. She couldn't make out the words, too fast and quiet. She treaded in the water. The sky was a perfect blue. It started spinning, confusing and distorting her vision. The shore was empty. The jungle swirled and stretched. She saw in her mind a dark staircase descending into thick blackness. Dark-gray stone walls enclosed the tunnel downward. She felt a stinging piercing cold, and frost puffed from her breath.

The vision dissipated and the distortions righted themselves. She spun around, confused. Her heart skipped a beat and a sudden devastating weight filled her. Her sisters swam clueless to the experience. They made it to the ship and its waiting ladder before noticing her stagnant position.

"What's wrong?" Jennet was still halfway in the water holding the ladder.

"Are you all right?" Tessa asked, descending a few steps.

There is nothing I wouldn't do for them, Acantha thought. She panicked, but controlled her breathing and face, refusing to reveal the signs of her distress. Her sisters already worried. She couldn't validate their concerns.

"Fine," she called out, swimming again. When they all were on deck, Jennings, Vaster, and Scar handed them their things. Basile stood at the base of the stairs itching for information.

Jennings's deep voice boomed, "What's the orders, Captain?"

"Take us to Woodmor."

It was a trip they made once a year at the same time, but this year they were early by several months. It heightened spirits onboard. The crew buzzed with excitement once the word got out. They worked harder than they had the entire trip to set their course.

◇◇◇

Basile listened in on their conversations. "Where are you going to spend your gold, Pole?" he asked the freakishly tall and skinny pirate.

"The only place I go is to the Red Dragon." Several men around him chuckled.

"What's so funny?" Basile asked.

Billings, the one with the crooked face, sneered at him. "They don't let babies into the Red Dragon."

Basile rolled his eyes, annoyed as the men continued chuckling. Half of them couldn't be much more than ten years older than him. Even Tessa had called him a puppy. *Even she was young!*

Most of the crew sat scattered around the deck that night with lanterns lit. Light seeped from the captain's door. Basile sat against the rail of the ship, in the shadow outside the nearest lantern's light.

Chanks, a man with a large nose, spoke. "This is the pirate's life. All you new ones will have a dirty field day when we reach Woodmor."

"What do you mean?" Billings asked. His face looked as though someone had stepped on it, crooked and flattened on one side.

"It's payday. Woodmor means we get our share and can do with it as we please." All the men who had spent more time on the ship than the newer recruits nodded, pleased.

"How long have you served?" Billings asked.

"Three years. It's the best job I had. You keep your head down, out of her way, and she pays."

"She always pays," confirmed Marco, a fatter chap sitting on the other side of them. "On other ships ye work like a dog and get almost nothing for it." He peered around at them as he smoked his pipe. "She gives all the gold to the crew."

"Not *all* the gold!" argued Carter, his deep voice booming. He stood in the shadows behind all of them. Carter had stayed out of his way since their scuffle, but he still harbored unfriendly feelings.

The crew members all shook their heads, contradicting the statement. Pole said, "I've been here five years and never seen her spend a single gold coin."

"Surely she takes some for herself," Carter argued.

"It's gone," said Marco. "It disappears."

Basile remembered the bagged gold and treasure that he himself helped put down below, that had vanished with no trace. Vaster had told him to leave it alone.

"Does she come off?" Carter asked while examining all their faces. "At Woodmor?"

Basile squinted, aware of his intent. He was there to steal from the captain. Protectiveness fill his chest.

"Captain doesn't stay on land long," said Pole. "She heads into the town for a time and then goes back to the ship the very same day."

"Don't worry!" Chanks barked. "She don't bother what you do in the town. It'll be the best week of your life."

"A week?" Carter asked surprised. "She sits in her ship for a week?"

"Oh no. *The Dark Eve* leaves," corrected Pole.

"What? That's nonsense. Then who crews her?"

Pole snorted. "It don't matter who crews her. You don't ask questions if you want to live and be paid the way we do." He looked at them as though they were ungrateful. "They say the Lady is cursed. She can't stay on land for long."

Basile listened intently. *Cursed.* He had watched her enough to know that she was troubled. A curse would explain her miserable and hateful existence.

"What do you mean 'cursed'?" choked Carter.

Pole grunted back at him. "What do you mean, what do I mean? Cursed is cursed. Dark evil cast over her! I've been on this ship long enough to know. She hardly gets off or stays any place besides Woodmor, where she disappears for a week. She never stays long anywhere on land. Otherwise, she does what she does! Kills! Raids. She's a treasure hunter, the treasure that she pays to us."

"What evil?" said Carter in a distrustful tone.

"Evil is evil, and you don't know none of it till you've seen it," Pole said, as though he was experienced in the matter. "How do you think she lives against all evils? She's sold her soul to the devil for power."

"What about the rest?" Billings asked.

"What rest?" Pole barked back.

"There was more than gold pieces on that wraith ship. I saws it on the deck with me own eyes."

"It don't matter to you, that's what. She takes her keep like any captain would." He scanned each of their faces, warning them. "Take your keep, and that's all. I've seen her gut too greedy a bloke." He twined the frayed edge of the rope he sat on. "You won't get any better anywhere else. She killed her own parents, they say, so she didn't have to share it anymore."

"She does with her two sisters," argued Carter.

"They add to the pile, don't they?" Chanks stated.

Vaster stormed into the circle of men from the shadows of the night. "What are ye, mad?" They all dodged their faces away, guilty. "Barkin' so close to the captain's door?"

Some glanced over to the door that stood a good ten steps away. Basile shrunk back into his hidden corner. They started to get up. Vaster watched each of them go and scanned around suspiciously before he left too.

Basile's mind worked on the words of the crew members. It would make sense that she was cursed. Never spending any time on land and treasure disappearing as soon as it hits the boat. Her sisters not daring to cross her —but maybe they were cursed as well? She must take the treasure to a hidden place, and Woodmor must be it or near about. He schemed to get to the bottom of these questions. The second they hit Woodmor, he would follow her. He would solve this mystery or die trying, which he hoped wouldn't be the case.

Woodmor stood just off shore. The town stretched a mile before them. Every building looked new, kept up from time and season. Basile could tell it was a nice place to live. Behind it, hills covered with lush pine forest rolled in the distance, and beyond those arose the snowcaps of two mountains.

It's beautiful country. Basile watched the sun rise over the hills. He compared the scene to the rolling endless dirt landscape of home. This was his first time to any of the Twelve Kingdoms. Woodmor sat at the very tip in the furthermost country of Goldcrest. A gentle fog flowed through the wooden town. He couldn't see a brick or stone building anywhere. The two other ships, *Le Voleur* and *The Deity*, were anchored just beyond the port.

Vaster rushed out of the captain's doors, eyeing him suspiciously. A pile of bags, each about the size of his head, stood on the deck of the ship. He went to them and jerked his head for Basile to come over. Basile obeyed. On the outside of the ship the ropes to go overboard readied the longboats. Basile measured the distance for their descent and wondered why they didn't port at the docks. A group of men worked the poles around the capstan dropping the anchor, while another group furled the sails. As the sun rose, the remaining crew appeared on the deck, ready for their trip to town. The three captains emerged and stood at the head of the line of men. Basile stayed in the back.

One by one, they gave each man a bag. They all stood in good spirits and thanked the captain, then passed her to find their places in the longboats, which, once full, lowered to the water. It felt like it would take forever as Basile waited his turn. Tessa looked to him and he tipped his head for her to join. She walked slowly to the end of the ship where he stood.

"Are you ready for your holiday?" she quietly asked.

He shrank back, wondering what bothered her. "Not so sure it'll be much of a holiday for me. It doesn't seem to be the type of things I would enjoy."

"What, you don't like a good time like the rest of them?" She nodded toward the crew.

"No," he said reassuringly. "I'll probably find a good piece of beach somewhere and camp out for my time. I like the outdoors. I've never seen country like this before. Maybe I'll go get some supplies and make my way through it for a bit."

Her eyebrows raised and she shook her head. "Well, don't get taken by any bears. Do you know how to use that sword?" She glanced at the blade strapped to his belt.

Basile touched his weapon. "Bears! Now that would be something. Yeah, I can use it well enough."

"We'll test that theory when you get back." She chuckled. "You are an adventurer. Enjoy it while you can." It was almost a warning.

"What about you? What will you do?"

"Oh, you know. Enjoy the quiet." She looked away with a faint smile.

His confidence grew. "You never go to town? For anything?"

Tessa darted her eyes back to him. "No. There are things I must do."

"Like what?"

Before she even had time to answer, Vaster cleared his throat. It was Basile's turn. All the other crew members were on the longboats. Acantha's heavy stare was on them both. How long had she been watching? Had she heard any of their conversation? He walked away from Tessa, who leaned against the opposite railing of the ship. As he neared Acantha, she picked up one of three bags left and held it out to him. He received the heavy bag in his hands. Gold coins clanged from it. Her eyes were emotionless. She jerked her head, motioning him to the boats. As he climbed in, she turned back to Jennet and Tessa. Vaster followed him with his own bag. Even Jennings and Scar manned two separate longboats.

Her closest three didn't even go with her.

"Get the ship ready. I'll be back tonight," Acantha said to her sisters. She twisted something off her finger and dropped it in the water. He tried to seem casual as he searched her actions. Both Jennet and Tessa had matching emerald rings, but not Acantha. Did she just throw hers overboard? His mind whirled. She picked up the two last bags of gold and got into the longboat as well. Tessa and Jennet turned the cranks to lower them. Tessa glanced to Basile only once.

It was early evening by the time they got to the shore. The other crew members tied up their longboats and disappeared into the town. Acantha kept to herself as usual.

"You have a week's time," she warned the sailors. They worked the boat right next to the dock, leaping out to tie it to the nearest post. They all left quickly. Basile held his bag of gold on his lap. Vaster climbed out along with the captain, leaving him alone.

He opened the bag, exposing the large gold coins. He let them fall between his fingers. *I am rich*, he thought, feeling suddenly alone in a strange place.

Acantha watched him from the dock. "Use it wisely."

Vaster cradled his bag of gold like a baby and talked to it as he went into town. She trailed after him, her two bags in her arms.

Basile steadied himself and crawled out onto the dock. Waiting for only a moment, he slowly followed her. When Acantha reached the shore, she headed down the road opposite of where most of the crew went.

Most of them had gone right, to the tavern district. Tavern signs displayed up and down the street and sailors poured into different ones. Women stood outdoors, baring their shoulders, and hissing at them. Some of the men jingled their bags of gold. Several others threw free coins at them. The women grabbed at them like vipers.

Basile looked back to Acantha. She kept walking. He drew closer to the buildings and followed. Keeping his distance, he always ensured himself a place to hide if she should turn around. He glanced back several times, making sure no one else trailed him. The darkness of night soon helped him hide. The town changed from market to housing neighborhoods. She never looked back, but remained steady with an obvious destination in mind. He could swear she had a bit of lightheartedness in her step.

In the end, she led him to a slummy part of town. Pubs connected to whorehouses and other undesirable businesses along the street. She crossed into an alley between a palm reader's shop and the Red Dragon. A large dragon cut out of wood and ornately painted sat above the door. Red light and smoke drifted out of its mouth. The windows were covered with high wall screens from the inside. He followed quickly to the front of the Red Dragon and peeked into the alley.

She disappeared around the back of the building. He walked the alley slowly and paused as he reached the rear. Knocking sounded on a door. He peeked his head around and saw the captain's back to him. She was knocking on the back door of the Red Dragon. The door opened, and the strange red lights glinted from inside. She entered and the door shut behind her.

There were no windows in the back of the building. Carefully he started out toward the other side of the door beyond the alley. It opened and he froze, still in sight, but the door blocked him for a moment. He jolted quietly back into the alley.

Leaning as close as could, he listened to the conversation. A lady spoke in a strange language. He peered around the corner. She was very short, with a flat face and slanted eyes. She wore a long patterned dress and had her hair pulled back in a tight bun. He guessed she was in her fifties.

"Nothing changes in our deal," Acantha said, and the woman bowed to her. Acantha closed the door and took off in the opposite direction, toward the hills. She only carried one bag of gold now. Basile walked out into the open when she got farther away. He went to the door and touched it. Maybe he needed to spend more time with Pole at the Red Dragon. Swiftly he continued, ducking in and out of the shadows. It reminded him of the times he would sneak into the kitchen at home. He got very good at stealing the sweet buns right out from under the servants' noses.

She led him out of town into some high grass. In the distance the rolling hills fanned out, covered in pine trees. A dirt road went along the shoreline, around the distant hills toward the mountains behind them. Acantha cut through the waist-high grass, putting her hands out to feel the tops of it. Basile slowly followed, hiding behind the nearby trees.

Where was she going? The suspense was building inside him.

Finally, she reached the nearest tree-covered hill. As he got closer, he could see a glowing light. A small cottage hid among the trees, lights flickering from its windows. The front door opened to Acantha. A lady holding a baby smiled and let her in, then yelled back into the house that she was there. Acantha gave her the second bag of gold.

Basile hid behind a tall tree, squinting and shaking his head. He crept to the side of the house next to a woodpile. There was a small window above it. He carefully climbed up and peered through. It was a bedroom, clean, bed made, and empty. Jumping down, he went to the back of the house. No lights were on in the windows, so he continued. On the other side stood a large, diamond-paned window. He followed close to the wall, peering through.

All he could see was the hallway back to the front door, so he got down and crawled under the window to the other side. He looked through the bottom corner of the window. A large armchair sat with its back to him, the hand of its occupant resting on its arm. The hand was wrinkled and spotted with time. A side table with a fancy lamp sat next to it. Acantha sat on the other side of the room in another armchair by a blazing fireplace.

She was smiling. Basile was shocked. He accidentally hit his forehead against the window. Quickly he pulled back from view and calmed himself. He listened for if they had heard the disturbance, but the pace of their voices remained the same.

He looked back inside. She still smiled at the person in the armchair, her expression heartbreakingly beautiful. She was so happy, but with sadness in her eyes. When this moment ended, so would her smile.

Then she laughed. She grabbed her stomach, gesturing to the person across from her to stop. Basile sat back down against the wood cottage. Her laughter muffled through the window, like sweet music ringing through his mind. It conflicted with everything he had seen since he had first laid eyes upon her. She was always alone, angry and hard on those around her.

But she was human, capable of laughter and a smile. Someone touched her enough to make her face glow and cast the darkness from her eyes. Basile's heart broke for her. He tried to make out their conversation. When the window rattled, he pulled himself closer to the wall of the cottage. The lady at the door opened the window right next to him.

"I'll let in some air for you," her kind voice spoke. When she walked away, he started breathing once again.

That was close. But now he could hear their words clearly.

"I have to go." Acantha's voice was soft with regret.

Basile rolled his eyes. Of course she would leave the second he could hear.

An old man's voice pleaded. "Must you?"

Basile peered through the corner window again. She held the old man's hand now as he sat forward. He had no hair, his scalp full of age spots. His skin looked thin and papery. He was much older than his hand had led Basile to believe.

This couldn't be her father. He had to be her grandfather or even great-grandfather by the appearance of him.

She held her guilt back. "You know I must go, old man." Lovingly she bent down, brushed her face against the back of his hand, and kissed it gently. "But I will be back next year."

"Soon there will be no next year." He shook with age as he spoke.

Acantha's face dropped. Her lips tightened and she gently let his hand go. She turned without hesitation to the hallway, and the front door opened. Basile crawled along the side of the house and watched the captain walk out toward the town. She stopped and stood at the edge of the tall grass. Then she spun around looking back. He swore there was a shimmer in her eyes, but nothing fell. For a moment, she took in the little cottage. Then, she turned back to the town.

She would head to the ship to leave for the week. As soon as she was out view, Basile jumped to his feet and stood at the cottage door. He hesitated there, pacing back and forth.

What will I say? He went through all the legitimate excuses for him to be there at night, so far from town. He raised his hand several times but lowered it again, thinking more. Finally, he just knocked and panicked, running his hand through his hair and straightening his shirt.

The lady he had seen earlier opened the door. "Yes, can I help you?" She looked him up and down and then relaxed. She was short, stocky, and had a square face. Her brown hair pinned up in a bun around her head. Her light brown eyes were friendly and her manner direct.

"I, uh." Basile's mind went blank. "I was..." He fumbled, searching for excuses. "Uh, hello," he finally said.

She squinted.

"Who is it, Marge?" croaked the old man.

"It's a young fellow on the porch," she yelled back.

"Oh, a young fellow! Is he a nice young fellow?"

Basile widened his eyes to the conversation.

"He looks good enough!" she shouted again as she watched Basile's behavior.

Basile nodded his agreement.

Marge lifted her eyebrows, scrutinizing him.

"Well, what does he want?" rumbled the old man.

"I don't quite know yet. He hasn't told me." She turned back to Basile. "What do you want, young man?"

"I, uh… went for a walk, you see." Basile pointed toward the forest. "And I got turned around." He examined her, sizing up whether or not she believed him. "I stumbled upon your house and saw the Lady—I mean a lady—leave here." He fidgeted with his hands. "Your home looked so safe that I thought I might see if I could get some assistance."

She glared at him through slanted eyes, judging his honesty. "Are you hungry?"

He almost jumped. "Yes, ma'am!"

"Well, let him come in!" shouted the old man.

"Come on with you." She moved from the door, opening the path for him to walk past. Basile stood in the entryway. A doorway led to a kitchen and another to the cozy sitting room where the old man sat. The last door must have led to the bedrooms, but it was closed. The fire blazed, warming the feet of the old man, who still remained in the chair against the window.

"Go on in. I'll get you something," Marge said.

Basile entered the sitting room. The cottage was just the right size to be comfortable but not overwhelming, crafted well and decorated with dark wood end tables, fancy lamps, and fresh flowers in a vase. The chairs were tall and restful looking. Books adorned a shelf against the wall. The old man sat in his chair, his eyes covered with a bandage. He was blind. He hunched in the chair and looked as though if he fell over, the distance would kill him.

Basile studied him, taking in the person that Acantha faithfully visited each year.

"Let me shake your hand." The old man lifted his wobbly hand. Basile grabbed it, and it was surprisingly firm. "Well, now, you are a young man." His old, wrinkled face smiled. "I know a good, strong pair of hands."

"Thank you, sir," Basile replied.

"Sit down while Marge gets you something to eat."

He sat in the chair where the captain had been. The old man had been tall once. He wore a nightshirt, with a blanket covering his legs. His poor shriveled feet wore house shoes. Even just sitting there, his hands trembled.

"What is your name?"

"I am Basile," he said with respect.

"I am Dagan, master of this cottage." He slightly lifted his hand.

"I thank you for letting me in."

"No problem, no problem at all. Can't say we get too many visitors out here."

Marge came in through the door next to the shelf of books. She held a tray with a bowl of soup and bread on it and placed it on the table next to Basile. He nodded in thanks and ate.

"It's almost time for your medicine." Marge looked at the clock ticking on the mantle of the fireplace. It was almost nine o'clock.

"I don't need any medicine." Dagan's face wrinkled in disdain.

"You know you take your medicine every night."

He shook his head. "There is no need to prolong the inevitable. I've lived my fill and now I wait to die."

"Don't make me tell *her* that you're not taking it," she said, as though talking to a child. Basile assumed this "her" to be Acantha.

The old man's hands shook more as he touched his mouth with his fingers, upset.

"Are you all right?" Basile asked him.

"Yes, yes. I'm just old. Filled with too much time and memory." The old man settled his hands again on his lap.

"Who is this lady?" Basile asked. "The one who just left?"

"Ahh," said the old man as if receiving insight. "Acantha." His voice was hoarse with marvel.

Marge squinted, suspicious of the conversation, but the sound of a crying baby called her away.

The old man listened for her footsteps. "Now that we're alone..." he said with measure. He sat still in his old chair and though he was blind his face took on an official expression.

Basile felt like he was in the presence of his own grandparent. He took a large bite of the soup. The comfort of the house and food reminded him of when his mother was alive.

"So, young man, how long have you been stationed on *The Dark Eve?*" Dagan's face was serious, but his voice was not cross.

Basile hesitated into his next bite, stunned. "I..." he faltered, "Uh."

"No need to worry. I won't tell her you visited." Dagan's face was smeared with humor. "You aren't the regular type of chap that signs up for that life."

"I'm sorry," Basile exclaimed with guilt. "I never meant to lead you on. I followed her here hoping to learn more about her. You see, when she brought me here I was dumbfounded—I just had to know why."

"Well, you are an educated chap, grown up in a good home, young, and curious. Curiosity killed the cat." Dagan still smiled.

"How do you know all of that?" Basile asked.

"I'm a very old man. I know when I'm being swindled, and by who." Dagan smiled even bigger. "You have some spirit to follow Acantha."

Basile sat back and scanned the old man again, but deeper this time.

"She would kill you if she knew." Small, old scars like veins edged out from the bandage over his eyes. His breaths were thin and sharp, as if each one could be his last. He didn't feel threatened by Basile or by anything. Basile calmly took in the room. The old man looked in every way like a fixture of it.

"Who are you?" Basile asked.

"I thought we already did introductions," the old man jested.

"I'm sorry, I mean—" Basile started again, but Dagan lifted his hands to quiet him.

"I know what you're asking."

"How do you know the Lady?" Basile tried again.

"Ahh." Dagan shook his head fervently. "That's a question." His voice sounded reflective.

"Are you her grandfather?"

Dagan coughed in surprise and swayed forward in his chair. Basile thought he would fall over due to his frailness. He put his arms out to catch him, but Dagan didn't fall. He gently leaned back to his comfortable position. His old hand shook and drew to cover his heart. "No, young man." He coughed. "Back when I was young, I loved her."

Basile shook his head and his eyes narrowed. Surely the old man was playing with him. *It couldn't possibly be so.*

Dagan sensed his hesitation and nodded.

"But that can't be," Basile said. "It's impossible."

Dagan still nodded. "There are many impossible things that have occurred in my lifetime, and all the lifetimes after me."

Was this a practical joke? But the old man's voice was steadfast, sincere, and earnest. He was telling the truth. This realization made Basile's mind plunge.

"How is that possible?" His voice escalated in his apprehension.

Dagan hushed him, listening for Marge. When he was sure that she had not heard them, he went on. "We shared good times up near those mountains in the distance." His voice lowered to a whisper.

Basile took that as a sign that they weren't to talk of such things and lowered his resolve. He pushed the tray of food on his lap aside onto the table and drew closer to the old man.

"When I was twenty-four, probably about your age, I had lived my entire life in the area. It was summer. The grass was high and the days were long. That summer the lake was full. We swam in it almost every day. She walked into town with only the clothes on her back and changed everything. I'm not saying she was responsible for everything. No one can have that much power. But she was a force of nature, only eighteen, more beautiful than any one person should be, with so much authority that she could take whatever challenged her. Wild, impulsive, untamable like an animal that had been caged its entire life and just been granted freedom. She had so much life in her. Her smile..." He paused as he remembered it with an affectionate yet devastating look upon his face. "She was the only person I could have ever loved." He said it with finality.

Basile tried to imagine the place he spoke of—Dagan as a young man running around with the captain, going swimming, and being in love—but there was no reality in which he could imagine that. The captain was dark, stern, and intolerant. He had never imagined he would see a smile on her face, but it was beautiful, perfect, and what made it even more picturesque was that it was genuine. Feelings for this old man had to exist for her to visit him every year. Everything inside Basile screamed that he shouldn't believe this story, but what else did he have to believe?

"You were lovers?" he asked doubtfully. "I'm sorry. I—" He tried to soften his voice. "But you are, and she is? And it's—?" He shook his head. "I'm sorry. I don't see how that is possible."

"You don't have to apologize." Dagan smiled at this. "I know how it all sounds." He rested his head against the armchair, revealing more of the scars beneath his bandage. They were more solid like burns. "If I hadn't lived it personally, I wouldn't believe it myself. All I have now are the memories of those days." Sorrow exposed itself through the old man's voice. Basile's heart dropped, and he reached to take his hand. Dagan accepted, lifting his head back up.

"How old are you?" Basile asked, trying not to be rude.

"Old," Dagan said. "Very, very old."

"But she is young—about my age, I'd say. How can that be? Surely you must be confused."

"Oh, no. I've lived longer than a man should. I don't know exactly how, but she keeps me along. She looks the same, doesn't she?" He paused with reflection. "Tall, proud, with long curly black hair down to her lower back, and full untouchable lips. Dark eyes that pierce straight into your soul. You feel completely exposed when she looks at you. Soft face, beautiful smile."

Dagan's words gave the same image that he knew, except for the friendliness. He tried to picture her softly walking through the grass with a woman's gentle appeal, dressed in a natural dress instead of her armor. She could have been that lovely woman once. She remained as beautiful and as fierce, but now she was deadly, with no hint of love or emotion to make her human to him.

"And no," Dagan interrupted his daydream.

"No, what?"

"We were not lovers."

Basile sat back, shocked. "I don't understand. You said she was the only woman you had ever loved."

"Yes, but she didn't love me back."

Basile's heart broke. He couldn't imagine the captain loving anyone, but it felt like this man in his youth would have been worth loving. *Still*, he considered, *the captain visits him every year, leaving a large portion of gold.* Maybe she really did love him, but too late. She must have regretted not loving him when she could have.

"Where does she come from, if not your village?"

"I don't know. She would never tell me about her home." Dagan wrung his hands. "She didn't talk about those things. She always told me that wherever she was, that was her home. But there was a problem that arose about a ring."

"What?" Basile was now utterly confused.

"It came from her home and she had lost it. She went through great troubles to get it back."

"But surely she talked to you about her family or past?"

"Nothing detailed. Maybe a story here or there, what she had been taught by a person and such things like that." Dagan's voice grew tired.

In the short time of being there, Basile felt concern and loyalty for the old man. "What happened? She doesn't seem to be this person you speak of."

This question took more pause for Dagan to answer. "I don't know, exactly. She disappeared for two weeks. It was hard to be responsible for her. You couldn't take to worrying, because she came and went as she pleased. The day she came back was the day this happened." He lifted his hands and brushed the bandage on his eyes. "It was just a regular day. We were working the fields outside town, the one that is now thriving among us. We were attacked with no warning. She saved my life. She fought like a dark angel. I've never seen anything so magnificent and horrifying at the same time. It was the last thing I saw." He coughed and shook uncontrollably. Basile picked up a small glass of water on the table and lifted it to his mouth.

Marge rushed in, assessing the scene. She took the water from Basile, nodding with gratitude. "I think you've had enough visiting for today."

Basile's heart dropped. He still had so much to understand.

Dagan sipped several times and rested his head.

"I'm glad to have met you," Basile said, disappointed that his visit was ending.

Dagan's voice was hoarse. "And I you, young Mr. Basile. Come visit me again next year."

"I will, I promise." Basile walked through the hallway to the front door.

"I believe you," Dagan said. "And!" Basile turned back. "Come the day *after* Acantha comes!"

Basile thanked Marge on his way out. He went to the border of the tall grass, stopping where the captain had. There, he took a final look at the cottage. It was tall, with a shingled roof, and warm glowing windows, a perfect place to live and grow up. He walked backward into the grass until he saw two ice-capped mountains in the distance beyond the hills. That was where Dagan had met her, fallen in love, and had his heart broken. The old man didn't blame her for what had happened to him, and she had taken care of him here. She must have felt guilt for whatever took place, to have taken him on his entire life.

Fireflies flitted near the tree lines. They made the cottage and surrounding forest look enchanted.

He walked along the forest line away from the cottage and town, toward the mountains in the distance.

The Lady was much older than she appeared. Maybe that was her curse, long life. It didn't sound too bad. Her sisters must be cursed too, though they didn't seem it. The Lady had a fury that raged silently inside her, but Tessa was gentle, beautiful, and full of life and spirit. He recalled her face, ivory and perfect amidst her golden hair. Her gentle hazel eyes made him freeze wherever he stood, unable to look away. He couldn't get her out of his mind.

He walked back to the coast away from the town. The countryside was breathtaking. He soaked it in while he debated what to do for a whole week. He could travel to the town Dagan spoke of. Someone there had to know more about the captain, but what would he get for asking? She had influence and authority wherever she went. It could get him into trouble.

Just then, he was snapped back into reality. *The Dark Eve* sailed through the waters, following the shoreline and curving toward a small island miles from Woodmor. They were leaving.

He panicked. He had to follow them, but how? In the distance he saw a dock. He sprinted. It was a good distance off. When he finally reached it he was out of breath and rested against a large post. Out at sea, *The Dark Eve* rounded the small island in the distance.

A small fisherman's boat with oars bobbed at the dock's end. Basile climbed onto the weathered dock, afraid of falling through, and made his way to the boat. He climbed in, but with sudden guilt. He was stealing. Almost angered by his moral principles, he returned to the shore and wrote a message in the mud with a stick. He pulled out some gold, leaving a small pile.

"There!" He spun to make sure no one else was around. He hurried back to the boat once again and started to row toward the island.

What if they can't read? He pinched the top of his nose in frustration. What was his problem? He was starting to resent his mother for making him so straight and narrow. This angered him even more. What would she think?

Stop. Stop! "I'm a pirate!" Basile yelled to the sea and land. "I've killed a man, spied on people, and stolen a boat." His proclamation filled him with firm determination. "I'm a pirate!" he repeated, and he started rowing.

Basile had never gauged how hard rowing a small boat a long distance by himself would be. Halfway there, he collapsed, his arms and legs burning. His back felt as though it could crack in two. Lying there catching his breath, he let his mind relax.

Just a moment, and then I will row more.

A cool breeze glided gently over him, cooling his sweaty face. He closed his eyes to a swarm of colors behind the lids. When he opened them again, his mind whirled with the bright stars gazing down at him. He sat up, gazing into the sky. It was brilliant against the darkness. He had never seen stars shine so bright. He sat himself farther back and his hand brushed against something hard and cold. It was a looking-glass.

This will come in handy. He rummaged for more hidden objects, but found only a sturdy rope, a wooden dagger, and a necklace made from string and a large tooth. A child must have recently been in the boat. Basile put the necklace around his neck and made a few swipes with the wooden dagger before placing it in his belt. He started to worry about food and water but shrugged it off.

The guilt rose again. He assumed his position and rowed.

It took him hours to reach the island. With barely enough energy to pull the boat ashore, he collapsed in the sand. The water flowed up, touching his toes. Sleep called to him, but a deeper nagging told him to get up. Slowly, he pulled himself up, stretching his body from the intense strain. The moonlight allowed him to see clearly.

There was little vegetation. The island was mostly a large hill, not too large to climb, but his legs didn't feel up to the task. So, he set out around the shore to where *The Dark Eve* had gone. Walking in the sand proved to be even more tiring. The shadows from the sparse vegetation played tricks with his exhausted mind. It was an endless trek to get around, and he started to worry that soon the sun would rise over the horizon.

"What am I doing? Why am I doing this?" He shook his head wearily. His mind felt as numb as his legs.

"I'm a stalker! I'm crazy!" He stopped. "What am I doing? They're probably long gone." He pinched his nose, frustrated, and turned on his heels to walk back. "Well, you've come this far. You might as well." He turned back again. "Wouldn't want to waste the energy." He skipped a step, increasing his pace, more determined. "Why, why do you care?" He threw his hands out. "Because," he slurred with hesitation as he deciphered his reasoning, "it doesn't make sense."

"But why does it have to make sense?"

He paused, searching for the answer before walking again. "Because it should." He squinted, unconvinced. There was more to it than that. He took a moment to genuinely think it out. Rubbing the dirt and sweat from his face, he cupped his mouth with his hand and massaged his jaw. Why did he care? The question plagued him as he remembered back to signing up for the ship, to seeing it on the dock and feeling the strange pull toward his destiny.

What if he had made it all up? Imagined it to propel him away from being nothing but an ordinary working sap who did everything that all the other ordinary saps did. Work in the store, get married, have kids, work, work, work, and then die. Die with nothing to show for him. No grand adventure, discovering new places, learning new things. Just another bee, droning around with no other purpose than to bring back to the hive.

Was this purpose?

He imagined seeing the ship as a small boy. The mirage glimmered in front of him again. The sun bore down, blurring his vision, and the music played again in his ears, propelling him.

He focused in his memory at the lone figure again.

It was Acantha. Her hair gently blew in the wind. It would always be her on the helm of that ship. He had watched her there in that exact place for over three months now. The music ringing in his ear lulled his focus. Its sad, low, rhythmic tune moved his feet forward.

Suddenly, his mind thrust back from this memory. He had continued walking and was hearing the familiar music again. He threw aside any apprehensions and ran to the other side of island, his legs energized as the music played louder and louder the closer he got. His lungs burned, but he didn't care. He pushed himself harder as his vision tunneled. The distance looked farther and farther away until he broke through some brush and tumbled out the other side.

The Dark Eve glistened in the moonlight just off shore, its sirens staring straight at him. The music in his ears immediately ceased. Panicking, he tossed himself back into the shelter of the brush. His heart thrummed like it would burst out of his chest. He rested, almost choking out his breath.

Once his chest relaxed, he peered out from the concealing brush. *The Dark Eve* sat roughly a hundred yards off the small island's shore. Moonlight reflected its silhouette in the water.

Basile grabbed the spyglass in his belt. Only one lantern glowed in his view, revealing the captain's door and not much else. Three dark figures emerged in the shadows on deck. They stood by the mast and hunched over, working on something. One of them stood and motioned overboard. A fourth overly tall figure inched out of the shadow of the mast. Basile drew his head back, startled at the giant. He did a double-take, squinting hard. The fourth figure unnaturally towered over the small captains. All of them stretched their necks up to the person—they were having a conversation.

A giant?

The sisters hunched over again, lifting large, bundled objects and threw them overboard. *The gold sacks!*

Basile's heart pounded. The sacks hit the water, sinking from his view. *They were just throwing it all overboard?* Baffled and disturbed, he watched as they tossed the bags. The tall figure, abnormally statuesque, towered over them. Basile counted forty-two sacks. He could only imagine how many actually lay at the bottom of this area, seeing that they visited every year. Maybe thousands and thousands! His mind blanked with the possibilities.

If they really did live forever, then who knows how much gold was down there.

A large stick broke behind him. He turned, only for the hilt of a rifle to connect to his face. The sharp pain turned everything black. He fell to the ground as darkness overtook his senses.

CHAPTER TEN
Digging up the Past

Basile stood on a high cliff with sheer drops in every direction. Even the smallest of breezes threatened his balance. Turning back, he looked at the dangerous switchback paths that led back to solid ground. How had he gotten so high?

He investigated the scenery, struck with awe at the rising sun over the valley. Patterns of villages and a city nestled amid rolling hills, the sea in the distance beyond them. Lush green forests sprayed out against the earthen ground. Mist filled the valley with a lulling blue while the sun, still invisible, grew from behind the hills. The mist slowly dissipated, revealing more of the landscape. And then, like the striking of a church bell, the first hint of fire-yellow sun burst over the horizon.

He forgot his wobbly circumstances, filled with amazement at the beautiful, cleansing moment. The wind brushed against his face and awakened his soul.

Then it was gone. The magic that had lit the morning leveled out and the sun shone on the world as he had always seen it. Rocks fell behind him. He twisted around, startled by the noise and the falling distance beneath him. Acantha stood not three feet from him. He gasped.

She looked out at the sunrise. Her hair flowed freely in the wind, revealing her sharp, elegant face. Though her expression was still firm, he could tell she had felt the enchantment of the moment. She did not wobble with worry over the height. Closing her eyes, she absorbed the caresses of the wind.

Suddenly, she turned her head and looked at him. He drew back, anticipating her anger, but found none. Her eyes were serious and her lips pursed closed. His chest rose and fell with suspense.

"What are you most afraid of, Basile?"

He flinched, surprised, unsettled that she even spoke to him. Her eyes bore into him. He felt shocked and exposed, with nowhere to turn, and no place to escape.

"I don't know," he answered. What could he possibly say that would be meaningful? She looked down on him harder. His heart pounded more. It thrummed in the air around him.

Quickly, she drew out her swords, crossing them as she pointed them at his chest. He surged backward, catching the edge of the cliff, and then pulled himself forward with his arms thrown out for balance. There was nowhere to go.

"Is death your worst fear?" Her voice was now enlightening.

He raised his hands protectively. "NO! No. I don't know what it is."

Her expression softened to almost a piteous look. "It's time to find out." She thrust her two swords, pushing him over the edge. His balance gave as he tried to divert from her blades. The fall happened suddenly. His stomach lurched into his chest.

He woke, jerking his face from the sandy beach. Panicked, he caught his breath from the nightmarish dream, struggling to open his eyes against the burning light of the sun. His head pounded. He reached up to the dry blood from his nose. Gentle ocean waves rushed the shore not too far away. His body felt heavy. He laid himself back down, looking at the ocean through covered eyes.

He could hardly process a thought, his head hurt so bad. Not only that, but he was starved. The last time he had eaten had been at Dagan's house. Immediately, he remembered.

The Dark Eve!

He scrambled unsteady to his feet, jutting through the brush like a drunken madman. It was gone. *The Dark Eve* no longer stood just off shore. He scanned his view, but the ship was completely out of sight.

He sank down in the sand, tired and overwhelmed. Someone had hit him last night, knocked him out, and left him defenseless. He was now grateful he had hidden his gold in the fisherman's boat. His chest flooded with anger that this mystery person had got the better of him. He didn't consider them a real danger or he would be dead.

They must have been looking for the same thing he was. He felt instantly relieved that the captain had finished throwing the treasure overboard before he had been attacked. Whoever had knocked him out would only have seen them on the ship. His suspicion pointed toward Carter.

His stomach cramped for food. He looked around for anything that might serve as a meal but found the limited greenery did not yield fruit. He decided to take a swim—eating would have to wait until he got back to the mainland.

The water was cool and refreshing as he dove in. He swam toward where *The Dark Eve* had been, feeling free and alive. He took his time floating out the distance that he had gauged the ship to be. Upon getting to a satisfactory point, he took out the spyglass and pointed it into the water. He expected to see the piles and piles of treasure bags sitting silently on the bottom of the ocean floor. He scanned the watery depths—the underwater terrain rolled with plant life and schools of fish, the view swarmed with blue tones. The sun's rays sparkled through the deep. He felt weightless in the water as he spied around on a world he didn't belong to.

He found nothing in the area. Looking back to the island he again gauged his distance. He spent the next hour swimming in a large circle, looking for any hint of the treasure. He found none.

Finally, he went back to shore, once again throwing himself down in utter exhaustion.

How could that be? He had seen them throw the bags of treasure overboard. They wouldn't have dumped the bags overboard and then dived to retrieve them again. His coordinates simply must be off. He would have to try again. But not now. He felt close to death with fatigue and starvation. He stood and walked back to the other side of the island, where thankfully his boat still sat in the spot he had dragged it on shore.

Long marks stood out in the sand where another boat had been shored by his. Several footprints were scattered about. Whoever had followed him had several people. For a moment, he panicked. *What if they had gotten aboard The Dark Eve and took the captain hostage?*

He remembered the tall giant coming out from the shadow of the mast, leery and unnatural. He quickly dismissed his feelings. There was no way the captain would lose in a fight. He was glad that his dream had not been real. The fear of just being in her presence swept over him.

What was his worst fear? It wasn't her, though he did fear what she was capable of. She appeared to be an unstoppable force, afraid of nothing, silent and alone. *Alone.* Was he afraid of being alone? He had felt alone the entire trip. He was always in the way of everybody else and not valued.

Until Tessa came. Once again he focused on her soft angelic features. He was so grateful for her gentleness. He thought back to his mother and her soft arms surrounding him, her warming voice telling him stories about adventure, creatures in the sea, heroes saving beautiful maidens, and overcoming great obstacles. As he rowed back to the mainland, these memories flooded him: mermaids granting wishes if you caught them and Perseus the hero who fought the kraken to save Andromeda; the gods that lived in the sky, water, and earth.

Back then he had been a young boy dreaming. Now he found himself half believing that stories like these could be true.

Acantha had some type of unseen powers. The exotic mural in *The Dark Eve* inspired him just as those stories of his boyhood had. Maybe she was under the control of this king that sat on the mountains. He pondered the possibility and then shook his head, unbelieving. Stories were just that, stories.

But Dagan talked of her being ageless. Maybe she was a god, cast from Heaven for her sins, and her sisters fell along with her. They wandered the seas searching for enough gold and treasure to buy their way back into heaven's good graces.

He seriously disbelieved this. Acantha wasn't getting into anyone's good graces with her reputation.

In their fight against the wraiths, she had all the proficiency of a warrior, with defined skill and movement. Pole had told Basile about how he saw her come upon a man beating a woman in the street. She instantly gutted him. The woman flung herself at her feet, thanking her for her mercy. But Acantha had kicked her from her path and continued walking. No person could receive grace for the indescribable horrors she was able to commit.

Basile neared the shore. It had taken him twice the amount of time to get back in his weakened state. A man and child stood near the dock where he had taken the dingy. *Great.* He shook his head shamefully, ready to face the reckoning. As he neared, the young boy ran up and down the shore, excited for his arrival. The older man stood like a grim figure waiting to pounce. Basile imagined a scolding like his father would give as punishment for stealing. He was shocked when the man's stance softened and he waved as the boat hit the dock. The boy ran to help tie the boat. Basile got out and went to meet the man whose boat he had stolen.

The man, common enough like his son, stretched out his hand to Basile with a wide smile.

"Boat! Your boat!"

The young boy skipped around.

"Yes," Basile replied skeptically.

The man had a flat face like the lady at the Red Dragon. His accent was quick and sharp, making his English hard to understand.

"I'm sorry I stole your boat. I have brought it back to you though, so no hard feelings."

But the man only shook his hand happily. "You name? You name?"

"I'm Basile, and I must go. I'm sorry." He turned toward the town. The man and his son watched him leave.

"Baaahseeel!" the man shouted after him, but he couldn't look back. He couldn't think of anything but food and sleep. He had half a mile to walk until he reached the town. He could veer toward Dagan's home, but he had already treaded on their hospitality. Each step was heavier and heavier, until he dragged each foot.

The first pub and boarding house he found was called The Cavern. He stumbled in unaware of anyone else, though blotches in his vision denoted figures scattered around the room. He rushed straight to the bar, barely able to hold himself up. A beautiful lady with scarlet lips stood behind the counter. His vision faded in and out.

"Please, I need a room and something to eat." His words sounded distant. He was afraid he hadn't spoken at all.

"You gotta pay for things like that." Her voice was not as nice or pleasant as he had expected it to be.

Reaching into his pocket, he pulled out a single gold coin and slapped it on the counter. She gave him a disgusted look.

He shoveled down hot stew. It burned his throat as he desperately ate.

"Slow down or you'll choke to death," she barked, placing a mug of ale beside him. He drained it, spilling over the sides of his face. After devouring three large bowls of stew and several mugs of ale, he sat back, relieved and beaten into submission by exhaustion. The woman behind the counter tugged harshly at his shoulder. Squinting up to her face, all he could see through his distorted vision was her red lips warping as she tried to talk. He couldn't understand a word. Finally, he moved to her tugging. She led him through the tavern.

His face hit a pillow.

His dreams were filled with confusion. He stood on the cliffs, attacked by Acantha again and again. She endlessly asked him what he feared the most. Memories of his life flashed violently. In a whirlwind of dust he saw his home, cattle scattered as his father rode his horse around them in a constant circle. The brown earth made up the only landscape around him. Then his mother's voice, "Be kind to him. He's just a boy. You expect too much from him." She rested in her bed, weak and pale.

His father sat beside her, holding her petite hand gingerly in his large, rough grip as the fire blazed beyond them. "In the end, we are all that we have. After the end we become the dust."

Her face smiled, free in the sun on the beach as they splashed in the water. Her laugh sounded like the sweet ringing of a bell, constant and forever in his mind.

"Your stupid ideas that the world can just be what you want it to be!" His father stormed like the dust. "There are more important things that matter." The swirling dust storm clouded his figure. He looked hunched and almost beaten. Basile felt to run to his side and hold him up. Once he stepped into the storm, his father's figure was gone. The wind and dirt lashed upon him, throwing him to the ground. The sun pierced through the storm, casting it off him. Light shone down like the glory of heaven, and a golden figure stepped from it. Her gentle face looked upon him with kindness. Then something called her from behind and she shrank back. His heart panicked. He reached out just as she disappeared into the blinding light.

"Wait," he pleaded. His desires played out in his mind. He sat on a tropical beach, decorated with lush vegetation, fruit everywhere, clear blue sea and sky in all directions around him. Piles of gold surrounded him. In the distance, a beautiful beach hut stood just like he had dreamed of his entire life. It was the same each time, warm, inviting, and peaceful. It was his heaven, taunting him with endless dreams. He had to find his treasure. All he needed was treasure.

The golden sun around him turned dim. The water clouded dark and gloomy. All the color of the life around him was sucked out. The clouds billowed and stormed; the gold changed into shadowy sand. The hut was blown to the ground by the wind.

"What are you afraid of?" Acantha's voice throbbed in the distance. "There is no place for you, because you do not have what it takes to make it exist."

A repeated banging penetrated his dream. It made the walls vibrate like ripples in water. The ripples increased and widened until it was all a blur in his mind.

He opened his eyes to the pounding on the door. He raised his head. Sunlight streamed into the gray room. He was sprawled on a large bed with little tables on both sides. He could hardly recall how he got there, remembering the lady with the red lips.

"Have you died in there?" It was her voice through the door.

Lifting himself up, he found strength in his sore arms. The memories of the last few days flashed before him. "No," he yelled, uncertain of how she would respond. He shook the strange dreams from his mind and rose, still wobbly. Slowly, he pulled the door open. The lady with the red lips held a basket of linens. He blinked. He must have been crazed, for he did not find her beautiful at all. Her nose was abnormally large, and her lips, still painted red, were two skim lines on her face. Her green eyes stared at him, narrowed with suspicion.

"I thought you were gonna die. You wobbled in here beaten. Black eyes and all." She wrinkled her forehead, jerking her eyebrow up.

He touched his face, still sore from his attack. "I got lost in the countryside. I'm not from here, you see." Why did he feel the need to explain himself?

"I know you come from the black ship."

"How do you know that?"

Her eyes popped open wide. "The gold coins, silly!" She shook her head. "Money pours into town when the black ship comes."

"Oh." He just wanted to crawl back into bed. "How long have I been here?"

"Two days. I thought you might have died in your sleep."

"Two days," he repeated. That meant he had four days left until he had to board *The Dark Eve* again. "Do I owe you more for the rest of the week?"

"Not unless you're thinking of being more kindly." She started to sway a little. "I'm Kella." She puckered her thin, red lips.

Basile stared. Was that supposed to seduce him? He looked at her chalky, pale skin. Her red lips made her look sickly, and she was too skinny. "Thank you for helping me out," he said quickly. "I'll be staying the rest of the week, and I'll be more orderly from now on, I promise." He stepped back into the room and closed the door, attempting not to be as rude as he felt like being.

A long mirror stood in the corner of the room. He caught sight of his face and almost fell over. Both eyes were pitch black and swollen. His clothes, once his best town clothes, were now worn, dirty and torn all over. He washed in a nearby washbasin and found a nightshirt in a wardrobe. Afterward, he climbed back into bed.

The next day he wandered the town, where he bought himself more clothes and better shoes. It was exciting, the buzz people made over him. He knew it was only because of the gold in his pocket, but he loved being treated like a king. Everything was hot and fresh, the best ale, and the people seemed genuinely nice. He didn't see any of the other sailors. Then again, he stayed clear of the roads that they had flocked to. He wasn't interested in indulging in their fun.

The next day, he packed up supplies for his trip back to the island. He planned to stay the rest of his time there to scout out the water for the treasure. The bags had to be down there. He would take them and find his piece of beach, somewhere he couldn't be found.

Guilt hit him again. He wasn't any better than Carter, who probably was the one that had hit him in the face. He remembered Tessa with a hint of regret. And then there was the captain. He thought of Dagan and his story. It was impossible.

He looked back to the countryside, to the two mountains in the distance. His feet itched for a different path. He could come back anytime and find the treasure now that he knew where it was. Whether he could actually steal some of it from the captain worried him.

Instead, he set his direction to the distant snowcapped mountains, taking the long, winding shore where he had stolen the boat. As he neared the small dock, he noticed a nice, large fishing boat. The man and his son stood on the ship working on some netting. Upon seeing him, they rushed to shore. Basile rolled his eyes with annoyance, but they came with wide smiles to shake his hand. The old fishing boat stood minuscule in size to the new one. Basile looked close and saw *BAHSEEL* painted on the rear of the smaller boat. He stopped, perplexed by the letters.

"You need you boat?" the man asked in choppy English.

The gears in Basile's head turned, understanding the situation.

"No, I'm not going out right now." He spoke slow and clearly. "I am walking this time."

The man bowed his head repeatedly with the same grin upon his face. "I am Cho Lee. I watch your boat for you."

"Thank you," Basile said loudly, though he realized that the man was not deaf.

"Thank you, thank you," repeated Cho Lee. "You buy my boat. Thank you, thank you."

Finally, Basile broke free from them and continued along his path. A dirt road led into the countryside. Grass grew tall and wild, spreading as far as he could see. Trees lined the fields in the distance and the two mountains loomed in the background. It took him hours to get to a small village. Dozens of dome huts spaced among the tall grass, made of sticks, straw, and mud. All were abandoned and most were crumbled. It had been a long time since they had been inhabited.

What could this deserted path possibly tell him about Acantha?

He approached the closest hut. The floor was dirt and heaps of shredded cloth lay in the back. It was large enough for three people to stay in. He inspected the inside. A large-legged spider crawled over his hand. He smacked it off, losing his balance and falling back against and through the wall to the outside again. His hand brushed something soft and solid. He sat up. He had fallen though the shredded cloth.

He pulled out a child's doll from the heap. It was old and worn, with a black mark painted across its head. Disturbed, Basile stood and looked beyond the dome huts into the distance. A road curved into the hills. He could faintly see yellowish structures.

He continued up the road until he rounded a hill and the city's view opened up. With the sun setting and bouncing its light off the yellow bricks, it gave an appearance of gold.

The road turned to cobblestone beneath his feet as he continued. An outer wall stood alone to protect the city, with the mountains just beyond. A palace jutted in the middle, desolate. He walked through the open gates and down the main road. All the buildings were made with yellow brick. At one time it had been a great city, but now all the doors were shut or broken, and every building abandoned with debris lying about. A hollow wind blew through the streets as he rounded a corner that revealed the palace entrance. A grand stone staircase flowed up to the large square castle, with two wings that lined it. As Basile walked up the staircase to the grand doors he could see over the city walls to the mountains in the distance. Marshlands stood between the city and the mountains.

Basile turned around to catch a rooftop view of the city. It glimmered golden in the setting sun. *This place couldn't be totally abandoned.* He continued to the top of the stairs. The palace was beautifully carved and the large doors at the entrance stood immovable. A long black mark like the one on the doll was painted across the threshold. A metal knocker stood just feet from him. *It couldn't hurt,* he thought as he lifted the knocker and released it.

The banging echoed within the palace walls. He put his ear to the door, listening for any movement within. When no answer came, he plopped down the top steps, staring out again.

What could have happened that would have deserted this whole city?

After a long time, shuffling sounded behind him. He stood quickly as the large wooden doors cracked open.

"What do you want?" an angry man shouted, concealed behind the doors.

Basile spoke quickly. "I found your city and was afraid that it was completely deserted."

"It is. You had best leave for your own sake."

"What's happened here?" Basile asked, peeking into the crack of the door, trying to view the person.

The man opened the door to reveal his face. He was older, maybe in his sixties. His clothes were plain and tattered. "This place is cursed."

"How? Why?"

The old man eyed him up and down. "Happened a long time ago to the family that lived here. People don't come here no more, unless they want the dark mark upon them. Even the men in the mountain pass are long gone."

Basile glanced up to the black mark above the door and then to the pathway between the mountains where the marsh spread from.

"You can't stay here!" the old man barked, "or the mark will come upon you."

"But what does that mean?" Basile asked.

"It means desolation, the end of your family line. Soon you'll see the mark upon your forehead and you'll go mad."

He started to close the door, but Basile wedged his foot in. "Please! I need to know."

The old man looked up with weary eyes, judging his request. "Come with me." As he opened the large doors and led him in, Basile noticed wrongness in the old man's physique. From the front he was normal, but his back protruded with a twisting curve of the spine, overly visible even through his clothing. He dragged his left leg as he walked through a large hallway into a grand room with a balcony and open floor. It had been a great hall once, but now, tattered banners hung from the ceilings and cobwebs draped. It had been a long time since any foot had walked through the piles of dust.

At the end of the hall stood two thrones and a staircase just beyond. The balcony decorated the left side of the room. As Basile looked in, he imagined ghostly guests dancing around, filling the hall with their dead laughter and celebration. Chills rolled up his spine. Two dead royal figures sat upon the thrones among the guests.

"This way." The old man led him into the hall. Their footprints tracked through the dust. "This was once a great hall where my ancestors lived. Their spirits still remain and sometimes you can see them dancing around."

Basile shook his head, wondering if he had made that up or saw them. "Are you the only one still here?"

"Yes. I am the last of the royal line."

Basile studied the old man's wrinkled face. "What's your name?"

The old man ushered him over to a large tapestry against the far wall. It was a lineage tree and at the very top names were woven in. *Lord James Edwin Bracket* and *Lady Martha Willis Bracket*. Underneath them they had two sons: *Edwin Hugh Bracket* and *Tucker Willis Bracket*. The line under the first son stopped, but the line under the second son sparsely continued for several generations until the last name, *James Tucker Bracket III*. Basile looked to the old man. "James?"

He nodded. "I am the last of the Bracket line."

Basile looked back up to the tapestry. "What about your ancestors before this?" He pointed to the top two names.

"Story says they ventured across the sea and found this land. After settling here, they built the great city you find yourself in now with a vast treasure they brought with them." His voice echoed through the room. "They lived in peace here for a long time till a darkness fell upon them."

"Darkness?" Basile asked. "What kind of darkness?"

"A curse. A black mark upon the head of those it claimed, making them barren and, in the end, mad." James walked him over to a cluster of portraits along the wall. "Lord and Lady Bracket." He pointed to the first canvas, faded and worn. A fat, pompous man sat on the throne with a larger woman standing beside him. "Lady Bracket went mad and died in the left wing of this castle by setting herself on fire. Lord Bracket followed soon after by hanging himself off the right wing." James continued on to the next portrait of the first son. "Edwin Hugh Bracket was the source of the curse."

Basile gazed upon the portrait. Edwin had an angular face with a pronounced jaw and nose. The portrait depicted a confident, proud man. "What happened to him?"

"They say that a dark witch seduced him. She transformed herself into a beautiful woman, hypnotizing him. She wanted to marry him to steal their treasures, but he saw her true form one night under the full moon and refused her. She laid an evil curse upon him and his family and all who should come after them to become barren and lose their minds. Edwin disappeared after that night. They say he went mad and jumped from the roof into the swamp. They presumed him dead. But the curse caused all the royal women to become barren, wiping out the line of Brackets."

Basile looked back to the ended line beneath Edwin's name. "But if the women were barren, then how does the line continue under Lord Tucker?" He asked skeptically.

"Bastards!" James spat out. "All noble blood that married into the Bracket line delivered dark, unnatural heirs that died soon after. Bastards are the only continuation."

Basile squinted back to James. "I don't see the dark mark on you."

"You have to be cursed to see it. And you won't be here long enough for that to happen." James led him back to the door. Basile hesitated, looking one last time on the pictures before following him out.

"So what happened to the rest of the city?"

"It was warned that the curse would spread. The people left after the first birth. All nobility left, along with the common folk. I am the last and when I die, hopefully the curse dies with me, ridding this land of the evil here." He pointed to the mountain pass and the marsh. "A band of thieves lived deep within the mountains and would raid the city through a secret path in the marsh." His hand wove a pathway through the land to the city. "Even they have disappeared." James looked to Basile. "It's time for you to leave." He went back through the large doors, abandoning him there.

Basile's mind flooded with questions. Somehow, the captain was here all those years ago, and whatever had happened—witch or not—this land was desolate because of it.

The sun had set. He made his way back to the dome village, where he camped overnight. After taking refuge in one of the huts and lighting a small fire outside, he sat down to eat his provisions. Afterward, he lay back, gazing up into the night sky. It was spotted with endless stars shining brighter than he could ever imagine. He felt closer to heaven in that moment.

It was a shame that such beautiful countryside was abandoned. He was surprised that the bordering kingdoms had not moved in claiming it. The crew had said the captain was cursed. It must have happened while she lived here. That was why the people all lived now at the seaside town. Nobody dared come for fear of the curse.

But Dagan had not mentioned anything about a curse. Basile itched for another chance to talk to him, but he had no right going back so soon.

After he thought about it, he was convinced that the captain couldn't be cursed. James said it was contagious, and that you had to have it to see it. If the captain was cursed, she would curse everyone around her. He shook his head. It was useless to try and figure it out without all the pieces.

He nodded off, drifting back into his recurring dreams.

CHAPTER ELEVEN
Point of No Return

The crew boarded *The Dark Eve* after the week. They emerged from all directions of town, dragging their feet. Their faces clenched, hungover from their week of pleasure. Vaster snapped them into shape as they sluggishly appeared, but even he squinted for relief from his own headache.

Basile jumped onboard, rejuvenated. He went straight to his mop and bucket, whistling a merry tune. Vaster restrained the urge to smack his head just for smiling, but his attention quickly diverted as the captain charged past him onto the helm.

"Take us to the southern ridge," she ordered Jennings.

"Captain?" Vaster blinked rapidly. "The southern ridge be the last known land mass south of us." No ship that had ventured past there had ever been seen or heard from again. It was just a small ridge of rocks barely standing out of the water and nothing grew there, but it stood as a warning to sail no farther. "What could we possibly get from the southern ridge?"

"It's past the southern ridge that we will find what we are looking for. Vaster, do we have enough supplies to last us?" Acantha asked.

Vaster stiffened. "For how long?"

She ignored him, turning to Jennings for his cooperation. Jennings nodded. All those present on the helm shifted, edgy about her instructions. Even Tessa and Jennet looked away, though they understood the reasons.

Basile tried his hardest to work around the ship without looking too conspicuous as he watched Tessa from afar. After his journey and learning all he could, he was dying to talk to her again. She might have some more insight.

Then again, he didn't know how far he could tread. Tessa followed Acantha everywhere and did whatever she asked. He focused on scrubbing down the deck of the ship and instantly remembered how much he disliked it.

"Why don't we teach you a little offense with that sword?"

He swirled. Tessa stood behind him, balancing her sword on her boot. The relief was apparent on his face.

After giving him a sword and testing some basic moves, she intervened.

"No." She flipped his wrist over. "Hold it like this, and make it mean something when you point it at me."

"I learned in school how to use a sword. It's a little difficult to mean it when it's pointed at you," Basile jeered back at her.

"Well, when will you mean it? Being taught how to use a sword all depends on your teacher."

"Maybe when someone is trying to run me though! Who taught you?"

"That doesn't seem like it would be too hard." She playfully threatened him with her sword. "My father taught me."

"Well, I've done all right so far." He thought of the dead wraith.

"You think you would make it past me?"

"No, because I would have a lot more to worry about if I did." He looked up to the helm.

She laughed. It was musical, like the ringing of a sweet bell. Basile's heart ached in that moment.

"That is very true," she said. "But I don't think you could get that far."

They crossed swords with each other. He soaked in every word she spoke as she took the time to correct his posture and grip. She even showed how tight he was supposed to hold it compared to different types of fighting. She pointed out the weak spots of another person and how to judge their skill level. Basile focused more as the lesson progressed. He was trying to make sense of her and this interesting situation. Whoever her father was, he was an expert and had rigorously trained his daughters.

"Did you enjoy your leave?" she asked.

He looked up, concentrating on the change of subject. "Yes. It was refreshing to be off the ship." He hesitated to mention anything he had done with his time off.

Can I trust her? Should I tell her? Will I die because I told her? But deep down, he wanted nothing else than to confess.

"I've done something," he finally spoke, casting his eyes down.

Tessa nodded. "The whole crew does it. It's the type of life they lead."

"No." He shook his head. "I've done something that I shouldn't have done."

Tessa squinted. "Do you need a priest?" she teased.

Basile stood straight, dropping his sword to his side. He walked directly up to her, close enough that no one else could hear. "I followed the captain when she got off the ship, to Dagan's house. I went in after she left and talked to him."

Tessa's eyes bulged. A warning and damning stare followed. Then her eyes softened with understanding. She pulled his arm, drawing him closer to the railing and away from any overhearing ears. "What have you done?"

"I didn't mean the captain any harm."

She looked around, hushing his voice.

"I just wanted to know more about her, more about you, and more about this." He motioned to the ship. "And Dagan was so nice. He let me in and told me the story."

"What did he say?" She spoke urgently, with great interest.

Now Basile was intrigued. The look on her face communicated that there were things even she didn't know. Silence grew between them.

"He told me a lot of things, and some I don't know if I believe." He met her gaze, gravely serious. "I was afraid to tell you."

"You should be."

"Are you going to tell her?"

Tessa deliberated. She ought to tell Acantha immediately, but she had a reserved feeling that she shouldn't. As she looked into Basile's eyes, she could see his intent and purpose were different from others. Not just that, but Acantha herself had expressed that Basile was important to their plan. Even if Acantha didn't know why, she had preserved him, which was one of the reasons Tessa found him so interesting. She had been distracted all week long trying to figure it out. Waiting for her next opportunity to talk with him and know more.

Why was he so important?

"No," she said. "I'm not going to tell her."

Basile released his breath with relief. "But why?"

"I don't know. Maybe because I want you to live a bit longer," she admitted. It wasn't often that she talked so freely with another person besides her sisters. Basile made things so much more complicated. In this moment, an internal struggle built inside her.

"You cannot tell anyone anything that you've learned about us," she threatened him.

He nodded. "I don't think I've actually learned anything about you."

"Tell me what Dagan told you."

He spent the rest of their brief time together relaying the story. He was disappointed when she didn't so much as comment but abruptly left as Acantha called her to the helm. With each step she walked away, his disappointment built higher and higher inside his chest. *What now?* He was a fool to have opened his mouth. He didn't know if he could trust anyone. He might have thrown everything away by trusting her.

◇◇◇

Night had fallen. Acantha stood at the helm, staring into the thick dark fog that covered the gloomy night water. It drifted smoothly, churning and hypnotizing her eyes. She had always enjoyed its calming effect that allowed her to open her mind and think clearly. She closed her eyes, breathing in the deep, fresh scent upon the moist air. Silently, she took in the sounds around her—the water flushing against the sides of the ship and the yelps of the crew. Raindrops fell, lightly touching her skin. Her stress melted away. She searched the men's faces, but was too occupied in her own mind to see any guarded behavior.

A thought popped into her head. She stood straight and rushed down the stairs to her quarters. Tessa, who saw the sudden movement and change of expression, followed her.

Acantha waited for her before going inside. Jennet sat up from the bed, brewing with boredom.

Tessa spoke first. "What?" she asked, folding her arms.

Acantha looked to Jennet, who tilted her head and widened her eyes in silent question.

"Did you lose it?" Acantha asked most seriously.

Tessa twitched her head, perking up. She peered over to Jennet, waiting for an answer, but neither of them needed one.

"Where is it?" Acantha asked like a parent.

Jennet stood defiantly and walked over to the desk. She sat in the chair, facing the both of them. "It's in the bottom of my ship."

Tessa closed her eyes at the strain that weighed on her. Acantha stared at the wall.

Tessa asked, "What if we just give it back?"

Jennet huffed and Acantha looked displeased at both of them.

"He could care less about his pendant now," she said.

Both Tessa and Jennet sulked. The underlying problem still existed regardless of the scaled pendant.

Jennet looked to Acantha for understanding. "You know I couldn't give it back to him after I got caught. He wouldn't have let me go."

Neither Acantha nor Tessa argued.

"Well," Tessa said, "don't you think we could have used it now?"

Jennet shrugged apathetically.

Acantha just rolled her eyes, jaded. There was no other course for them. Jennet had doomed them the second she was caught by the wraiths. Hiding the pendant was probably her only chance of living. She served her time for a year on the dirty island just waiting for them to show up and find her.

Tessa disturbed the silence among them. "What happened to the others of your crew?"

"He slowly fed them to that beast." Jennet casted her eyes to the floor with a blameworthy look. "I had to watch all of them die." It was a rare moment in which she sounded remorseful. She went into a trance, remembering her captivity on the blood-red island. The cement prison they kept her in had a wooden door locked from the outside. The jungle was thick, separating the other prisons spaced around the area. Her crew was divided among them. Every night they came with scraps from who-knows-what. She demanded better food.

"I am not some common person! I need more than this muck!" She threw the food back at the delivering wraiths. "You tell that fat pig that I won't eat any more until I receive some decent food," she shouted as they scurried back through the door and fastened it shut behind them.

Naulkiendum paraded down the mountain the next day. Her prison doors were opened and she was bound, arms in front with a rope that served as a leash for the wraiths to pull her along the trail. Several of her men were brought along too. A dozen or more wraiths carried Naulkiendum in a large wooden chair. Every once in a while, he would peer back at her and laugh as he devoured a tray of meats and fruits.

They hiked up and around to almost the other side of the mountain. Finally, the jungle broke and a large lake spread into view. An island stood in the middle of it. Several of her men were tied to posts that stood straight out of the ground ten yards off. Each looked to her for deliverance, but Naulkiendum took her to the dock.

"So, Mizz Jennet, great thief!" He peered down at her with drool running from his full mouth. He swallowed and pointed to the lake. "You're not so great of a thief, are you now?" He laughed.

Jennet refused to talk to him. Instead she glared, completely irritated and disgusted.

He laughed and motioned to the wraith holding a horn. The wraith blew the instrument three times. Something large moved into the water from the island. She didn't see it, but the ripples reached the shore. She stood taller and more alert, along with her crew. They watched the water, waiting on edge for the unforeseen. Hesitancy made her back off the dock as far as the rope would allow. Naulkiendum smiled crookedly.

The head of the snake flew out of the water, spraying those closest to Naulkiendum. Fear struck her chest as the massive serpent stood at least twenty feet out of the rippling surface. Its scales, large and thick, glistened in the sun with a brownish green tint. The head bobbed back and forth, turning to look closer with its large yellow eyes. It spotted the men on the posts.

Naulkiendum laughed heartily. "You give me back my pendant now?"

Jennet spat at him.

He laughed more as he motioned the snake toward the tied crew. "Go ahead, my baby!" He laughed. The snake shot to the feeding poles. The crew members screamed and fought against their ropes, but it was no use. The snake ripped them one by one from their posts and either swallowed them whole or broke them and threw them into the lake and jungle.

The violence only lasted seconds, and the whole time, the wraiths bobbed nervously. The large serpent slithered back to the dock, eyeing Jennet. Its large head lowered as if to smell her.

Naulkiendum laughed again. "Not yet, my beauty! Not yet."

Then the questioning started. He summoned her to eat with him and would pry with questions about her family and life. She refused to speak.

She would be abandoned for weeks in her cell until he called for her again. On the next day, they would take the walk again. She was down to her last four crew members when Acantha showed up. She knew the second she arrived. The wraiths scattered crazily around and the sails of *The Dark Eve* could be seen.

Her eyes closed with relief. She had faced that snake so many times. It had crawled around her, coveting the moment it would eat her.

The entire mood on the ship diminished after they ventured beyond the last known landmark of life. The southern ridge floated out of view and the crew looked bitterly into the unknown sea that lay ahead of them. The captains watched closely at the helm, taking turns commanding the ship. The scenery around the ship never changed, endless water to beyond where the eye could see, with no familiar landmarks or land to gauge their course or progress. The crew itched with restlessness.

It felt like the sun was drifting closer to them, heating up the days. The nights were worse as thick clouds covered the moon and ship. All was silent. Those standing watch at night were always on edge waiting for some unknown evil to come upon them. As they drifted farther and farther away from civilization, it only worsened.

Tessa manned the helm and for the first time in weeks allowed herself to look back at Basile.

He caught her eye, having continually watched her. He had waited forever for a good moment to talk. It consumed his mind, making it impossible to focus on anything else. She covertly sauntered to the deck railing, looking out into the darkness, and signaled for him to join.

"I didn't tell Acantha," she spoke, breaking the silence.

Basile nodded. "I know. If you had I would be dead by now." For the first time he felt awkward in her presence. "Why didn't you tell her?"

"I don't know."

"I don't understand," he said, searching her face.

"What's there to understand?"

"Why didn't you tell her?" The question had haunted him. Why would she go against her sister?

"I don't know," she barked quietly.

"Is any of it true?" he probed.

She shrugged, unwilling to divulge any information.

Basile rolled his eyes, and the pressure in his head compounded.

"I don't know all the story," she admitted. "Yes, there are things I don't know. Woodmor is Acantha's town. We aren't to meddle in its affairs and I've hardly been ashore there."

He searched around for anyone who might be listening and hushed her.

She put the pressure back on him. "The real question is what does it matter to you? Why do you care?"

He searched his reasoning, but everything he came up with was lame, selfish, and pitiful. Did he simply want to solve the mystery picking away in the back of his mind? Would it matter if his only reason for being there were to steal from her and leave?

Tessa stared at him.

"I have no reasonable explanation," he admitted, shrugging bleakly. He thought hard again searching for anything to say. "I need to know."

Tessa shook her head, unbelieving. "So? What does it matter?"

"I don't know why it matters, it just does." He seethed, closing his eyes tight. He opened them again and shifted his weight.

Tessa looked up, noticing his change. The darkness of the night filtered in around them. Jennings stood on the helm, but the deck was empty for the moment. They stood motionless, staring at each other. Basile felt anticipation rise inside. It built slowly as he searched her soft face. His whole body screamed for movement, but he didn't dare budge.

Then, without warning, he acted.

Pushing her back against the helm wall, he kissed her. He expected her to push back, fight, be angry and reject him. But the only thing that returned against him was the pressure of her soft lips answering his. His eyes closed.

A momentary fear swept inside him. At any moment they could be caught. He didn't care. For a few brief seconds, he melted, totally released from all his worries. Her hands touched his face, sending chills down his spine.

In the blink of an eye, she pulled away, rigid with apprehension. She looked around and took a step back. Basile glanced over his shoulder, understanding her fear, and then returned with more questions building up inside him. She took a deep breath and stepped back further, disconnecting from what happened.

Before he could say anything, she turned on her heels and bolted to the helm. He stood there for a moment just blinking.

What did this mean? Revelation, questions, doubts and anticipation filled him at the same time. *What did it mean? What would it mean? She had kissed him back.* The thought revolved in his mind.

◇◇◇

"Changes ahead," warned the sailor from the crow's nest. Every man's attention diverted to where he pointed. The ship bustled, alive again for the first time in weeks. Basile looked out ahead from the railing. Gray clouds covered the ocean and air like a wall.

Vaster ran into the captain's quarters to report. Acantha and Tessa directly emerged and went straight to the helm. Basile and Tessa shared a small glance as she passed. All three captains stood alert, looking into the distance. The clouds, dark and gray, towered like a wall overcoming the sky and sea. All three sisters furrowed their brows.

Acantha looked back at Jennings. "Take us in."

Jennet and Tessa jolted their heads back.

"We can't go in there," Jennet argued.

Tessa nervously bit her thumb. "We don't have a choice, Jennet, thanks to you."

Jennet glared back. "That," she pointed to the storm in the distance, "is a static storm. We will all die the second we set foot into it."

Every person onboard stared into the distant scene. Those on the helm watched as the tension built between the captains.

"You, sister, have never seen a static storm," accused Acantha.

Jennet whipped her head around. "You weren't the only person on that ship." Resentment built in her voice.

Tessa stood in the background. Nervously she glanced from her sisters to the storm. The crew, hearing the commotion on the helm, did the same.

"That might be so," Acantha said, "but I saw the storm."

Anger built inside Jennet. She stood like a statue, fuming. "This is a warning. They do not want us to go in there."

Acantha and Tessa looked back at their sister with construed expressions. "Do not speak any more," Acantha warned. "You know that is a lie. They do not interfere with us and our agreement stays as is. If you don't like it, you can swim back to your boat and serve yourself on a platter to that snake."

Jennet's only answer was a contemptuous scowl. She turned her focus on the storm ahead.

"Move us!" Acantha yelled.

As they traveled closer to the billowing storm, the water beneath them darkened. It resembled murky swamp water. The clouds looked almost solid in position. There was a black line in the water, like a veil in the sea.

Tessa and Acantha shared looks.

"We didn't come all this way not to go through with it," said Acantha.

Tessa whispered, "Are you sure that it isn't a static storm? And they aren't trying to stop us?"

Acantha had always protected her younger sister, when she had been around to do so. She reflected back to the surging storm Tessa referred to.

"I'm sure," she replied, firm.

The fog thickened and the air felt unbreathable. As they neared the cloud face, the crew eyed it. Most held their breaths as the bow of the ship seeped through.

Crossing over the line revealed pitch-black water impenetrable to the eye. They had sailed into a completely new world. When the ship crossed all the way, a gushing wind smote them. Ghostly figures reached out from the fog, howling through the air, engulfing the ship. The crew dodged, batting them off as they fled. The sky was dark and gray.

The haunted figures swirled around Acantha like a typhoon. Their tortured faces howled. Then, as quickly as they had come, they vanished back into the fog, and the wind ceased. The ship stood still, waiting for another attack, but none came.

"What was that?" Vaster yelled from a corner of the helm where he had fallen. Each crew member peered from their hiding places.

"A warning," Acantha said as she reached down to help him up. Tessa and Jennet stood near her. "Don't be afraid of what can't touch you."

Vaster yelled the crew back to their posts. The sails drooped lifelessly and then fluttered. Acantha and her sisters looked overboard at the black water. It was like tar.

"What is it?" Jennet asked, crinkling her nose.

"Water," answered Acantha as she scanned around them and set her eyes toward where they were headed. Her arm rose almost involuntarily and pointed to their destination. "There," she commanded, creasing her forehead.

The wind once again blew in the direction where she pointed. The sails fluttered not properly set.

Jennings booming voice yelled over all their heads. "Set the sails!" The maneuvering teams bustled to grapple the braces. The crew hauled and slackened to turn the sails and then trimmed the yards.

"Haul up the spanker!" Jennings bellowed.

The sails filled, pushing them in the direction thirty degrees port. The movement was so strong and sudden they all had to catch their balance.

"What was that?" Jennet examined the wind.

"How did you do that?" Tessa muttered.

"I'm not sure," she said suspiciously. She felt a pulling feeling in that direction, almost magnetic. In her mind she saw the dead mountain the Oracle had shown her, its base covered with fog. A winding gray path led to the top, but she could not see an opening.

A circle of fog floated at a distance, moving along with the ship through the cursed water. It was hard to tell at times if they were even making progress. Deeper in the haze, the haunted spirits fluttered. *The Dark Eve* sailed like this for hours, not seeing where they were headed. The compass on the table spun endlessly and the sun never penetrated the fog.

They had sailed into an endless night.

Acantha and Jennet went below, and the night crew was set to guard their path.

Tessa found herself once again on the deck, at the same spot near the railing, just waiting. Waiting—that was her life. Waiting for the next thing to happen, the next plan to execute, the next drop to make.

But this waiting was different.

He slipped next to her. For a moment they stood silently looking out into the darkness. Under the surface, however, questions waited to be answered. She grasped for words, but for the first time her mind was blank.

He finally looked at her. Her face was no longer shielded and worry wrinkled her forehead. Basile had spent the last week torturing himself over their moment, both relishing the memory and condemning them for it.

"How does this work?" he asked in all seriousness.

"I don't know," she calmly answered. "We don't have…" She stopped and retracted her words. "I don't know."

He gently touched her hand on the balcony. "You kissed me back."

She slid her hand away. "I know." She looked at him for the first time. "I don't know. In my world, *this* doesn't work."

She walked away to the helm. He watched, struggling with disappointment. Suddenly he followed, desperate for some response. "Please," he whispered. She stopped, pressing to the shadows against the wall, and covered her face.

"Are you afraid?" Basile asked, trying to see her.

Her hands dropped to her side. "Yes. And I have great reason to be."

"Over this? A kiss?"

She paused, blinking, and coughed. "If that's all it was, then no."

It wasn't *just* a kiss. The weeks leading up to this moment had been filled with anxiety. He hadn't been able to get her face out of his mind. It was torturous to be in close proximity to her and not act the way he wanted. His eyes widened. Did he love her? Or was it merely a moment that happened due to attraction and circumstance? He hardly knew her or what he was getting himself into.

As they stood there, he guessed she was struggling with the same things. Then there were the dreams. All the crazy, consistent dreams that he had been having since being on *The Dark Eve*. The recurring sun casting the storm off him, and the golden figure appearing and then drawing back. He would reach out for her every time. Everything else was meaningless. His treasure piled on the beach turned dark and dusty.

Then there was always Acantha pushing him off the mountain, testing him. As the dreams advanced, the golden figure appeared more and more like Tessa. Her soft ringing laugh haunted him, making him miss home and feel near it at the same time.

But what was he doing now? He was here as a means to an end. He intended to leave, find his island, and to not worry about anyone else, to live off the land with no one telling him what to do. Now it tormented him. Every time he daydreamed about his island, he would see her face there smiling back.

"We'll figure it out," he blurted.

She searched his face. "We'll see," she said before walking back up the stairs.

◇◇◇

Acantha lay in her bed, staring out into the void. She closed her eyes picturing it in her mind. Every day, she lived her life a thousand times over again in the same beautiful picture of the sea. The wind was blowing her hair, with the smell of salt and the premonition of something new around the corner.

The dark mountain rose in her mind. And here it was, *maybe the end*. She repeated this thought over and over, searching for some sign to confirm the verdict. It was hard to believe with the terms of her contract.

She sat straight in her bed, gazing out the windows into the haunted fog that followed them—like the past that constantly haunted her. So much blame lived inside, fueling her course and objectives.

Walking over to the window, she took deep breaths. She would know if her end was near. It would reveal itself to her. Right now, her intuition said nothing.

I would know.

What would it mean for her sisters if she died? Would *they* let them continue if she was not there to lead? *Would their contract dissolve? What would they do without her?*

She reflected on the green glow in her dreams. Anger built, pushing against her chest. *No. I won't leave till I find you.*

Her anger faded and more memories flooded out: sitting on the water tower, watching the stars fall out of the black canvas. They streaked across the sky as if heaven were falling in all its glory. She had never seen them shower like that before.

"This is the most beautiful thing I have ever seen." His familiar voice spoke. Acantha turned her head from the sky to his face. Her jester was not looking at the sky, but at her with his deep blue eyes, shining with feelings that she was aware of. Fear welled up inside, and she held her breath. She turned back to the sky not answering his stare.

"Yes, it is the most beautiful thing I have seen, so far."

Acantha drew back from her memory, feeling emptier. She hated hindsight; it wasn't worth anything until it was too late.

A muffled call sounded outside her doors. "Land!" shouted the sailor in the crow's nest.

Through the fog, the silhouette of a sharp, jagged mountain appeared. Acantha felt a bitter sting in her heart.

She quickly walked out onto the deck. The crew rushed, working to slow the ship and navigate it around the cutting shores of the island. As they neared it, the fog dissipated, showing the gloomy, dead landscape of the harsh mountain.

CHAPTER TWELVE
A Dark Path

The mountain, a twisting pile of volcanic rock, sharpened its point straight into the sky. The water was deep enough that they could pull straight up to the shore. They maneuvered the ship into a half-moon opening. The path stood just off shore without a single footprint on it.

"The Oracle said we had to go to the very top, and that there would be a way in." Acantha pointed up.

Jennet leaned in examining. "What kind of a way?"

"She didn't specify," said Tessa. "Weren't you paying attention?"

"She never does," Acantha said. "Maybe I should just go."

Tessa instantly protested. "No. She said it would take all three of us to succeed. Plus, I'm sure there's more up there that we don't know about."

"I'm not taking any crew up with me," Acantha said. "And I'm not sure that we should leave *The Dark Eve* without a captain."

"I'm not staying behind. It's too boring," Jennet said.

"Leave the ship with your three. You trust them," Tessa pointed out.

She trusted all three of them, but then she looked upon her crew. That is where she doubted—she eyed Basile, who stood at the railing examining the scenery.

He caught her stare and glanced at Tessa. Acantha followed his eyes, and he quickly diverted his attention back up to the mountain.

"Fine. The three of us will go up. I suppose at least one of us will come back. Tessa, get some torches and strap them to your back. Both of you armor up."

The hike was slippery. Rocks crumbled under their feet, sending them three steps back each time. It was eerily silent— no birds or sounds of life, but only an empty, solemn stillness. Even conversation felt wrong.

Acantha looked back several times to the ship as is grew farther away. After hours of struggling up the mountain, they rolled onto a landing just before the summit. A small hole large enough for them to crawl through was in the face of the mountain.

"That's the way in. I'm not interested in being born again." Jennet went to examine the hole. "This cannot be it."

"It is small," Tessa agreed right behind her. "It'll be tight, but doable."

Acantha rolled her eyes. "Let's go." She led the way headfirst into the hole. At first she crawled on her belly to get through, with the other two on her heels. The narrow rock tunnel widened, allowing them to crawl on their hands and knees. Finally, it opened into a large cavern. The smell was stale and musty.

"Get out the torches," Acantha commanded. Tessa fumbled, twisting and turning to getting them off her back.

"Will you just hold still?" Jennet barked as she helped her.

The lit torches illuminated the area. The height of the cavern had to be over a hundred feet and its length looked a little shorter. Stalactites hung down from the ceiling, and some even connected to the floor. Along the left side, all the way back to the wall, was an eerie black pool of stagnant water.

They wandered over to the pool. "I wonder how deep it is?" Tessa peered down. She picked up a stone and dropped it in.

Something moved. A small creature resembling a tadpole started glowing. Tessa pointed. "Look!"

All three of them peered down. The glowing creature flicked around. More of them lit up, swimming all over, giving the faintest illumination to the cavern.

"There has to be a way this water is coming in," Tessa said.

At the far end stood a tall black door. Acantha pointed, barely seeing it in the darkness. "There. That's the door."

"This is it?" Jennet moaned. "Does anyone else feel like this is not as bad as we were expecting?" She peered around the cavern and then at the black door.

"Let's just get there and not press our luck," Tessa said wearily as she stepped past Acantha.

Something crunched and broke under Jennet's boot. She nearly twisted her ankle, but caught her step and spun around. As she lowered the torch to the ground, a human skull stared back. Her boot had crushed one side of its face in, but the other side leered up at her. Shivers jolted up her spine. She checked the floor, revealing more human and animal bones. They were piled, half-crushed, and scattered all over the cave.

"Uh." She backed up toward the black door, ducking down as she looked up at the pitch-black ceiling. Tiny black objects stirred. "I think we had best move quickly."

Acantha looked toward her. "What's wrong?" She looked up.

Jennet's hand touched the hilt of her sword.

Through the water, Tessa saw a large portion of the cavern wall move in the reflection behind them. "Stop!" She held her arm out. They froze, staring suspiciously into the ceiling.

"Please tell me it's not a dragon," Acantha whispered.

A boulder unfolded from the wall. Dark red eyes opened and squinted at them. It was at least fifteen feet high and curled up, hanging from the wall. Its blood-red eyes clenched and focused. Tessa stepped toward Acantha and a piece of bone snapped under her foot. The beast shook, unraveling its wings that had to be at least twenty feet in length. Its lips curled back, revealing long fangs.

"Run," Tessa said. "Run!" Her urgent warning sent them into a dead sprint to the door, too far away. The light from their torches flickered over piles of human remains covered with a white residue.

The creature sprang from the wall into the air, soaring in their direction. Piercing shrieks vibrated off the cavern. All three of them covered their ears as it swooped above their heads. They hid on the other side of a stalagmite. Small creatures on the ceiling unfolded and dropped into the air.

"Bats." Tessa's voice vibrated.

"That's not a bat," Jennet protested.

Tessa moaned. "It's a huge, man-eating, son of a——"

"Here it comes!" Acantha pointed at the massive, airborne creature as it dove down at them. Tessa flew backward into the glowing water, barely escaping its razor claws. Her torch snuffed out. Jennet and Acantha dove in opposite directions, landing in piles of bones.

Tessa lifted her arms and the liquid oozed off her. "This isn't water!" She scrambled out of the pool. Both Jennet and Acantha were already on their feet, helping her. The colossal bat soared above them in a stream of smaller bats. They dropped off the ceiling and flocked around the huge beast.

"We've got to get to the door," Acantha said, "but there aren't any more of these pillars to hide behind." In the distance, the bat clung to one of the stalactites and snapped its jaws, sending off shrieks.

"We'll have to make a run for it." Acantha looked back at them.

They both nodded.

"Ready?" She peered at the beast. The smaller bats spiraled around it.

"NOW!" They sprinted. Dust flew from under them, choking their lungs, but they kept their pace. The beast flung itself back into the air, cracking the pillar it had perched on. Their eyes flickered back over their shoulders. They ran as hard as they could, but their progress was slow.

"We aren't going to make it!" Tessa was in the rear. She halted and drew her sword as the beast fell upon her. She thrust her blade into the bottom of its wing as its claw grabbed her thigh. It dug into her leg and lifted off, but the sudden injury caused it to drop her, flinging her though the air and crashing into the dirt. The bat flapped sideways, crashing a little way off and flopping around.

"Tessa!" Acantha ran to her side as she scurried onto her feet. A cut gashed her leg. "Can you walk?"

"Yeah." Her voice was hesitant.

The bat flipped over and started crawling toward them.

"Jennet!" they both said in unison.

Jennet drew her pistol and walked out in front as Acantha helped Tessa toward the door.

"You want to play?" she asked, and her pistol fired. She walked backward, keeping up with Acantha and Tessa. She reached into a pouch and pulled out some fire rocks, which she threw at the floor in front of the bat. Fire sparked into the bat's face, stopping its advance toward them. The creature snapped and tried to work its way around the flames.

Acantha and Tessa reached the door. Several smaller bats circled and snapped at their heads. Tessa waved them off with her sword, killing several that darted close. "Hurry with the door, Acantha!" She knocked a bat down and crushed its skull with the heel of her boot.

The door was pitch black, its surface smooth like polished rock. Acantha placed both her hands on it, remembering the words the Oracle had put into her mind. "I have come to face the flames. I give myself to be tested and be proven worthy. If I don't, then I accept the consequences forever in the flames… I give myself to the flames…" Her heart skipped a beat. A heavy weight fell on her shoulders.

Upon finishing her pledge, her hands sucked to the door like magnets. Her words echoed in the cave around them, and small engravings wove up the door, lit by a blue glow. She tried to pull away, but her hands were immovable. A frost crept up the face of the door, making it shine and glimmer as if alive. The engravings resembled an unknown language that burned in the frosted flames.

Inside her head, a voice spoke, like the wind whistling in her ears.
Push!

She looked down at the skin on her arms. The frost climbed up them to her shoulders. The bitter, stinging cold penetrated her entire body. Her breath frosted in the air. She swallowed the lump in her throat and pushed as hard as she could. The door barely budged. She pushed harder. Behind her, the bat shrieked and the screams of her sisters echoed.

"I give myself," she grunted as she thrust all her weight and energy into the door. "I give myself!"

The door cracked.

Tessa flew from behind, crashing into door to help. With her aid, it pried open enough for them to squeeze though.

"Jennet, come on!" Tessa yelled.

Jennet dodged, frantically slashing her sword at the bat as it clawed at her. She threw her last three firestones into its face and dashed away as they burst into flames. The bat thrashed, rolling around the floor. She sprinted with all her strength to the door. They squeezed through the tiny opening and fell onto the floor. The door sealed shut behind them, silencing the shrieking cries of the bat.

The room was still. Acantha held their last torch and looked tensely around. They were in an open stone room, not like that of the mountain, but of actual stone blocks. It was circular in shape and constructed perfectly. At the other side a huge stone archway framed an opening to a tunnel, its entrance guarded with stone gargoyles.

"What is this place?" Jennet asked.

Acantha ripped a piece of cloth off her already torn sleeve and tied it tight around Tessa's bleeding leg. "There is blue blood." Acantha lifted her hand showing the light blue steak of color in red smeared on her hand.

Jennet hovered over them.

"You will get a slight fever and chills." Acantha said. "Can you make it, because I don't want to leave you behind?"

"I'll be fine," Tessa grunted. "Nothing I haven't done before."

The three walked to the archway, gazing at the ornate stone gargoyles. The tunnel revealed a downward spiraling staircase.

"This is unnatural," Tessa warned.

They all shared looks as they cautiously entered the stairway. They took every turn with caution, waiting for danger ahead. The tunnel felt endless. Even the rock walls had a perfect pattern with every turn.

"Are you sure we're going anywhere at all?" Jennet bellowed.

Flames from their torch flickered as a wind blew up from the bottom.

A chill went up Acantha's spine. She glanced back at her two sisters, who both looked weary. "Jennet, you watch our backs. We aren't getting taken by surprise anymore."

Jennet walked slowly backward. "Do you think there will be anything else?" she whispered.

"Of course," Acantha said.

"Have we thought about how we're getting out?"

Acantha peered back at them. "If we don't succeed, there's really no point in getting out."

With each neverending turn, she felt more on edge, tired of imagining what awaited her at the bottom. It was a tad unfair that she would be the only one to face hell. She must have drawn the short stick in life.

She shook her head to clear those thoughts. "We don't even know if we'll survive whatever we expect to succeed at."

"Can we take a break?" Tessa begged, sullen.

Acantha turned back to her younger sister and Jennet threw her hands up and sat down where she stood. They settled on the stairs and sat quietly for a long time.

Then Tessa stirred uncomfortably. She spoke with worry. "What if this doesn't work? What if you die?"

The moment weighed heavy. All eyes looked to Acantha, and she turned her head from them, gazing down the winding staircase.

"I guess you should go back to Solon," she finally answered, disconnecting from the conversation. "You can come up with your own plans."

They once again fell silent.

"We could hide," Tessa's said, her voice strained. Jennet and Acantha glared. "Naulkiendum will die eventually, and then we can come back out of hiding and continue on."

Her sisters huffed at the solution.

Tessa quickly added, "We could go back just for a little while."

"No," Acantha stated. "I'm unwilling to waste another day of my life on that island."

"It's not that bad!" Tessa argued. Once again, both Jennet and Acantha moaned.

"It's already started," Acantha said.

"What has?" Jennet asked.

"The test." Acantha stared down the cold stairway, feeling the pull upon her body. It coaxed her down. Her sisters watched hopelessly. "Whatever's down there, we have no choice but to find out. My life is entwined with it."

"Acantha!" Tessa protested.

She looked at her little sister. She had always watched over her. Then her gaze shifted to Jennet, and while she could see the regret in her eyes, her face remained solemn. Jennet and she knew a harsher world than Tessa did, as the younger siblings escaped most of the wrath of growing up.

A sudden gust of wind blew up through the tunnel, its force so strong that they had to hold themselves against the steps. A deep, dark, sinister voice beckoned to them, vibrating in their minds.

"Deeper."

"Acantha!" Tessa screamed, covering her ears. The direction of the wind's current changed downward. All three scraped for something to hold on to, but there was nothing. It pushed them from their sitting places, rolling them down the rock staircase.

"Deeper!" thundered the voice again. They slipped along with the current, until they fell on flat ground. They laid tangled in each other.

"Is everybody alive?" Acantha spoke, breathless. Moans answered. Her head was bleeding and a burning pain throbbed from her hip.

It had been the same voice after visiting the Oracle for the second time. The recognition sent alarm reeling up her as she realized that whatever waited was more powerful than she had suspected.

Tessa stood, steadying herself. She sidled to the wall and hung onto it. "What the hell was that?" she panted. "I think I've cracked a rib!" She bent over and then straightened again. "Jennet? Are you okay?"

Jennet rested on her knees. "I've dislocated two of my fingers." She held her hand in the air. "Acantha, fix them for me."

In one fluid motion Acantha bent over and straightened her fingers. Jennet clenched her face and hit her own legs several times. She curled her fingers back into a fist and held it tight as her eyes glowed with anger. "Ahhhhhggh," she growled with the urge to hit her sister in the face. "You idiot!"

Acantha and Tessa glanced at each other and laughed. The laughter started small and then built uncontrollably.

"I hate both of you!" Jennet bellowed. But then she smiled, giving a little laugh as well.

Acantha threw back her head and stretched her neck. "Let's move faster. Tessa are your ribs okay?"

Tessa nodded yes, but discomfort was apparent on her face. Acantha worried about her more than Jennet. They stood in a circular room again, another downward staircase on the opposite side. They picked up their pace, still traveling with care. Again the tunnel spiraled. Around every corner was another corner, always flowing down.

Thirty minutes later, they stopped. "This is never going to end!" Tessa panted, holding her side and leaning against the wall to catch her breath.

"We are going to die in here!" Jennet complained. "This is a boring death! It's going to blow us down again if we stop!"

"Wait, can you feel it?" Acantha put her hand up. "It's getting colder." Their trip down had been anything but warm, but this was a different type of cold. It was the same as the door, frost-biting cold that pierced to the bone.

Tessa and Jennet put their hands out to feel the air.

"I don't feel anything!" Jennet complained, dropping her arm. Tessa still held hers out, but it was evident she didn't feel anything either.

Acantha started downward again, with Jennet and Tessa on her heels. Around six more corners, finally, the passage opened up. Through another archway twelve gargoyles hunched, with six on each side lining the long hallway. At the other end was another archway adorned with small stone creatures. They did not resemble any that Acantha had ever seen.

A faint blue light radiated from the opening, giving off a humming noise. Her senses lulled as she drew closer. She felt exhausted. Her heart raced inside her chest and an unnatural panic filled her mind. Something was drawing her down. The gentle tugging escalated, now almost a dragging sensation. Every step she took felt as though she could not pick her foot up fast enough for the next step to come.

"Are you all right?" Tessa asked.

"Yes." Acantha staggered, and Jennet steadied her. "I just feel strange."

They crept past each statue. The archway opened up into a giant circular room. The sides of the walls again had the same statues and stone creatures. A large round hole was cut out of the center of the room, endlessly deep as they looked down into the pit. A large round platform floated above the gaping hole, connected by a walkway on the opposite side. A metal gate blocked the path. They crossed around the entire room to the gated pathway. Acantha peered over the side, uneasy.

"How deep do you think it is?" Tessa asked.

"This doesn't feel right," Jennet interjected.

Tessa shook the gate. "It's locked. Do you think we could jump?" She motioned to the platform. A good twenty-foot gap spread between them.

"No." Acantha approached the gate. The stone creatures of its decorative arch curved around like shadows in the rock. The platform through the gate had a surface like the door, smooth and black.

Just then, from the middle of the platform, part of the floor rose to construct a black table. At its center, a small round hole appeared. Frost frothed out, billowing down the table and platform into the endless pit.

Acantha tried the gate. When she touched the metal, it glowed and then opened. She tested the strength of the bridge leading to the platform. It held firm, so she stepped through to the other side. Instantly, the gate shut, locking her in. She shook it. Tessa and Jennet did the same from the other side.

Acantha spoke to them through the gate. "I guess this is it. If anything happens, get out of here and take my ship. Do what Tessa suggests and go back for as long as it takes."

Tessa nodded. Jennet shook her head.

Acantha glared. "Then be snake food!"

She whirled, walking straight over the bridge to the table, glancing back only once. On the table, a fine-stemmed glass had risen out of the frost. It held a thick, silvery substance. The frost flickered like blue flames coming up from under the platform.

Her chest tightened. The dark voice that haunted her whispered for her to drink. As she picked up the glass, the frost traveled up her fingers. The eyes of the stone gargoyles and creatures turned the same color blue. Shivers ran up and down her spine. The blue flames covered the areas around her, stretching down to the gate. Her mind swarmed with apprehension, but ultimately, there was no escape. There never had been.

There has to be an end to everything. She couldn't expect it all to go on forever.

She focused on her unfinished dealings, feeling cheated if this was to be her end.

No. I won't leave till I find you.

But what consequences followed her by succeeding at this? Slowly, she brought the glass to her nose, but the liquid had no smell. The frost spread over her body. Her lungs were starting to chill. As she drew it to her lips, her mind went crazy, flashing through her life: their journey here, Naulkiendum's demands, Jennet's carelessness, Tessa and Basile. Endless years of living on the sea, battles, storms, images of her childhood, an old castle covered by the darkness of night, the footsteps of a child rushing down the stairs, and three large ships in the harbor. An island, with mountains of treasure piled on the shore and sea lions barking in the distance. Images of all her crazy, treasure-seeking plans flooded her. Demons, vampires, and dragons. Love.

She took in one last, deep breath for life and lifted the glass again to her lips.

She poured the silver down her throat like a shot of rum. It burned like fire. The blue flames around her burst into red and flooded her with heat. She clenched her throat, collapsing to her knees. The glass shattered on the ground as the fire scalded and tore her flesh from the inside, like liquid fire inching down into her system. She opened her mouth to scream, but nothing sounded out. As the liquid hit her heart, it jolted her chest like it had combusted. The burning solution pumped through her entire body. Her heart burst with every beat. She writhed in pain on the floor, shaking uncontrollably. She couldn't hear anything and all she saw was red flames. Every nerve frayed with the heat.

Suddenly, her bones slowly cracked, like glass splaying into small shards. In pain, she rolled onto her back. Her heart jerked in slow, hard thrusts inside her chest, making her pulse vibrate excruciatingly through her body. The hammering of her heart slowed and the sound bounced off the walls, echoing in her ears. Her breath followed the pounding, slowing with every moment.

Then there was silence, and her last breath surged out of her chest. Her eyes were covered in darkness that blotted out the light.

◇◇◇

"She's dead! She's dead! She's dead!" Tessa paced helplessly outside the gate. Acantha lay motionless. Jennet was curled up on the floor with her palms branded by the iron of the gate.

While Acantha had thrashed in pain, the flames combusted into a raging fire. Jennet had grabbed onto the gate to pry it open, scalding her hands. Tessa pulled her off and threw her to the ground protectively.

The gargoyles' eyes glowed alive with red. Each one broke away from their stone basins, shaking their heads and stretching their wings before standing tall. Their eyes watched Acantha closely.

Tessa left Jennet and paced the length of the gate, calling Acantha's name.

◇◇◇

Force pulled Acantha from every part of her body. At first, she resisted, struggling against the power, but the pull seized stronger. Darkness shrouded everything. Nothing existed around her except her consciousness. Pressure filled her. She struggled against the weight, but with the urge to just let go. The constant fight in her mind naturally defied the feeling. Indifference struck. She relinquished her will and relaxed, giving in to the pulling strength.

A bell rang in her ears. She looked around at the familiar stone room. The fire was gone. She stood alone on the platform with the gate melted shut behind her. The table that once held the frosted glass lowered into the floor again. She reached out to it, and her fingers moved through the solid surface. Quickly, she drew back, examining her hand closer. It gave off a translucent shimmer. She tried touching her hands together, but they floated through each other, having no physical boundaries.

Suddenly, the wind blew again, howling for her attention, and the voice returned. "Come to me." It resonated in her mind. "Join me."

She wasn't touching the floor, but hovered just above it. Her spirit body flowed gently like the blue flame.

Once again she heard the silver bell, a muffled musical noise.

The dark voice called again. "Acantha…" Her mind spun unable to concentrate on anything else. The wind surged up from the pit beneath her. The gust latched onto her, like minuscule fissuring hooks attaching to her soul. It yanked her down.

The voice beckoned again. "Come to me."

The earth-rock walls bore writing in strange languages. They whispered gibberish to her as she passed. Pictures stained in the walls—of armies and battles, beasts, demons, and angels—came alive, presenting their tumultuous fates. A ledge appeared below her and a cave sank into the rock face of the pit.

She stood before it and stepped toward the cave into the darkness. She traveled into the void until a black sinister throne loomed. Sitting on it was a tall, dark figure. Unnatural shadows flowed from the hem of its cloak. A skeleton's hand pointed out from its draped sleeve straight at her.

Death. The wind spilled from the figure. Creatures fell out from the surrounding darkness and stone gargoyles crept from behind the throne, their eyes glowing red.

Death pointed behind her. Acantha turned to a large portrait stained into the wall. The man was pale, and the whites of his eyes were black. His features were sharp, almost boney. She studied his face and felt a strange connection to him. The portrait distorted, almost melting off the rock face. A new image slowly brightened into view.

Acantha fell back, alarmed, when her own face appeared. For the first time fear struck her mind. She spun around to face the cloaked figure.

"No." Her voice resonated like the ringing bell. She covered her mouth, startled by the sound.

The hoarse voice spoke again. "Join me. Take a place by my side…"

She shook her head. The creatures at Death's feet shrieked and howled, clawing at the ground. Death sat undeterred from their reaction. She again examined the portrait. It was back to the picture of the pale, black-eyed man. Relief flooded her.

The throned figure lifted his bone-hand, splaying his fingers in her direction. Once again the wind grasped her, binding her. Unable to move, she felt trapped and frozen in Death's grip.

The dark shadows combined from the hem of his cloak to form a cloud in front of her. The hand of Death thrust the cloud forward, striking her.

It entered her, filling her spirit with darkness. Her mind expanded as the shadows connected to her soul.

Death spoke again. "Join me. I will teach you to use it."

Acantha firmly shook her head. For a brief second she worried about what refusing him would mean, but then she was sucked out of the cave. Her vision blackened.

The ringing bell vibrated again and again, calling louder each time. A numbness swept up her body. Her eyes fluttered, and only a smear of color waved in front of them. A deep cold seeped beneath her, a heavy pressure on her chest.

Her eyes flew open and she touched her face. The fire was gone. All that remained was smoke. The bell rang again, and she followed the sound to the gate, where a fuzzy figure motioned her to come.

"Tessa?" Her throat burned as she spoke.

"Acantha!" Her sister's musical voice rang out again. "You're alive!" Tessa sobbed in relief.

Extreme pain throbbed through her. *I'm alive, I passed the test*, she thought over and over again. Deep breaths sent relief spreading like a warm blanket through her body.

She rose, feeling lighter than ever. Through the gate, Jennet was collapsed on the floor and Tessa stood with her arms between the bars, reaching out for her.

Acantha spoke to calm her. "I'm all right. I'm here."

The gate opened and Tessa fell through. Acantha helped her up and went to Jennet, whose hands were burned, the skin severely blistered.

"It's all right." Acantha reached for Jennet's hands. They would heal, though slowly.

Death's voice blew up from the darkness. "Touch them."

Acantha hesitated. When she took a hold of them, Jennet yelped. A coldness seeped from her palms to Jennet's. The pain on her sister's face melted away, and she opened her eyes.

Jennet sat up and looked at her hands. They were not completely healed, but the pain was gone and smooth surface scars remained.

"What the hell are you?" she asked in disbelief.

"I don't know, but I feel different."

"At least you don't have to go through the fever to heal," Tessa admitted. Sweat beaded on her own head. Her leg and side was throbbing. The healing fever was draining her energy.

The gargoyles howled into the air around them, causing the walls to shake. "That's our cue to get out of here," Acantha said. Rocks fell from the ceiling and crashed around them, shattering into pieces. The three sisters ran toward the long hallway as the room collapsed. They climbed the tunnel staircase as the rock structures crumbled into a dark void. Screeches and howls lamented, but nothing was visible when they glanced back.

"I hope we don't have to deal with that bat again!" huffed Tessa.

Sadness possessed Acantha as the place crumbled behind her. She sensed a strange connection. Then she remembered the man in the portrait on the wall. He must have shared her fate but chose to serve Death. She shuddered. Someday she sensed she would come face-to-face with him.

Every step reminded her that her life had been prolonged again. Finally they reached the top. The destruction stopped. Acantha turned back to the stairs. There was nothing but endless darkness through the archway.

The dark voice blew up around her again in sinister laughter. It rumbled from the space before it faded away.

"Acantha?" Jennet called to her. "What about the bat?"

CHAPTER THIRTEEN
Murky Water

"Ahoy! Ahoy!" called the crow's nest. The mountain shook, sending boulders and debris rolling down its sides. Strange creatures flew out into the darkness.

Basile watched the path. "What's going on, Vaster?"

Vaster had the looking glass up.

"Any sign of them?" Basile asked.

"No, not yet," Vaster replied.

"Give me the scope." Basile grabbed the looking glass from his hands. "I think that some of those are bats…"

Vaster snatched the glass back. "Some?" He squinted at the swarming cloud above the mountaintop.

Basile stole the scope again. Through it, he saw the oversized monster crawl out from the opening. He panicked. "Uh, a little problem."

Vaster seized the scope and looked. His eyes bulged. "All men on deck!" He ran to the bell and rang it, summoning the crew. The huge bat flew straight toward them as crew members flooded the deck.

"Arm yourselves!" Vaster yelled. The bat crashed into the side of the ship and rolled down it. The collision rocked the ship.

Basile stumbled, landing near some long boat hook poles. He grabbed one. For a moment everything was still, then a scratching scraped up the side of the ship. The bat emerged, climbing the railing. Its strength rocked the ship. With its long claws it swiped at the crew. Sailors dodged its attacks.

The bat snatched Barton, a tall, chubby man. His pain-stricken cry pierced the air. The bat disconnected, flying back to shore with its captive in hand. The crew ran to the railing. On shore, the bat rapidly ate the sailor, silencing his cries in an instant. It turned back to *The Dark Eve*.

This time, it flew straight into the sails, snapping the ropes. The boat swayed. The monster thrashed at the white canvas, tearing it as it descended, breaking everything in its path. It screeched out, trying to move closer to the darting crew. It took flight again, working its way back to the railing. Basile held the hook out to keep the bat from coming aboard. Several more men grabbed long hooks, following his lead. Large spikes on the bottom of the bat's wings dug into the floor as it crawled onto the deck. The bat snapped at the attacking hooks. Its claws gripped deeper into the railing.

"Vaster!" Basile yelled. Vaster stumbled over to him. "The cannons."

Vaster ran for the arsenal deck below. The men bustled defensively.

"Hold it back!" Basile yelled to the crew, and they all stepped forward. The bat reared and then retaliated, striking violently. With its great jaws it broke one of the long poles in half. Another sailor got clawed across the face and fell to the ground screaming. Some of the men backed away. The monstrous bat latched onto the pole held by Watson and lifted him up in the air. Basile struck the bat with the sharp point of his hook, lodging it into its chest. The creature screeched and dropped Watson to the ground.

The sound of a cannon burst through the air. The bat, whose lower half was still on the side of the ship, was launched off. It took a piece of the railing with it as it flew backward onto the shore, a cannonball lodged in its belly. The bat screamed and flopped before collapsing. All the men on deck breathed heavily, looking out toward the carcass.

Vaster rushed out of the deck doors. Basile's chest heaved with adrenaline. The crew yelled in triumph.

Vaster stood tall. "Get those sails down and start patching them. Get all spare materials below and fix the deck and… get out there and get those rails." He pointed at the dead bat.

Basile followed the crowd, but Vaster grabbed him by the collar, yanking him back. "Oh, no. Ye get back to the helm and watch for the captain. Let me know the second she's back in sight."

For hours, Basile kept watch. A large group of sailors sat on the deck sewing the sails. Others fixed the railing. After what felt like forever, all three captains walked down from the top.

Basile sank with relief upon seeing the flowing blond hair. "I see them!" he shouted.

"Let me look!" Vaster grabbed for the scope, but Basile dodged away. "All three of them?"

"Yes," Basile confirmed.

Vaster ran to the edge of the railing. "Prepare yerselves! The captain comes!" The men hastened their work.

Something unsettling overwhelmed Basile as the three sisters descended. He had expected at least one to be left behind. After the bat, he had anticipated that Tessa wouldn't come back, and the entire time he felt tortured.

The crew stood ready as the small figures moved down the mountain.

As they neared, Vaster positioned himself at the stairs leading to the helm.

All three captains had been through a great deal: clothes torn, covered in dirt, with bruises and scratches bleeding all over. Jennet's vain, smug face was gone, replaced with exhaustion as she assisted Tessa to walk. She cradled the left side of her torso.

Then there was Acantha.

Vaster peered down on edge, but he restrained himself. She looked like the life had been sucked from her, ghostly pale. He wondered how she had strength to stand. Dark bruises covered her face and arms, with a dry, bloody gash on her forehead.

Her eyes widened as she looked up at them. "What happened?" Her voice was hard.

Vaster straightened. "We got attacked by a monster bat." He pointed out to where the dead creature lay.

Her voice softened. "Are we able to sail?"

"Yes, Captain." Vaster saluted.

Acantha glanced to the helm. "Take us back to familiar waters, Mr. Jennings," she commanded.

Basile tried to catch Tessa's eyes, but she focused on Jennet and Acantha. Jennet escorted her hobbling into the captain's quarters. His heart sank as the door latched shut, but it burst open again.

Basile jumped back as Jennet plowed out. "You! Deck boy."

He shook his head, stunned. "Me?"

"Tell the cook to bring boiling water and a washing tub."

He fumbled into action, disappearing into the ship.

◇◇◇

As Acantha stood on the helm, she could almost hear the questions in her crew's minds: *Did they find what they had been looking for? Were they successful? Could they defend themselves against the Sea Snake?*

She had no words to explain what had happened, or if it would help them in their upcoming confrontation.

"Captain?" Vaster called. "What happened? Did you get what you wanted?"

As the dark mountain floated farther away, the frosty feeling inside of her faded.

"Yes," she answered, even though she wasn't sure. The Oracle had said she would be put to the test and had to pass it.

I passed it. She could hardly stand, but it was important to stay visible so that the crew knew she was still in control.

What she was supposed to do now? She had died, of that she was certain. Her heart had stopped as she stood before the throne of Death. She had to have passed the test to be alive now. But what did it all mean? She wavered, tempted to fall down where she stood.

"So…" Vaster prodded for more information.

"We'll discuss it later." Her voice was final. "I'm leaving you in charge." She turned, thankful that "later" would probably never come. She walked as quickly as she could to her quarters. As soon as the door was closed she collapsed against the wall. In the mirror across from her, she saw herself sliding to the ground. As her eyes closed, Jennet reached down for her.

◇◇◇

Vaster ran back and forth giving orders. Basile stood by with his mop and bucket. He had been down to the kitchen three times. Mort, the old cook, passed with buckets of boiling water. Then he passed again with plates of food. Whenever he opened the door to the captain's quarters, Basile tried to look in. Every time, he was unable to see anything.

After several days, Tessa finally emerged. She looked well rested, but the happy sparkle in her eyes was dim. She glanced at him and then turned to the helm. Basile's heart and shoulders dropped.

What was he thinking? He had been convinced that there was

176

something between them, but now all he felt was naïve. The memory of her soft lips against his own sent a flood of warmth through him. It ended with emptiness.

The connection would only be a haunting memory.

As he returned to his mop and bucket, a hard realization hit him

This is my life. The grayness around him mocked his mood. His father's words echoed in his mind. *You are the most ungrateful, unworthy, lackadaisical boy! You've been given the paved road and you don't want it.*

It was all true. He looked back to Tessa on the helm, amazed that she wasn't still hobbling. Maybe she hadn't been as hurt as they thought. Squinting closer, he swore she had a cut on her face, but her skin was smooth and flawless. She gazed out to sea, showing her profile. Her gray suit enhanced the soft curves of her body.

I am ungrateful. My head is stuck in the clouds and all I want…" He looked back to the gloomy gray fog.

All I want is her. I want her to want me.

◇◇◇

Acantha struggled to wake up, paralyzed and trapped in her own mind. She willed her eyes to open—and she thought they had—only to realize she was still lying frozen in her bed. A painful tingling crawled up her legs. Inside she screamed, wishing for someone to touch her, determined that it would be the key to unlocking her mental prison.

Jennet's voice called her name and hands shook her. Finally her eyes flew open.

Jennet hovered. "Are you all right?" She stepped back as Acantha sat up.

Acantha's head pounded. "I couldn't wake up."

"Couldn't wake up? You were surrounded by a dark cloud."

Acantha shook her head. "I don't understand."

"I came in and there was darkness around your bed covering you." Jennet waved her arms in the air. I shouted your name several times, and then it disappeared, and I saw you sleeping."

"I think you're losing your mind." Acantha stood.

Jennet nodded. "I need a drink."

It was probably the only thing they agreed about. Acantha opened her desk drawer and pulled out the bottle of rum. "I only have one glass."

"I don't need a glass." Jennet grabbed the bottle from her and took a desperate drink.

Acantha shrugged and put the glass back into the drawer.

Hours later both were laughing uncontrollably. "Do—do you remember that time I punched you in the nose?" Jennet shook.

"Yes." Acantha's face was serious. "I told you not to." She rubbed her nose.

"I didn't mean to." Jennet continued to laugh. "I was practicing the moves Father had shown me."

"Yeah, well, not on my nose. That was a long time ago." Acantha took the last drink out of the bottle. She snickered. "Do you remember when I choked you?"

Now Jennet's face was serious. "Mother had to tear you off to get you to stop."

"I told you not to touch me!" A wicked smile grew upon Acantha's face. "Yeah, she loved that!"

Both of them chuckled.

"We sure did like to torture her." Acantha rolled the bottle away as a bitterness rose inside her. "I hated them."

Jennet drastically raised her eyebrows and then pouted her lips, nodding. "It was harder for us, because we were the eldest. We got most of the backlash because of their disappointments."

"I was a disappointment!" Acantha raised her hand.

"Me too!" Jennet raised hers. "That's why Tessa is not as good with the sword left-handed."

"What?"

Jennet looked like she was going to pass out, "Because the younger ones didn't get as many 'lessons' as we did."

Acantha nodded. "Can Ruella even use a sword?"

"I don't think so. She just uses her lips."

They both snickered.

The door flung open and Tessa squinted hard at them. Her eyes bulged. "Are you two drunk?"

"Are we talking and laughing?" Jennet furrowed her brows. "Hurry and ask Acantha something before she comes to her senses!" She burst into laughter.

Tessa looked down piteously. "What happened when you first escaped?"

Jennet's eyes bulged. "I don't know if she's that drunk."

Acantha's gaze went glossy and a long moment passed.

Tessa rolled her eyes. "Well, I'm tired it's time to switch." She flopped down on the bed.

Jennet collapsed on the ground. "I can't go. The room is moving too much."

Acantha rested her head against the wall. "Give me a minute."

"Are we going to talk about what happened and what we're going to do next?" Tessa asked.

"Acantha can obviously heal people, so now she's god or something like that." Jennet waved her hand into the air.

"I didn't know what I was doing. I don't feel like a god." Acantha stated, bobbing her head. "I feel like I was broken into little pieces and then put back together again. With a strange bond."

"What did happen when you drank that vile stuff?" Jennet muffled out.

"I died." She paused, waiting for a response from them, but none came. "I burned from the inside out. Then my heart stopped. I stood before the throne of Death."

"What?" Tessa interjected.

"I stood before Death," Acantha reiterated.

"We need to get you drunk more often," Jennet said.

Acantha continued. "He asked me to join him, but I refused."

"You refused him?" Jennet sat up straight and rigid. "What if you were supposed to accept?"

"Then there's no way we'll succeed, because I'm not going to do yet another person's bidding. Besides, there was already someone doing it."

"What do you mean?" Tessa asked, inching forward off the bed. "You chose to serve Solon? How do you know someone else is doing Death's bidding?"

"Serving Solon serves my own serving, or something like that." Acantha felt confused. "There was a face of a man on the wall in Death's throne room. He wanted to replace him with me." The man's face was familiar. She scanned her memory, but could not pinpoint where she knew that face.

"So what was the point?" Tessa snorted. "Why did we go there?" she stood and paced the floor. "How the hell was this supposed to help us? Did we even do what we were supposed to do?"

"You're making me dizzy. Stop moving," Jennet said.

"We did what we were supposed to do. I just don't know how it's going to help us," Acantha answered.

"How mysterious," Tessa shouted. "I'm sick of it!"

179

Jennet sat up. "Let's stop trying to fix it. We're doomed! Look at us! We're falling apart. We have serious issues."

"I wouldn't have serious issues if it weren't for you," Acantha said.

Jennet glared back. "Maybe it's time to end this. We've been at it for how many years now?" She looked to Tessa, who shrugged. "Maybe it's time."

"Speak for yourself," Acantha said.

"I am speaking for myself. I'm tired. I think I'm ready to die."

They were all silent again.

"Where would you like to be buried?" Acantha asked.

They all looked at each other and busted out laughing.

After the laughter died and feelings dimmed, Acantha spoke. "I made the deal for all of you so you could escape. I haven't forced you into this life. Go make your own deals with Solon." She stood and steadied herself.

"We could always go back to the Oracle," Tessa noted quietly.

"No," Acantha said. "We've been there twice. Twice in one year is way too much. She doesn't see everything. We were instructed where to go and what to do to defeat Naulkiendum. It's time to let things play out and see what unfolds."

"But we don't know anything," Tessa protested again.

"Then it's time to have faith in our instructions." Acantha countered. A new headache was forming as she left. "Like Father would say, work with what information you have and then pool your resources and be as prepared as you possibly can."

"Faith? Father?" Tessa questioned, bewildered. "Is she kidding?"

"No," Jennet said. "She's drunk."

"Acantha." Tessa stopped her from leaving. "Why can't you let this go?"

Acantha turned, unwilling to talk. "I have unfinished business. I will not leave until it's resolved. Only then will I die."

◇◇◇

Days later, they finally hit clear water again. The darkness lifted. When the sun peeked out from the fog for the first time, the crew basked in its divine warmth, like hell had been dispersed. All three captains stood on deck.

"Back to Woodmor," Acantha ordered.

Jennet studied the faint scars that covered her hands. Tessa stared at the perfect blue water. For the first time in months they could see the sun set. It sizzled into the sea, illuminating the sky with a parade of colors.

"Tessa, you have the night watch," Acantha said.

Tessa confirmed with a nod, but did not look to them as they left. Scar stood silently at the wheel, navigating their course. In the twilight she looked down to the deck and what few men remained. Basile was not one of them. Never had she felt more longing for the comfort of home than she did now. Her world strained on a breaking point. Fear grew in her chest: it was only a matter of time until all the safety she enjoyed would crash down. Endless uncertainty revolved around her mind.

She relied too much on Acantha.

The light faded from the sky, sending out the stars and slivered moon.

A throat cleared behind her. Tessa looked back to find Basile on the helm. Scar paid no attention to his presence. Basile had a concerned look.

"Can I have a word with the present captain?" He sounded indifferent. Scar looked to Tessa and she nodded. Scar gave her the wheel before leaving.

"I'm glad you're all right," Basile said, stepping closer.

She glanced at him but said nothing.

"Tessa." He stood on the other side of the wheel, blocking her vision.

She spoke harshly. "What do you need?"

He stepped back, furrowing his eyebrows. "Please," he coaxed her.

"This doesn't happen, not in my world."

"Why? What is so wrong with it?"

"Nothing's wrong with it if you're anyone normal. I'm not the same as you." She held his gaze. "I don't belong here."

He squinted. "You are normal. We'll go wherever you want to. We can escape. I'm willing to go and never come back."

She read his desperate expression. "You don't know what you're talking about."

"Then tell me!" His voice escalated. "I want to know."

"It's not things that you can understand," she said.

"Does it have to do with what I told you about Dagan and his story?" His eyes searched her face.

Tessa grabbed the rope and put it on one of the handles of the wheel. She walked around it and fell into his arms.

Basile held her tight, unwilling to let her escape as relief flooded his entire body. She reached up and kissed him. Her gentleness morphed into a desperate firmness. He felt her soft, golden hair and held tightly to her shoulders. He glided his hands down her back.

In an instant it was over. She stepped away from him and held her arm out for distance. Her face was flushed, her eyes closed as she controlled her breathing. Basile remained still.

"You don't get to choose to know," she said. "You have to be worthy to know secrets, because they affect more than just the three of us." She scrutinized him. "Who are you Mr. Basile? And what makes you able to change everything?" Her voice was genuine.

He shook his head confused. "I don't know, but I'll do whatever it takes."

But she looked tired again. "I won't be the judge of that. Acantha will." She called out to Scar. He unfolded out of the shadows of the deck below and returned to the wheel.

Tessa spoke heartlessly. "Thank you for your concern, Mr. Basile."

Inside she was dying. She had never wanted to let someone in until now. Every rule and reason seemed insignificant. Her connection to him felt unreal, making everything unstable. From the moment she first saw him, an invisible force tugged her in his direction. Now fighting against it was destroying her.

She needed to get away, on her own ship. The distance would tear her back into a familiar world, one that she had control over. He would become as meaningless as all the others in her lifetime, a fleeting moment. But an undeniable connection crept up.

I don't know how to make it work, she silently admitted.

CHAPTER FOURTEEN
The Fool's Errand

"What now?" asked Jennet.

After arriving at Woodmor, they had relieved the crew, but only for a couple of days. They crowded around the long mess hall table—Tessa with her first mate Monier, Jennet and the remainder of her original crew. Along with Acantha, Vaster, Scar, and Jennings, all stood waiting to hear their next step.

Acantha slouched in a wooden chair, her legs crossed and propped on the table. The dark circles under her eyes made everyone more on edge. Not even Vaster dared tread near. Since returning from Death's mountain, she couldn't shake her foul mood and always wanted to stay in during the day.

She spoke and the room listened. "We meet Naulkiendum at the Gates of Hell. We'll anchor our ships to the south of the island and hike in to high ground to set up our defenses. They'll have to come to us. If we arrive *first*, then we'll set up traps through the canyon path." She pictured the narrow trail up to the small, flat mesa. On one side was sheer cliffs, a steady drop down to thrashing water below. On the other side of the water, another cliff face created a narrow waterway between them, leaving little room for any ship to sail through. "If we get there first, we'll have the advantage."

"We'll be outnumbered," said Falke, Jennet's second-in-command, in his

French accent. If there was anything more annoying than Jennet, it was the remainder of her crew.

"Yeah," added one of the twins. "They have millions and millions." He looked to the other twin, who nodded.

The other twin added, "We've been on their island. There is no escape because of their numbers."

Tessa said, "Yes, but he won't be able to bring all of them."

"But!" added the first twin. "He can bring shiploads of them."

No one could ever tell the difference between the twins, and they never corrected anyone.

Jennet rolled her eyes. "That's why we have to get there first. Shut up unless you have something smart to say."

One twin hit the other, who elbowed him back.

Acantha spoke. "He could have been shipping them over since we left. But, where we're meeting, there's little room. If too many come, it's down the cliffs they go."

"We can't bet that he'll keep his word, can we?" Jennet asked.

"No, but we have an advantage over him," Tessa said.

All eyes few to her.

"What advantage, Captain?" Monier asked.

"Acantha!" she stated.

Acantha greeted their curious gazes with no hint of resolution. The members of the meeting shifted nervously. She was so tired of everyone doubting her. What had she not proven to them in the time they were together?

"It'll take us at least a week to get there, and we weren't supposed to meet until two weeks from now. We need to assume that he's done all these things and prepare for them." She looked to Tessa. The youngest sister's mood had changed since their trip to Death's Mountain. She was tired and on edge. After Scar's report, Acantha pondered her stability.

"Send your first mates into town and buy supplies," Acantha said. "We sail in two days." She turned to Vaster. "Get Basile." She carefully watched Tessa to see if her expression changed, but it didn't.

The men shuffled out of the room, leaving the three captains behind.

"What do we do now?" Tessa asked solemnly.

"I don't know." She studied Tessa's face. There were so many questions that she wanted to ask, but she wouldn't get truthful answers.

"You really have no idea how going to that island has helped us?" Jennet glared suspiciously at her.

"Sometimes it's about not knowing everything. We've done what we were told."

"Have you gone soft in your head?" Jennet asked. "Death didn't give you anything?"

Acantha switched thoughts, tired of answering the same questions. "Tessa, do you have anything to add?"

"No, I don't have anything to add."

Acantha stared long and hard. Tessa reciprocated. Acantha tried again. "Do you have anything to report to us?"

Jennet's interest piqued. "What's going on now?"

"Change is coming," Acantha said. "I have a feeling that this battle will take a lot out of us. Tessa's eyes look guilty."

Jennet looked closely at her and nodded.

"Will you two leave me alone?" Tessa grumbled.

Acantha sat up, disappointed. "This is your last chance right now to go back. Either you both are in or you're out."

"I'm in. You know I'm not going back," Jennet stated.

Tessa looked more apprehensive, but she nodded. "I'm in."

"Then prepare your ships and pick your commanders. Hopefully, we get enough recruits in town to fill all three ships," Acantha said. "I don't want to go into town, but if I have to, I will." She stood and paced the floor. "I have connections here that can benefit us if we need them. But I'd rather not stir things up. I like them the way they are."

Tessa scowled. "What's so special about this town?"

Acantha glared until Tessa drew her eyes away. "This town runs the way I want it to. I don't need to explain why."

Tessa sat back, defeated.

"Naulkiendum knows who we are," Acantha confessed. Jennet and Tessa squinted at her. "He knows."

Jennet asked, "How do you know that?"

"I just do, I feel it."

Jennet raised her eyebrows. "Is this one of your crazy dreams again? Are you going all Oracle on us too?"

Tessa just looked away.

"Call it intuition," said Acantha.

"That doesn't prove he knows who we are!" cried Jennet.

"He knows we live long lives. He might not know our lineage, but he knows," Acantha said. "I've been killing wraiths from the beginning, and his island is well preserved. He comes from a heritage—a line of kings. We've probably killed at least three generations in his family line." She shuddered at the memory of her first wraith battle and its consequences.

"Still, that doesn't mean he knows," Tessa said.

"It doesn't matter if he does," Jennet argued. "We'll kill him and end whatever he knows." She stood, shrugging her shoulders. "It's not like he can get to the treasure anyway."

"Maybe it's not about the treasure," Tessa interjected.

Acantha rolled her eyes. "We don't need to worry about the treasure. They're perfectly capable of defending themselves and the treasure. It's us I'm worried about. Solon is only interested in himself, and if we—through fault or not—reveal them, I'm not sure what will happen to the rest of the family."

"Since when did you worry about them?" Tessa asked gloomily.

Acantha scrunched her eyebrows. "I might not agree and follow them, but I do still recognize them. Naulkiendum doesn't need treasure. He has piles of gold in his stinky cave."

"Then what?" Tessa protested.

"Do I have to point everything out to you?" Acantha asked, annoyed. "We've killed generations of them. What's the one thing that every man wishes will never come?"

"Death," Jennet said blatantly.

Tessa pieced together the information. "But we cannot give him long life."

Acantha took a deep breath. "He doesn't know that, just as much as he doesn't know that we can die."

"But you did just die," Jennet said.

Basile dangled in his hammock, facing the window and a portion of the horizon. They were back in Woodmor and as much as his heart desired to get off the ship and roam the town like the rest of the crew, he couldn't will himself to go. The sky was clear and occasionally, a seagull soared by. He reminisced of his time in the backcountry, with the scent of pines and fresh air, and all the gold in his pocket. That had been freedom, with no one to confuse his thoughts and feelings. He could wander forever in this newfound world.

He had thought that Tessa would agree to come with him, that together they could leave. Frustration and confusion built inside him. He would be better off without her plaguing his mind, but no matter how much he tried she always crept back in.

All he needed was time. If he could get off the ship, her hazel eyes would fade from his memory, along with the soft touch of her lips. But every time he closed his eyes, he saw the sun glistening through her golden hair, with a gentle breeze in the background.

If Dagan's words about Acantha were true, he had to assume it was the same for her sisters. *What would it be like to live forever? And why do they possess this power?*

As much as Basile tried to convince himself that he could leave, he didn't want to. Everything he had once valued felt worthless if she was not willing to be part of it.

He was trapped *again*, but this time in a cage that he did not have the key to open.

Feet shuffled behind him. He turned quickly. Vaster leaned against the opposite hammock. Basile rolled his eyes and looked to his escape window.

"Captain wants to see ya," Vaster stated.

Basile looked back with surprise. "Why?"

"It doesn't matter why. She's called."

Basile sat up from his hammock, nodding, but his mind reeled. *She knows. What would she do?*

Possible escape routes opened up to him. Cowardice built inside his chest. The first time he had stood in front of her, he had decided to become someone of consequence. He couldn't run now. Something bigger was going on here. He could only see bits and pieces of an intricate puzzle. This was where he belonged—prison or not—until every last portion was revealed.

But he might not ever escape. This could very well be the end of him.

"I'll be there right away," he said.

◇◇◇

A knock pounded at the door.

"Come in," Acantha called.

Vaster and Basile shuffled through door. "Finally," Acantha said. "I'm putting you two in charge of recruits. We need as many as we can to fill all three ships." Basile and Vaster nodded. Basile briefly glanced toward Tessa, whose back faced him. "Vaster, promise them the usual wage.

You'll get resistance from this town. They've been a little more *sheltered* than the others we pull from, so expect it."

Vaster nodded.

Acantha looked to Tessa. "You'll join them."

Tessa sat alert and twisted her head, wide-eyed. She opened her mouth to protest, but she shut it again. She stood, clearing her face, and walked out the door. Basile and Vaster shuffled after her.

Jennet tapped on the table until the door shut behind them. "Why did you send Tessa on a fool's chore?"

"Because right now she's a fool," Acantha said.

Acantha's dreams spun in her mind. One second she was in the darkness of the mountain with the cold all around her. Then she flashed to a murky swamp where she ran in the rainy night. Her heart pounded. She scraped for earth, branches, and rocks to help her move. Dogs bayed in the distance. She was barely covered in her torn and bloody under garment and corset, wet and muddy. Bitter, angry tear streaks smeared down her face as she fought her way through.

Finally, she found solid ground. Climbing out of the swampy muck, she could feel scrapes and pain all over her body. There was no direct path. She charged through the thick brush, putting distance between her and the assailants following. Her lungs burned as sweat dripped down her face.

Her mind flashed again. She spun in the circle on the dance floor of the masquerade ball. The masked faces around her laughed grotesquely. She looked up, but it was not Lord Edwin's face staring back at her. It was a masked devil sneering with a crooked smile. The room swirled with blurred colors and she shifted to the sand in her familiar tunic. The gloomy sea stretched on forever; the boundless prison held her right where she sat. Her hair flowed gently in the wind. She wished for change on the horizon.

Seagulls screeched in the sky and waves rushed onto the shore. The laughter of children echoed behind her. Dark clouds billowed above, shrouding her in thick darkness.

Once again she stood before Death in his mountain, his bone hand pointing to her face on the wall.

The soft blue eyes that she remembered brightened. For just a moment, she reveled in both her hate and love of them. Everthing faded away, and her eyes fluttered open.

She lay in her room staring up at the wooden ceiling. It was dark outside. Ever since her journey, she could not rid herself of the cold. She stood and moved to the window, where she looked hard—as if seeing their end destination past the water to the shores of Hell's Gate. A wraith ship circled the island. Wraiths covered every inch like the sand on the beach, their faces covered in bone piercings. They bobbed back and forth, waiting patiently with jagged swords.

She could see it all clearly as though she stood there. Her mind flashed to a large ship splitting through the water. A giant skeleton gaped around its helm, along with three serrated spikes sticking out through the rib cage. Its coat of red dust mixed with the water, so that the whole ship looked as though it were covered in blood. Bones, both human and beast, lined every inch of its surface. In the background, the blood-red mountains loomed.

◇◇◇

"Vaster," Tessa said, "you spread the word through the taverns on the east side of town."

Vaster saluted, confirming her orders.

"Let them meet at the docks in the morning, any who wish to serve. I'll take the west side of town. Basile…" She paused, turning back. He stood without emotion, waiting for her order. "You take the north."

Basile nodded and walked straight past. She watched him walk away, disappointed. *What am I doing?* She spun around to the west side.

The first tavern she ventured upon was named The White Stag. She had never walked this town, but they all knew Acantha. She opened the wooden tavern doors and walked in. Her eyes adjusted to the change of light. At least fifteen men filled the room. A small dancing stage draped with red velvet and gold tasseled curtains took the right side of the bar, but there was no one on stage.

All eyes fixed on her as she walked through the tables to the tavern's bar. A burly man with a thick beard and a red-and-white striped apron tended. She had everyone's attention, even the ladies who sauntered around the floor half-dressed with their white-painted faces and rouged cheeks.

"We're looking for men," she stated to the barkeep, loud enough for the whole room to hear. "Anyone interested in sailing with *The Deity*, *Le Voleur*, and *The Dark Eve* can report tomorrow at the docks. Payment is a bag of gold each."

Murmurs whispered around the room.

"And who might you be?" asked the tavern man.

"I'm captain of *The Deity*."

The room was quiet.

"And we are to believe that?" the barkeep asked as his eyes grazed down the front of her.

Several men stood from the tables behind her. As two rushed, she drew her sword, swiping it around to strike both across the face. Two more charged. She pulled her pistol and shot one in the chest while the other jumped at her. She quickly dodged, and he fell into the bar. Two more men stood. She thrust the dagger from her belt into the belly of one. Then she pushed him against the last man, throwing them both backward onto a table.

For a second the bar was quiet. Tessa waited, poised for another attack, but the other customers blinked with wide eyes. She stared at the barkeep, whose eyebrows furrowed.

The tavern doors opened and a light burst through. The figure hesitated. It was Basile.

Tessa struck the barkeep across the head with the end of her pistol. He nearly fell over. His eyes bulged like they would pop out of his head. No one defended him as she grabbed his collar and dragged him out from behind the bar. He waved his hands. She turned back to the people in the tavern and spoke firmly to them all.

"Spread the word."

The tavern man's voice shook. "But the black ship has never asked for crew here."

Tessa glowered down at him. "I guess it's time for you to earn your gold instead of it just being spent among you."

Basile gaped at Tessa transformed to a version of her sister.

Once released, the barkeep placed a rag to his bleeding scalp. He jerked his head to some of the men in the crowd. Basile eyed them suspiciously. They sneered at him as they left.

Had the people been so vicious?

Tessa started toward the door and he followed her out. Once in the alley she turned on him. "What do you think you're doing?"

Basile stepped back. "I heard a gunshot. I saw you go in there, but I wasn't following you."

"Then what were you doing? I told you to take the north."

He no longer saw anything fragile in her. "I was only making sure you were all right."

"I don't need your help to do my job."

"I'm not saying you do. I just thought that you might want my help." He tried his hardest not to raise his voice.

She pressed her lips together and looked around.

"Tessa, will you meet me tonight outside of town?"

She glared at him like he was out of his mind. "This cannot continue."

"Please, just meet me and just talk. Nothing else," he begged.

She squinted hard.

"Just meet me." He backed up to leave.

She kept her eyes on him. Basile spun and ran to the main road. He glanced back only once before turning north at the fork.

He had to convince her to leave with him. After hearing the gunshot and seeing her in The White Stag, his instincts took over.

She will come.

He hit every tavern along the north side. All the while, he worked on answers for all her imagined excuses. Most men in the taverns looked at him skeptically as he explained the recruitment. He got into several scuffles, but he could better defend himself now.

As the sun set, he found himself in front of the Red Dragon. He peered carefully into the windows as the dragon sign emanated its crimson light and smoke. Decorative screens prevented him from seeing inside.

He hesitated. Maybe he should skip this one, but Acantha visited it. She would probably know if he did.

Basile walked up the steps and opened the door. A bell rang above his head. Red decorative wall dressing with a pattern of golden dragons lined the entry. Globe-lanterns hung from the ceiling, strung from one side of the room to the other. None of the few people who sat within bothered to look his direction. A man similar to Cho Lee from the docks stood behind the bar, but he glanced at Basile and then returned to wiping the counter.

"I'm supposed to give you a message." Basile whispered while creeping over to the bar.

The man looked up with a squinting face.

Basile remembered the language barrier and talked slowly. "From the black ship, in the harbor. A message."

"I heard you," the bartender snapped. "Wait here."

He left through a door behind the bar. Basile glanced around the room. The guests, who were all the same countrymen as the bartender, spared him quick looks. He had studied a little on the Dynasty Kingdoms, but didn't know them well enough to know which land they hailed from. He wondered how they had managed to establish themselves here.

The man returned and motioned Basile to go into the back. Basile passed through to an empty kitchen. A winding staircase led up to the next floor. He followed it up hesitantly.

The second level opened into a large room decorated in a vibrant red. In the middle were pillows heaped onto the floor. A woman whose face was painted white sat among them with a bright fan hiding her nose and mouth. Her raven-black hair was pinned in a bun on top of her head. She had a flat face and dark eyes.

"Who speaks for the Dark Lady?" Her accent was pronounced.

"I'm Basile, crew member of *The Dark Eve*. She calls for aid."

"She's never sent a messenger before." The woman spoke suspiciously. "Why now would she send one?"

"I don't know. I just know I was sent into town with a message to deliver to every tavern. *The Dark Eve* is recruiting and needs help in their next battle."

"The Dark Lady has never asked for help from here."

"She does now."

"You are very bold in my presence."

"I'm sorry," Basile said. "But I only know what has been spoken to me."

The woman closed her fan, revealing the rest of her face. Her long, pointed fingernails looked razor sharp. "Do you know who I am?"

He shook his head.

"I am Lady Yang and this is my town. Nothing happens here without me knowing about it." She shook one of her long, pointy fingers at him.

His eyes widened. *How could this be her town if it was the captain's town?* "I don't understand."

She lit a long, slim pipe and smoked in front of him. "You can tell the Lady I will send men to her." She released the smoke through her nose like a dragon.

Basile bowed his head and started to back away to the staircase.

"Tell me, Basile," she spoke, stopping him. "Did you find anyone still alive at the old golden city?"

His heart stuttered.

"Yes," he spoke truthfully. "One man remains alive."

"Did he tell you anything?"

Basile felt instantly guarded about James's information, but found no reason why he should be. "Just about a curse over the Bracket family line."

"Do you believe him?" Her face did not change—much like the captain.

"I don't know, Madam. I'm not so sure I believe in curses."

"Don't believe!" Lady Yang laughed. "Just because you don't know of them doesn't make them unreal!" She puffed again on her pipe. "I have seen dark evils that your eyes could never imagine."

Basile had seen plenty since being aboard the dark ship: the sirens and tucaranda at the Oracle's maze, their trip in the dark water, with the ghostly fog, and the dead mountain.

Yes, he knew evil existed.

"Is the curse real?" he asked, moving closer.

Lady Yang smiled a wicked smile. "Yes. My family has been here since the beginning and has been granted this land to watch over. If you had not reported that life still lives in the city, I would have sent one of my own to find out. We've waited a long time for the land to be cleansed from the evil there."

"Is the story the same that you have heard? About a witch cursing the Bracket line?" Basile asked looking for a place to sit, but decided against pillows on the ground.

She nodded. "Dark evil touched that place long ago, burning the mark into anyone who stayed."

"But why?" Basile asked.

Lady Yang's eyes widened. "Evil needs its place to live as well. You must watch closely, Mr. Basile, for the evil that lives among you."

Was she referring to the captain? But before he could ask, she spoke again. "I will send my men tomorrow to the docks."

"Thank you." He turned quickly, down the staircase and out the back kitchen doors into the alley.

Night was falling. He hurried out of town to meet Tessa. His heart pounded with hope that she would come. As he rounded the edge of town, a long figure waited in the twilight. A breath of relief surged from him. As he approached she turned.

"I thought you wouldn't come," he said.

"I wasn't sure I would," she admitted.

He took her hand and led her out into the tall grass, relieved when she followed without resistance. They sat, sheltering themselves from view. He itched to pull her close but knew it would be too much.

"Before you start talking," Tessa said, "I can't answer any questions about my sisters or myself. So please, don't ask."

His heart sank. "It doesn't matter. I don't know what to ask anymore."

She tilted her head. "Someday, you'll know everything you look for. If you choose it."

"Whatever that means," he said. "I don't know how to prove myself to you—or to anybody else, for that matter."

"Time always does it."

"Why does everyone say that? That's the worst." He rolled back in the grass, looking at the emerging stars overhead. *"I'm sorry, I know you want the information, and I have the information, but I can't tell you, because I'm dark and secretive and it's something you have to earn, but I can't tell you how to earn it. You just have to wait till the stars fall out of the sky and magically reveal it to you."*

"I don't know everything," Tessa barked.

"Good to know," he snapped.

They sat in silence for a long time. She eventually positioned herself next to him, sharing his view of the sky.

"It is beautiful here," she said.

Basile had spent the silent moments cooling his temper. "I can't believe that you never got off the ship here."

"This is Acantha's territory. We split up to cover more ground and never enter each other's unless necessary."

"Until you meet here?" Basile probed.

"Yes," she replied.

"But, doesn't your crew get off here too for the week?"

"No. I have another holiday harbor for them," She smirked.

"And then you take your portion of the treasure and pile it high in some cave for no good reason?"

"Something like that."

"Why?" He rolled to his side, looking at her. "You three are probably the richest people alive."

She rolled to face him as well. All the reasons floated across her face. He would give everything to be able to read her mind.

"Why do *you* do it?" she countered.

It was just like her to turn the question around. "I told you, I want my fortune to escape and leave."

"Oh, yes, far from any worries or cares. Void of anyone else, with mountains of gold piled around you, but useless because you can't spend it. At least not on an uninhabited island."

Basile acknowledged the silliness of his dreams. "You're right. I don't need the treasure. I could leave now and find my island. Live my stupid, idiotic dream."

"What keeps you?" she asked.

His anger flustered inside. He wanted to shout out at her, *"You! You have destroyed me, and I won't live without YOU!"*

But the words wouldn't come. He just gazed at her perfect hazel eyes.

He changed the subject. "What'll happen when we reach Hell's Gate?"

"I don't know. We're in unknown territory."

"Do you believe Acantha can pull us through this?" He searched her face for any hint of doubt.

"Acantha's an unnatural force. I believe she can accomplish anything if she determines to do it," Tessa said. She shivered.

Basile took off his jacket and laid it over her. She smiled, faintly thanking him. "She's saved me before."

He stilled, afraid of saying anything that would stop her from speaking.

"She was the first of us to go off on her own." Tessa rolled on her back again, staring up at the stars. "She was always braver than the rest of us." She smiled. "Our parents couldn't handle her. I don't think anyone can."

A quiet moment passed. Basile itched for more.

"I tried to be like her," Tessa admitted.

"You are sort of," he said.

"No, not really. Everything I am she's helped me to be."

Basile searched her face. *She was nothing like Acantha.*

"I love you." As soon as the words slipped from his mouth, he regretted them.

Tessa sat up, rigid.

"Please," he begged. "I'm sorry. I know you can't feel the same for me. Or at least show it." He propped himself up on his knees, reaching out to her. "I choose you. I don't know how to choose you, but I do. But I need to know if you choose me."

Tessa stared back with a closed expression.

"I'll give up all the treasure in the world to choose you," he said.

She pulled him down with her. Their lips met, gliding unrestrained. They rolled in the grass, tangling as the dark night seeped protectively around them.

CHAPTER FIFTEEN
Hell's Gate

The next morning, Basile stirred from the best night's sleep he'd had since boarding *The Dark Eve*. He reached over, only to find the spot next to him empty. His jacket remained where Tessa had curled up. The grass still bore her indent. His heart sank.

Last night was unrivaled in his life. He at last felt whole with her asleep by his side. Now a chill of uncertainty ran up his spine.

After trudging back to town and helping Vaster with the new recruits, his hope of speaking to her died. She had boarded her own ship, *The Deity*, and he returned to *The Dark Eve*.

All three warring vessels sailed toward their doomed destination. As the pending moment drew closer, anxiety increased in his chest.

Vaster enlisted him in the task of arming all on board, a step up from his mop and the trimming the ropes. He ran from deck to deck with a special case of guns, dispersing the arsenal to direct leaders. He relinquished one to Vaster, who in return offered one to him.

"Don't use it unless it is a dire emergency," Vaster warned.

Afterward, he issued swords in the mess hall to the extra sailors. Mort worked in the back as usual and Mr. Kinkles pecked in the corner. Pole inspected every sword before Basile handed them out.

"Are you nervous?" Basile asked.

Pole eyed him with a wrinkled forehead.

"About the fight? The wraiths and their king? The big snake?" Basile waved his hands around.

"Haven't thought about it," Pole said.

"How could that be?" They were possibly traveling to their deaths.

"I live in the here and now," Pole stated calmly. "And in the here and now, there's no need for worry." He spun the blade in his hand before passing it.

Basile blinked at the absurdity. "What if you die?"

Pole puffed his cheeks and blew out a slow breath. "Then I'll be dead and have nothing to worry about."

"But don't you have anything to live for? Doesn't the loss of your potential future worry you?"

Pole scoffed. "What future? I'm a pirate. I live for my next pay and week of folly. I do what I'm told—kill, eat, work, and sleep." He squinted at Basile. "What is it that you have to live for?"

Basile fell silent as another group of men shuffled in for weapons. This ship was exactly like the people back home. He had left one useless hive for another. Was there no other form of existence than that?

"Have ye seen The Lady?" one man said nudging another in line. The second bloke did not reply.

"Don't think I've ever seen a woman like that before!" the new sailor whispered.

Basile and Pole shared glances and the banging from the kitchen ceased. Old Mort poked his head up through the kitchen window. The talker stepped up to receive his weapon. Basile proffered a sword but held tight as the man went to take it.

"What the—?" the man barked.

Basile glared. "If I were you, I'd watch what I said about the captain."

A grunt sounded from the kitchen. Pole stared up with a firm face.

"And if I don't?" the man asked, jutting his chin out.

Pole shot up and the sailor lost his bravado. Basile released his weapon, allowing him to sit with the rest of his group.

Just then, Mr. Kinkles hopped onto his table and pecked its surface. The man grimaced. He backhanded the bird right off the board. Basile's and Pole's eyes bulged. Old Mort shuffled out from the kitchen with his butcher's knife. He stalked toward the table, gaining attention with every step. The sailor glanced up just as Mort hacked his knife down, severing his fingers. The recruit screamed in pain, jolting backward, holding his bleeding hand.

The old cook sneered. "Don't talk about the Lady," he warned, "and keep your hands off my chicken!"

"Are you crazy?" the man bellowed. He screamed profanities at Mort, but the old dog only turned to the rest of the new crew.

"You think you can take the fury of the sea?" He spat on the ground.

Basile and Pole dragged the injured sailor toward the door as Mort continued. "She was born with the mark of darkness upon her. She's a vixen, a horror of the seas!" he yelled grotesquely. The room stared with wide eyes. "She'll kill every last one of you!" He laughed and coughed. "She's your worst nightmare!"

Pole and Basile managed to get the man out of the mess and up to the deck.

"What's happened?" Vaster shouted at them.

"Mort cut off his fingers for touching his chicken," Pole said.

Vaster slapped his head with irritation. "This is not somethin' I need to deal with right now."

"I need a doctor!" the man bellowed, holding his hand tight. "Where's your doctor?"

"He just cut off yer fingers," Vaster replied.

The man wailed.

Vaster looked to Pole. "Take him below, and fix this." When Basile turned to go with, he spun him back around. "Oh, no, not you."

"I thought I would help," Basile suggested.

"No. Captain wants to see ya in her quarters."

Basile's eyes widened. "Me? Why? I haven't done anything."

"Ye've been called. Now get!" Vaster shoved him in the right direction.

Basile stumbled and caught himself. He walked as slow as he could toward the captain's door while straightening his clothes and hair. Vaster shook his head, embarrassed, and followed after Pole to deal with the new commotion.

Basile's mind raced. *Did she know he had followed her? Or about Tessa and him? Had Lady Yang told Acantha about his visit? Or maybe she just had a job for him to do?*

When he had first come on board, Vaster had warned him. *"The helm is the captain's throne. She be sensitive about her area. Best not go up there unless it's urgent or you are summoned. In the second case, I would probably just throw myself overboard, 'cuz that's likely why she be callin' ya."* He looked to the railing of the ship, tempted to follow the advice.

A throat cleared behind him. Mort stood with a silver-domed tray. Basile looked back to the door, finding more courage. If he wanted Tessa, he would have to deal with Acantha. He stood straight and knocked.

"Come in," her voice answered.

He allowed Old Mort to go through first, figuring she was less likely to kill him during her supper. Old Mort growled at him as he shuffled into the room.

What would it take for him to win some ground with these people?

Acantha, at her desk, faced them both. It was the first time he had been in her chambers. He tried not to look at the extravagant furnishings, but stared straight ahead through the windows to their wonderful view. Old Mort shakily placed the silver tray in front of her. He waited a breath and then dramatically took off the lid, revealing the presentation. The dinner was magnificent: a whole herb-roasted chicken garnished with onions, carrot, and potatoes.

She looked over the food, nodding her approval. He hunched in a bow. From a small cupboard on the opposite wall retrieved a decanter of wine and a silver goblet. He poured her a glass and left the decanter with her. Then he shuffled out, shutting the door behind him.

And the crew always ate common stew. *I guess being captain has its perks,* Basile thought.

Acantha sat back in her chair, looking at him blankly. The delicious aroma melted in his nose.

"Tell me about yourself and where you're from," she said.

Basile shook his head, confused. "Uh… I grew up outside of Montville. My father owns the land and raises mostly cattle, but he rents land to farmers. He has several stores in the region."

Acantha, with proper etiquette, ate her feast. "And your mother?"

"She died when I was ten." Strangely enough, it had been a long time since he had thought about her. "I was sent to boarding schools after her death till I was eighteen."

"It seems your father is quite accomplished and intelligent."

Her statement shocked him. He was not sure if he agreed. "I suppose so."

"You suppose so?" She pointed her silver knife at him. "He manages other people successfully while spreading his knowledge among them to enrich their lives."

It was true. His father was a hard man, but fair to those he worked with. He made it a point for Basile to teach the things he had learned in school to those that worked for them. His father had helped Benny and his family to earn their own lands.

"My father runs his trade well," Basile said. *Why did she care? And why was she bringing this up now?*

"What brought you aboard my ship?" she asked as she continued to eat.

Basile swallowed. "I…" he hesitated. In his mind the answer flowed freely. *I planned on finding a vast treasure, which I was going to steal from you, and live alone, not worrying about anyone but myself.* "For adventure," he finally said, knowing she would not accept that alone. "And to find a great treasure."

"I see. What's wrong with the lands and wealth you have at home?"

"It's not mine."

"But it will be when your father dies."

"It's not for me. I mean—" He felt trapped. "I don't want to be in charge of everyone else's lives. I want to be in charge of my own."

And Tessa's.

A cryptic expression crossed Acantha's face. Though it was hard to read, it resembled disappointment.

She finally spoke after a long moment. "That is all."

Basile's heart dropped. He had been in a test and didn't know it until the end. What kind of image had he given Acantha about himself? He stood frozen, helpless for the words to change what he had just done.

Defeated, he turned slowly and left.

◇◇◇

As the island spread into view, the crew anxiously scanned the shores. Acantha, at the helm, peered through the spyglass and searched the island. The shores had not even a single footprint in the sand.

"I don't see anything." She handed the glass to Vaster, who looked but lowered it again.

"Jennings!" Acantha shouted. "Take us as close as you can." All three ships lined the cove. The small boats were loaded and then dropped into the water. Vaster organized the men into groups, determining who would lead up the front, middle, and rear of the battle.

Acantha called to him from the helm.

He ran to her. "Yes, Captain?"

She eyed Basile in the back of the crowd as the others bustled around.

"I want Basile in the front line," she said.

Vaster shook his head, shocked. "The frontline, Captain? They'll take more hit than the rear."

"I know how it works." Acantha turned back to the island.

Vaster hesitated. He returned down the stairs, shaking his head. "Basile! Ye're in the group loading right now with Jennings."

"All right," Basile confirmed.

Half of them had already loaded. Jennings stood by the railing. As Basile passed into the longboat, he noticed the strange glances between him and Vaster. Even Pole squinted as the boat slowly dropped into the water. Basile's stomach twisted in knots. This was not going to end well for him.

As the men rowed closer to the shore and the wind brushed over him, he wished for the power to change what was coming. There were so many boats in the water. How many men would die?

Once ashore, they hiked. "Make for high ground," shouted Jennet.

They all started up the winding path to a large plateau, where stone pillars stood in an unnatural circle. The jungle was sparse and patchy in between the sand and rocks.

By noon they reached a narrow canyon that led to the other side of the island. "Take a rest!" yelled Vaster.

The sun burned down, making them all sweat. Basile continually looked for Tessa's blonde hair. So far he had been unable to find her among the mess of men. A sinking feeling hit him.

They were all going to die.

◇◇◇

Acantha sat between Tessa and Jennet, looking up through the rocky path.

"What do you think?" Jennet asked leaning in the shade.

"Well," Tessa said, "we haven't seen any sign of them. That's good."

Acantha looked back to them. "He's here. They all are."

"How do you know?" Jennet disputed.

"I can feel that they're here." The impression sickened her gut. "And they've been here for a while."

"What do we do?" Tessa asked.

Her sisters looked to her with wrinkled foreheads. "Our chances are the same in this place. That's why I chose it," Acantha said.

"Let's push on!" Jennet signaled the leaders to start the trek again. "I'm going to the front," she stated as she left.

The rough road made it hard to move quickly with a large group. Acantha was pleased with their numbers. Tessa dragged along beside her. Every once in a while, she would scan the crowd.

"You've been quiet lately," Acantha said.

"Is that a crime now?" Tessa asked, irritated.

"No, just unlike you. Ever since we got Jennet back you've been different."

"Well, she is annoying," Tessa said with a slight smile.

Acantha stopped their pace to look at her. "Is this still what you want?"

Tessa stared blankly at her. "What else is there?" Despairing truth infused her voice.

"This might not be for you anymore," Acantha said, trying to help her. "You could go back."

"To what? And why? There's no point. No continuation. It's a dead end, just like you said."

"Don't blame me, Tessa," Acantha warned. "I didn't control everything that happened." She scanned the men, making sure no one listened. "This was my method of escape. You can find your own way."

Tessa looked to her forlornly. "I've tried that. You of all people know I've already tried that."

"You're not the same person anymore. It was your first time. Give yourself a break. You have it in you to do or have whatever you want."

"Yeah," she responded, "then how come you can't say the same and how do you know it won't come crashing down on you in the end?"

Acantha closed her eyes, remembering the sound of pistols booming through the air toward her. She'd huddled on the rooftop of the palace as the rain poured down, slipping and sliding in her escape. The swamp to her left brimmed with water from the storm. She panicked, searching for a way down the palace walls.

"Acantha?" Tessa spoke, shaking her from her trance. "Are you all right?"

She looked back with deadly seriousness. "It's not the same for everyone. If you want something, you had better be willing to lose everything to have it."

Tessa blinked several times before they started walking again.

After several hours, they finally cleared the canyon. A narrow road led up around the cliff face, winding to the top where it plateaued against a sheer drop on the other side. From the point they now stood, it was a forty-foot drop onto jagged rock and sea. An opposite cliff protruded out of the water, forming a canal between the islands. The only directions were up or back down. They started the treacherous march, moving carefully while watching for falling rocks.

A shout went back among the men. "Acantha!" It was Jennet.

Acantha moved through the crowd to the front, with Tessa close to her side. The men made way for her, their faces blank. A thick figure towered above their heads: Naulkiendum blocked the path.

The massive wraith had a large headdress and a breastplate made of bones, but no army in sight. Acantha was astonished he was able to stand on his own feet.

"Captain!" Naulkiendum called out.

Acantha whispered to Jennings and Scar. "They'll attack us from behind. Go hold up the rear and be ready for them." They nodded and melted into the column of men.

◇◇◇

Basile's heart sank as he took in the monstrous size of the towering Wraith King.

Not even an army could take the likes of him.

"My Lady!" Naulkiendum shouted. "I wait for you."

The captain removed herself from the crowd and walked to him, insignificant in size by comparison. Tessa and Jennet took a position several feet in front of the men.

"I am here!" Acantha yelled back.

He laughed. "I was afraid you would not come."

"I always keep my word."

"So I see." Naulkiendum looked over to Jennet and Tessa. "You are all together now. She didn't bother you enough to kill her?" he asked, mocking Jennet.

"She still has her charms," Acantha said.

Jennet glowered. Basile slowly moved through the crowd, positioning himself a few men behind Tessa. When the battle started he would be by her side.

"So, Lady Captains, do you have my pendant?" Naulkiendum puckered his fat lips.

Acantha looked back to her sisters and faintly nodded. They responded in kind.

She spun. "Well, that's quite a story. You see, we found your pendant," Acantha said so all could hear. Naulkiendum's eyes glinted with excitement. "But my sister here," she motioned back to Jennet, "accidentally dropped it into the sea while we were sailing here to give it to you."

A wide smile crept up Jennet's face.

Naulkiendum, on the other hand, was not so amused. He lowered his face toward Acantha, his expression livid.

"You lie! You didn't even go find it."

Acantha raised her hands in the air. "I did, I promise. But did you really think I was dumb enough to find something that you could use against me?"

The tension grew so thick in the air that Basile found it hard to stand still.

"I am not so naïve!" Naulkiendum spat at her. "I know who you are." He pointed a finger in her direction.

"Naïve?" Acantha scoffed. "I'm surprised you know what the word means. Who are we, then?"

"Demons." The Wraith King cursed, pointing to the three sisters. "Witches from the depths of Hell! My own grandfather told me stories of the three witches that roamed the ocean's surface. Cursed, he said they were." He spat on the ground and continued. "Always destroying all ships. Collapsing them from the inside out!"

Basile looked closely at each of their faces, watching for any sign to confirm the accusations.

"I don't believe in fairytales," Acantha said.

"I know it's you! When I first caught her," Naulkiendum pointed to Jennet, who looked smug, "I knew I had captured one of the three witches. Beautiful like the treasures they steal, powerful enough to kill any man, and treasure hunters that curse everyone around them. But there is one thing I don't believe!"

"And what would that be?" Acantha asked.

He reached for the hilt at his waist and fluidly pulled his massive, thick blade from its sheath. The sword might slice several men in half with one swing. Basile swallowed at the sight of it. Inwardly he panicked, tempted to grab Tessa and run. But there was nowhere to go, and she would not follow him anyway. She chose Acantha.

Naulkiendum pointed the sword at Acantha. She stood like a rock, immovable and undaunted.

"I believe that you can die, witch!"

From around the corner behind him, a flood of wraiths surged. They attacked from the rear as well. Acantha drew both swords, but the wraiths veered around her, keeping their distance as Naulkiendum moved forward. Clashes echoed off the cliff face. Basile ripped out his sword, taking a breath of strength as the oncoming horde slipped through. Three blasts of a horn sounded from a nearby wraith.

◇◇◇

"Jennet, you're with me!" Acantha yelled back in the chaos. "I can't take him by myself."

Jennet stood shoulder to shoulder with her.

"Tessa—" Before she could finish, a piercing shriek echoed through the air.

"What was that?" Tessa asked, looking back.

"There is no way he brought that snake with him here!" Jennet said, disbelieving.

The snake shot out of the water. It straightened its back, scaling the side of the cliff with the length of its body. Its massive diamond-shaped head hovered over them. The combined crews stared with wide, frozen eyes. Acantha scanned the enormous snake in awe. Its thick green scales shimmered, its yellow eyes venomous as it examined the movement upon the cliffside.

It attacked, crushing those closest to the edge with its head and mouth, throwing bodies in every direction.

Acantha grabbed Tessa's arm, yanking her attention back. "Tessa, grab the others in command and kill that thing!" she said, feeling as though she had just ordered a death sentence.

Tessa bolted into the crowd, and Basile followed.

Acantha and Jennet turned and found Naulkiendum lingering for them.

"I've been waiting for this my entire life!" he said reverently. He weaved his heavy sword through the air. "All my life I've heard stories of you three, and now I will be the one to kill you."

"Fat chance!" Jennet yelled.

Acantha whispered to her. "Let him move first. He'll be slower, but only one swipe from him and we're dead."

They separated, gaining some space around him. Jennet had her sword and long dagger out. The first swipe of his sword flew at their heads.

They each bent backward as the heavy air rushed over them with the weight of his sword. It sent them spinning into action. They twisted and turned in a circle as they dodged his sword and inched to get close enough to touch him. His broad radius created quite the challenge.

◇◇◇

Basile followed behind Tessa as she picked off wraiths. Half of the men ran around crazily dodging the snake's attacks. The rest fought with the heathens, a never-ending horde. Every direction Basile turned, another was ready to run him through. Tessa spun just feet from him, taking on three wraiths. One lurched. She blocked his sword and threw him toward Basile, who kicked the weapon from his hand and lodged his own in his belly. Tessa dodged a flying knife and slashed her sword across the second wraith's face. The third wraith swung a large club down at her. She side-stepped, and it struck the ground. She grabbed the club and kicked the wraith over the edge of the cliff.

Finally, they made it to the middle.

"Vaster!" Tessa yelled. He fought a group of wraiths. She decapitated one and cut off the leg of another. Vaster lodged his sword in the belly of one wraith, pushed him back into another, and sent them both over the edge. Basile reached them as another wave of wraiths progressed. All three stood back-to-back-to-back against the oncoming attack, picking them off one by one.

"We need to kill that snake!" Tessa yelled.

Basile's eyes almost bulged out of his head. "We can't kill that thing. We have no ground to work with." He pushed back a crowd of wraiths with his sword.

Vaster glanced to the two of them. "I don't think we have anythin' strong enough to pierce through its armor."

Tessa looked around for any resources they might use, but it was useless.

The snake's attack shifted toward them. They pulled their pistols and fired. The snake reared its head, thrashing at the sky, giving them a chance to move farther back. The creature straightened again, attacking more viciously into the crowd.

"This isn't working. We just pissed it off," Tessa yelled. "We need a brigade of cannons!" The snake struck at her. She barely dodged, falling to the ground and rolling out of the way. Basile shot it again on the side of the head at close range. It screamed.

"We need the ship's cannons to kill this," he yelled.

"We can't bring the ship. Think of somethin' else," Vaster yelled battling two stray wraiths.

"The sword!" Tessa pointed at Naulkiendum, who held his oversized sword above his head, about to bring it down on Acantha. The three exchanged a glance and bolted back through the fighting.

◇◇◇

Naulkiendum brought his sword down. Acantha barely caught the weight with both of her swords, but it still sent her buckling. Jennet, thrown several feet back, raced to help. Even with the two of them, each blow pushed them back. He bore down, moving them foot by foot toward the cliff's edge.

"Acantha!" Jennet waned under the pressure.

"Hold him!" Acantha yelled as she spun around the side of him. He reached for her but missed. She slashed the back of his forward leg. He released Jennet, who fell in the change of weight.

His sword swung back after Acantha. She ducked, rolling out of the way as the weapon hit the dirt where she had stood. Naulkiendum returned to Jennet, who was barely back on her feet. She crossed her dagger and sword to catch his blow, but the weight broke her blade from the hilt. Jennet threw his weight to the side and tossed the hilt of her sword at his face. He scarcely dodged.

She shifted, armed only with her long dagger, a toothpick in comparison with his monstrous weapon.

Naulkiendum swung his sword down on her again. Jennet dodged while trying to block with her dagger, but the force was too great. The dagger flew from her hand off the side of the cliff. He smiled at her defenselessness.

Acantha charged his back, but he blocked her easily, using the momentum to throw her into the crowd of wraiths. He circled his sword, aiming for Jennet's belly. Just as he released all his force, Acantha jumped through the crowd, firing a shot into his leg. He buckled, diverting the direction of his sword's path. It swerved away from Jennet, relaying its energy toward Acantha.

The blade speared her through the chest.

Jennet screamed. "No!"

In that moment, time stopped. Acantha stared at the end of the huge sword, with Naulkiendum's hand still on the hilt. Basile, Tessa, and Vaster broke through the crowd into view. Acantha looked up slowly at

Naulkiendum's face.

His broad smile revealed decayed teeth. "I told you, witch," he sneered. "You can die."

Pain infused her, but it wasn't from the sword. Something moved inside her, like her blood flowing from all extremities to pool around the sword. The fire from the dark mountain seared through her again. Her head fell back from the intense pain, but then cold filled her insides, encompassing every part of her. Frost puffed from her breath. Her mind spun to the shadowy cave and the figure of Death thrusting darkness into her soul. That darkness roiled inside her now.

A black cloud billowed out around the sword in her chest. It flowed like a storm, circling around the blade and up onto Naulkiendum's arm. He wrenched back in horror, pulling his oversized sword from her chest as the darkness frothed upon him.

"The devil's magic!" he yelled.

Acantha, painless now, dropped to her knees. The ghostly force fastened around the Wraith King's ankle like a rope. Naulkiendum stumbled in panic as the darkness consumed him. His sword clanged to the ground. The cloud traveled up his body, and he tried to bat it off. The darkness surged into his nose and through his mouth. The energy behind it tingled though Acantha. She could feel it searching for his source of life—his beating heart. Her red stone pendant vibrated against her neck and pulsed a low crimson light.

The nearby wraiths fled from the supernatural event. Naulkiendum fell to his knees. His purpling face bulged. Choking for air, he seized and violently shook. A noise cracked from him as his ribcage collapsed.

He fell forward, dead.

The dark cloud swarmed around him. It drew his soul from his crumpled body, which disappeared like a vapor. The darkness flowed like a river back into Acantha's chest. She looked down at the site of the wound. It had sealed.

Her mind spun, stunned and confused.

"What the hell was that?" Jennet yelled.

Everyone stared at Acantha in horror.

Just then, the snake's attack turned on them. The crew picked off wraiths as they tried to retreat. Tessa ran to Naulkiendum's sword, but it was too heavy. Basile ran to help, taking hold of the oversized sword.

The snake crashed down violently knocking more men off the cliffside.

"We need to aim it at him as he strikes," Basile said.

Tessa nodded, wide-eyed.

Acantha frowned, observing them. The snake snapped at her. She rolled out of the way behind Basile and Tessa, diverting the creature to them.

They drew the sword up together as the massive snake dove down at them. The blade pierced through its open mouth up into its head. The snake jerked hard toward the cliff yanking the two of them to the edge. Basile pushed Tessa back with all his strength, taking most of the hit. She screamed. His feet skidded against the ground, and he flew backward over the cliff.

It was all in slow motion for Acantha. Tessa cried out as she reached for Basile. Acantha' body reacted instantly. She ran in the same movement of Basile's fall and jumped headfirst over the cliff after him. The writhing, dying snake whipped and descended with the two figures, one fuming in black smoke toward the ocean's surface.

CHAPTER SIXTEEN
A Life of Servitude

Pots clanking though the walls sounded in his ears. Basile could hardly move, feeling like someone was sitting on his chest. A bright light fluttered through a nearby window, blinding his vision. He reached up and touched his face. His every movement shot unbearable pain through his body. He yelled out as his hand searched his surroundings and his eyes adjusted to the blinding light. A rock wall brushed under his fingertips. He held tight to it.

Through his slanted vision, a silhouette came to his bedside.

"Lie back down, son," his father's familiar voice coaxed him.

Basile panicked. Screaming with pain, he tried to open his eyes and sit up, but found himself restrained—not only by his father's arms, but by the pain.

"Audim, sit back! You've almost died. Give yourself a rest. You're safe here," his father assured.

"No, I'm not here. What is going on?" Basile continued to struggle.

"Son, you're home, you're home!" his father yelled.

"Where is she? Is she safe? Did she die?" Basile ranted in a panic. "I don't know what happened. The black smoke covered me before I hit the water." He still couldn't see. His arms and legs gave in against the struggle. Every part of his body felt crushed.

He finally heard his father's words. "She's not here, son."

"Where did she go?" Basile asked as his consciousness slipped.

"The dark lady didn't come to the door, but her crew brought you here in a wagon. I thought you were dead. When they told me you weren't, I just about died from shock." His father sounded thankful.

This isn't right. "Where's Tessa?" Basile asked, quivering as cold moved through him.

"I don't know anything about her. But you have been calling out her name in your sleep." His father held him.

Basile did not have the strength to refuse. "How long have I been here?"

"About a week. You've been asleep. We weren't sure you would wake."

"A week," Basile whispered. The room spun. The night table was covered with strange tools.

His father noticed his view. "They had you connected to these." He picked up a long hose with a point at one end. At the other was a bulb with the residue of a blue liquid.

Basile squinted. "What is this?"

"I don't know, but it's kept you alive."

◇◇◇

In his dreams, Basile relived the fight with the wraiths. Endless bodies littered the ground, Pole's dead, gaping face among them. The snake snapped out continuously after him. Tessa was always fighting in the distance.

The scene replayed over and over, different every time, but in the end he always fell. His stomach would lurch into his chest as the water below came closer. Before the collision, darkness shrouded him with arms so tight he couldn't breathe. Next, his lungs filled with water and he was thrashed about by waves. He couldn't see anything. Tessa's voice rang through the dark, calling his name.

Basile opened his eyes, seeing clearly. His father stood above him with a tray of food. "Audim? Are you all right?" He brushed a wet cloth along his burning head.

Basile blinked. The familiar surroundings of his room brightened. "Yes," he responded bleakly.

His father set the tray on the table beside him. Basile looked to the food and then back to his father's face, almost scared. He didn't know what to say.

"Just eat. I know we have a lot to talk about, but don't worry about it now."

Basile shook his head. His father took care of him—feeding him, changing his clothes, making him feel like a baby. He had never acted so concerned and hospitable.

Basile obeyed, even though he was uncomfortable with the service.

He thought back to the events he last remembered. *If I survived the fall, then why did the captain bring me home? Maybe she found out about Tessa and me?*

He resolved to leave, to get a ship and find them. But that was impossible. He could hardly move, like every part of him had been crushed.

He looked to his father, who watched him closely. "Just focus on getting better," he stated as if reading his mind.

"What's wrong with me?" Basile asked.

"The doctor said nothing was broken. You suffered some dislocations, but they were set before you arrived. Every part of you experienced a massive pressure. You were bruised both inside and out. The doctor said there was nothing to be done except to wait and see if you woke up. What happened?" His father's worry was a foreign expression to Basile.

"I fell off a cliff."

"A cliff!" His eyes bulged. He didn't get angry the way Basile expected, but only sat confused.

"I don't know why I'm alive," Basile admitted.

◇◇◇

It took a long month for Basile to recover, but he would never be the same. The doctor said it was a miracle, that it should have taken him six months to a year to ever walk again. His left leg was still stiff. He was lucky it was the only lingering effect of the fall, and it got better every day. His father remained by his side the entire time, like he had become a new person while Basile was gone. They had regular conversations about the town and people. Benny visited often, elevating his mood.

But it all felt wrong. He wasn't supposed to be there.

Basile sat in the living room with the grand stone fireplace blazing. His father, in the chair next to him, smoked his pipe. Basile fidgeted with the blanket that covered him. Should he even try to speak? His father had been so pleasant.

But it was only a matter of time until the yelling began again. Basile had to clear things between them.

"You know why I left, right?" he asked, staring at the flickering flames.

His father grunted. "I suppose I do."

"I'm sorry I didn't tell you I was leaving."

His father bore none of the anger he expected. "Will you leave again?"

Tessa's whereabouts haunted him. How could he find her? He had never heard of them before signing up. He felt hopeless about tracking them down.

He looked up at the picture of his mother. He had never thought he would return here. Now, the comfort of his home enveloped him. Every day he remembered more and more. In his mind played the haunting image of Acantha, with the black river of smoke from her chest that attacked and killed the oversized Wraith King. But as he reflected back on it, he recognized surprise and shock on her face as well. She hadn't known what was happening.

Naulkiendum had called the three captains witches, demons that cursed people everywhere they went.

He thought of the Bracket family, with their empty golden city in the mountains and the dark mark above the palace doors. He imagined old James Bracket, the last of the Bracket line, dead in the middle of the grand hall with a dark streak on his forehead.

Was this why Tessa could not love him? What if it was true? What if she lived forever? He would age, while she stayed young and beautiful.

But as hard as Basile tried, he could not picture Tessa being evil and causing so much damage upon the world.

"Where will you go? What will you do?" His father asked, drawing him from his mind.

"I don't know." He was fully healed besides his sore leg.

"And this person, Tessa? Do you love her?" his father asked.

It was hard to relay his feelings. He was not used to having such cordial conversation.

"More than I want to. But I don't know where she is or if she's even alive anymore, or if she cares the same way I do." He looked to his father and they shared a moment of understanding. "And even if she does care the same way about me, she has a complicated life. I don't know if I can be part of it." Relief came in honestly divulging his feelings.

His father didn't speak for a long time, but in the end he admitted, "I know I've done wrong by you. Ever since your mother died. I wasn't the same as her, and the best I knew was to teach you how to live in the world. So I sent you to schools, and I made you work for the best that I knew. But now as I look at you, I see you have your own course to follow."

He stood, putting his pipe on the mantle right by his wife's picture. He reflected on her face the same way Basile had so many times.

"Good night," he said, turning to go upstairs.

"Good night," Basile called back to him, dizzy from his father's confession. He had never expected that.

He fell asleep where he sat, warmed by the fire. His dreams were more real than he had ever experienced, almost like a memory. The captain stood in her quarters. He lay immovable on the bed.

Jennet stormed in through the door. "He's still alive?" She stalked straight to him, darkening his vision.

"Yes. Satyr's been to see him."

"How did you two live?" Jennet asked.

"It's not my first dive off a cliff, but I didn't break my neck or he would have died. I think we've discovered what our trip to the dark mountain gave us. I think it protected him."

There was a quiet moment. "So that cloud thing protected you and killed that fat pig for you?" Another silent moment. "Are you saying there's no way you can die now?" Jennet moved away toward the desk. "Did you know that when you jumped off the cliff?"

Acantha mused. "I felt Naulkiendum's blade go in me, but there was darkness instead of blood. Or maybe it was my blood. I don't know."

Jennet hovered, waiting for her to finish.

"And then the wound closed. The healing was not as bad as I expected."

"I wonder. If he'd chopped you in half, would it have been the same?" Jennet twisted her head, looking at him.

They both contemplated the question.

"Is Tessa's ship gone?" Acantha asked.

Jennet nodded. "Are you sure this is what she wants?"

"Yes. I know why it was so hard for her to admit her feelings. There's so much to risk. But she knew the moment he fell, just as I knew the moment I saw her reach out for him."

"Rough experience for enlightenment." Jennet snorted. "I feel sorry for him." She looked to the bed. "So you're really taking him home?"

"*Yes.*"

The word pounded inside Basile's head.

He woke to a banging noise. He sat up, disoriented, as the persistent thumping echoed throughout the house. His father flew down in his nightshirt, unsettled.

"Are you all right?" he asked, checking the room.

Basile nodded. "Someone's at the door."

His father looked up to the clock. It was two in the morning.

"Who would be here at this hour?" he grumbled. He carefully opened the large wooden doors. "What do you want?" he shouted out.

"Audim Basile," the voice spoke.

Basile instantly jumped to his feet, running over. Vaster stood outside with a lantern in his hands. Basile was flooded with relief, but Vaster's face remained serious.

"Ye have been called."

"Called?" Basile asked, squinting.

Vaster raised his lantern toward the hillside in the distance. Another lantern flickered in the darkness.

"Will ye come?" Vaster asked.

Basile ignored his request and spoke urgently. "Is Tessa there?" He no longer cared about secrecy. "Do you know where she is? Is she all right?"

Vaster's face remained serious, and he asked again, "Will ye come?"

Basile nodded. *But why was Vaster acting so weird?* In only moments, he ran upstairs and dressed, slipping on his shoes quickly. He darted back down. His father stood looking at his mother's picture on the mantle. The door was ajar, and Vaster walked into the outer yard.

"I have to go," Basile said.

"I know you do." He looked up with tears in his eyes. It was the first time Basile had ever seen his father cry. "I tried to make you the way I am, but your spirit comes from your mother, and that can't be helped."

For the first time in his life, Basile embraced his father. They held each other and, for the first time, understood each other's differences. Tears fell down Basile's face.

"I have to go," he said. He needed to escape from the moment before he had time to change his mind. He ran out the door into the dark night.

Vaster led the way through the familiar countryside. The distant lantern flickered in the darkness of the hills where Basile and Benny used to play. Montville lay over the ridge, where a dark ship would lurk in its harbor.

Vaster remained silent. When they reached the top of the hillside, it was pitch black. The lantern signal was gone, but Vaster led him to a large, crooked tree, its branches bent down to the earth. Acantha sat upon one of them, looking out at the Montville view.

"Mr. Basile," she said, her voice just the same, "I see you survived."

Basile stood shoulder to shoulder with Vaster. "Yes, Captain. Though I don't know how." His mind raced with questions, but the most important one leapt to the forefront. "Captain?"

Acantha looked to him, her face firm as usual.

"Is Tessa all right?"

She tilted her head. "I thought that you, Mr. Basile, did not care about anyone's welfare but your own." She arose from the tree, staring down to the sea. "And your treasure? Your chance to escape this hole of dirt?" She pointed back to the valley where his home was.

He remained silent. *Was this one of her tests?* "I was mistaken."

"Well, it looks to me like you have two choices."

Basile looked up, hopeful.

"Vaster," she called. He stepped forward with a rolled-up parchment paper. When he unfurled it, Basile looked at the familiar contract he had signed months ago. The top name was his, written elegantly. Basile remembered the intuition that his life was about to change. Now hindsight told him what that meant. He looked back to the captain, waiting for her to speak, afraid of what she would say.

"Because you saved my sister, I have preserved your life and brought you home. You have a choice. You can stay here, at home, and be free of this contract," she pointed at the parchment, "or you can come back aboard *The Dark Eve* and resume your position."

He opened his mouth to speak, but something in her expression waylaid him.

Acantha stared. "Don't take this decision lightly. Your name on this paper means a life of servitude on *The Dark Eve*. I've never pardoned someone like this before. You have the chance to get your life back." She nodded to his home. "On *The Dark Eve*, the only way to get off is to die." She paused. "Or to be retired. Which doesn't happen often."

Basile reflected on old Mort, the oldest on board, and his crazy speech after cutting off the fingers of the sailor in the mess hall. Mort was mad —and completely loyal to Acantha. Was that what Basile would be before she retired him?

"And Tessa?" he asked.

Acantha glanced to Vaster. "She's back on her ship."

Basile's mind swam. He wanted to be with Tessa. If he chose home, she would have to come to him. But Tessa had said her life chose her. Did that mean that he needed to choose the life closest to her? Even on *The*

Dark Eve he would only see her occasionally. Once a year at the drop-off, at least. Could they ever be together?

His mind was getting fuzzy. Tessa had said *he had to be found worthy*. Maybe the only way was to be in servitude to Acantha. Maybe then, he would be let into their secrets and live forever.

"I choose…" Basile said, looking back to the lights of his home in the distance. He imagined his father in the great room, holding his mother's picture. He imagined the piles of treasure on the shore of his island, gray and useless. "I choose you," he whispered for only her to hear.

Acantha's eyes narrowed. "Take him!" she commanded.

Men rushed the top of the hill. Basile was tackled and bound. "What?" he yelled out to her, but she already strode down the hill toward the sea. A fist delivered a blow to his face, knocking him out.

◇◇◇

Basile woke the next morning with a sore face in the prison cell in the belly of *The Dark Eve*. He looked around for anyone that might answer why he was there. It didn't make sense. Hadn't he shown loyalty by choosing her? What had he done to deserve this?

A noise shuffled from above. Old Mort took each step slowly down. A small opening in the bottom of the cage allowed him to slide in a tray of food.

"Mort! Mort, what have I done?" Basile cried out.

Old Mort grunted.

"Come on, Mort. Tell her I need to see her. Tell her I haven't done anything wrong. Can you call Vaster for me? This is a mistake."

But he remembered the two prisoners from when he first signed up. *Their crime was simply talking about her.* Would Scar and Jennings come for him? Would the crew cheer as he was thrown overboard?

No. He shook the thought from his mind.

Old Mort returned up the stairs. Basile sank down the wall, crushed. *I should have stayed. Tessa didn't choose me, or else she would have come.* She would have been by his side when he first woke up from his fall.

Anger welled inside his chest. Acantha had condemned him for whatever reason, and now he was going to die.

◇◇◇

He remained inside his cell for the week. The only person he saw was Old Mort, for every meal. Basile stopped asking him questions after only receiving the same grunting answers.

The scruff of his face thickened. Would he ever see daylight again? Finally, footsteps thudded down for him. Basile looked to the grim faces of Jennings and Scar.

Jennings's deep voice boomed. "You can walk or be dragged. Your choice."

"I'll walk," Basile answered miserably.

Scar opened the cell door and placed his hands in metal cuffs. Basile went without a fight.

Sunlight blinded him as he stepped onto the deck. The critical faces of the crew stared at him. Behind them, loomed a small, familiar hill of an island.

They were near Woodmor, where the captains and a strange figure had dropped treasure into the sea.

But why were they here?

Basile looked around. Sailors had removed the railing from a portion of the ship. A long wooden plank led out to the water. He gulped.

Acantha emerged from her chambers, with Vaster behind her. Jennings and Scar led Basile to the plank and turned him around to face captain and crew. Vaster did not look at him, but out to the sea.

"I don't understand," Basile said.

"There's not much to be understood," Acantha admitted.

She took his hand and slid something onto his middle finger. Basile looked down upon a ring with sea carvings around a large, green stone. He looked back to her, absolutely confused.

Acantha addressed the men, smirking. "When you sign up for a place on *The Dark Eve*, there are no deserters! Basile has chosen his path. Let us wish him well on his way!"

All the nearby sailors raised their hands in unison shouting, "Arghhhhh!"

"What?" Basile's eyes bulged. "I chose to stay!" He thought of Tessa, trying to picture her peaceful face and golden hair, but his mind panicked. He was going to die.

Acantha drew her sword and pointed it straight at him, pushing him farther and farther onto the plank. Basile held his balance above the crystal-blue water.

"You know that I chose right!" he yelled at her. He scanned the crowd catching Carter's smug face. "There are people you can't trust on board. I heard them say they were going to try to steal from you."

"Everyone has the intention to steal from me. I imagine even you."

Basile glanced away, instantly shamed.

Acantha smiled and brought her sword up to his neck. "Basile," she whispered. Mischief built in her eyes. "Take a deep breath and hold it for as long as you can."

"What?" Basile responded, confused. Her face changed from her constant seriousness. It revealed something to him, something he didn't understand.

"It only works if you trust me." She moved back toward the ship once again, pointing her sword at him.

He hated her. In that moment he hated her so much he wished he could tackle her and beat the life out of her.

But even as his anger built, he felt restraint—like he *should* trust her.

This didn't make sense. If he were smart he wouldn't take a breath. He would get it over quickly. Doubt filled him.

He didn't want to die.

He searched her face for any other sign that what was happening would not lead to his death.

Acantha waited. Basile looked past her to the crew.

"Do I need to push you?" she asked. "Or can you make the jump on your own?"

His constant dreams of her pushing him off the tall mountain flashed through his mind. She would push without hesitation. He hadn't taken any steps of his own, besides saving Tessa.

His worst fear was trusting the captain. Trusting someone besides himself. Losing Tessa. Living a common life.

He stared at the water below. *What did it matter anymore?* The crew on the ship cheered and snarled. His stomach hardened against any camaraderie for them. Vaster stood in the center with a serious face—perhaps even a little sad.

The mystery would die with him. The building desperation made his mind swirl. What did he have to lose? "Did you curse the people in the golden city?" He blurted out.

Acantha's solemn face now flashed a lethal glare. She pulled her blade back and stabbed him in the shoulder. Basile yelled and clenched the bleeding wound. The cut was shallow.

Basile blinked, shocked, and backed up to the end of the plank. *No one will save me, and death is not my worst fear.*

Basile sucked in a deep breath and jumped off the plank.

◇◇◇

The drop was clean and painless, but as he hit the ice-cold water, his mind panicked. A strong current grabbed him, like a hand pulling him straight down to the ocean floor. He had jumped into a whirlpool. He flailed as the pressure grew in his lungs. He tried to release his breath, to welcome death, but he couldn't make himself do it.

Her voice pulsed in his head. *Trust me.*

His throat choked for air. A green glow caught his attention: Acantha's ring. His finger throbbed as the ring tightened more and more the lower he went. His hand felt like iron. It weighed him down, pulling him closer and closer to the ocean floor.

Just then, the current flowed so fast that he shot down to the bottom, where he was thrust through an opening of a cave.

A shimmering of shell walls glittered around him as he spun helplessly through the torrent. His lungs burned and ached for another breath. He struggled, trying not to breathe.

Suddenly, he hit a hard surface, knocking the air out of his lungs. Water poured in, choking him. The current switched directions, thrusting him every which way. The flow pulled him faster and faster, launching him forward. Darkness filled his sight.

Just as he was about to pass out, he shot out of the water and landed on wet sand. He choked and gagged, unable to see anything. His stomach heaved violently, sending water up as he gripped the sand beneath him. Finally, he collapsed on his side, desperately breathing the air.

He opened his eyes. They burned from the salt, making everything fuzzy. In the distance, a gray figure moved toward him with gentle blond hair.

His heart skipped with relief. *It was her.*

But he couldn't move. His hands were still bound and the ring on his finger throbbed.

An opaque pair of large feet stepped in front of him. He squinted, trying to see them better. They were faintly translucent and shimmered strangely. He strained harder and unclearly discerned the webbed toes just before losing consciousness.

◇◇◇

"Basile." Tessa's voice rang in his ears.

Everything was a blur except her perfect hazel eyes staring down at him.

He felt instantly relieved.

"I'm not dead." The words escaped with trembling breath.

She smiled.

He looked past her to the pillar of a person standing near them. Blinking several times to clear his vision, he observed an overly tall white man, unlike any man Basile had ever seen. Was he indeed a man at all? Pure white hair fell straight past his broad shoulders, his skin glimmered like an opal, and his face was oblong with a flat nose. Large slits in his skin traveled down his neck from behind his ears. His clothes consisted of shimmering robes and layers of scale-like chainmail.

And the toes of his feet were webbed.

Tessa's voice echoed. "Basile, meet Irvern."

Irvern lowered an oversized hand. Basile took it reluctantly. Before he knew it, he stood next to the ghostly-white person. It was impossible not to stare.

Irvern bowed toward him. Basile replied by ducking slightly in shock.

"Tessa, where am I?" His eyes darted around the cavern.

"I guess this is the place my family calls home."

He turned back to her, but it was Irvern that spoke in a deep solid voice. "Welcome to Atlantis."

The End

About the Author

One thing to know about T.K. Thompson is that she has a few FREE BOOKS to start out her series, so visit this link to grab an entertaining read for FREE. (Click Here)

If you love to read and review books, then consider joining my review team (Click Here).

Now that you know these awesome fact, let's continue

T.K. Thompson is author of YA fantasy series, The Dark Eve, epic adventure packed novels with an endless amount of fun. She also enjoys co-staring in The Ride Home Review Podcast, where film pundit Dustin Thompson and she do their best to improve movies by rewriting the story on the fly.

She's a huge fan of Thrillers, Genre Movies, Dancing with the Stars, Stranger Things, and Gerard Butler... sing to me, Phantom. She loves chocolate milk... mmm...good, steak, and I am pretty sure she eats a whole Costco apple pie in December.

As a mother of three awesome children, T.K. is usually helping out with homework, dropping kids off at (dance, gymnastics, and soccer), or cooking some awesome concoctions with her hubs. Thank you Food Network. She loves writing entertaining reads filled with deep characters and stories littered with twists and turn leaving everyone on the edge of their seats. She dabbles in sewing stuff...note it doesn't always work out. She is a fierce writer with Netflix always playing in the background. A girl has got to have some noise in her life.

Email: TKTHOMPSONBOOKS@GMAIL.COM

Thank You for Reading
We invite you to share your thoughts and reactions.

I liked this book. - Click Here
http://tkthompson.com/review/

I don't like this book. - Click Here
http://tkthompson.com/feedback/

To get more FREE books from T.K. Thompson, learn more about *The Dark Eve* **book series,** get updates on future book releases, and more.

Subscribe to our newsletter at TKThompson.com

Acknowledgements

I want to thank all my family and friends, they believed in me before I did, and each and every single one of them did great things to support and encourage me. I also want to give recognition to the personalities from my life that made their way into this book, especially my sisters, you are all special to me. I want to thank my husband, Dustin Thompson, for being the man I needed in order to fall madly in love and believe in a life that I never thought existed. He is my partner in the creation of this story. His talents and skills have created the images for the imaginations that read this book. I want to thank God, for giving me the hard times that inspired this story. To those who understand that I plant my own garden instead of waiting for someone to bring me flowers. I don't believe in white knights on noble steeds. I believe in my own will power and strength to carry me beyond time and circumstance as long as God's guidance still favors me.